Fortunes of the Black Hills

SHADOW

OF

LEGENDS

a novel

There will be six books in this series
FORTUNES OF THE BLACK HILLS
by STEPHEN BLY
Book #1
Beneath a Dakota Cross
Book #2
Shadow of Legends
For a list of other books by
Stephen Bly

write:
Stephen Bly
Winchester, Idaho 83555

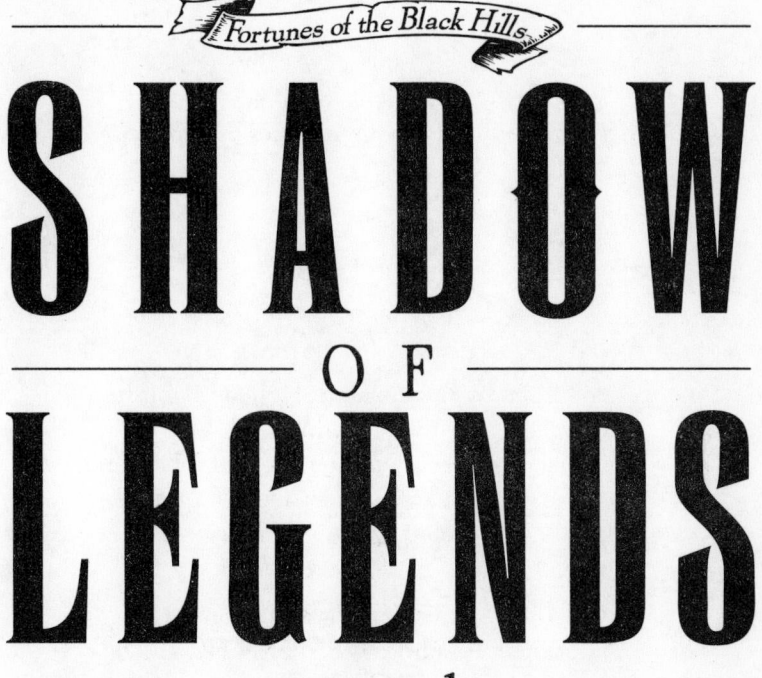

Fortunes of the Black Hills

SHADOW OF LEGENDS

a novel

STEPHEN BLY

BROADMAN
& HOLMAN
PUBLISHERS

Nashville, Tennessee

© 2000
by Stephen A. Bly
Printed in the United States of America

0–8054–2174–2

Published by Broadman & Holman Publishers,
Nashville, Tennessee
Editorial Team: Leonard G. Goss and John Landers
Page Design and Typesetting: TF Designs,
Mount Juliet, Tennessee

Dewey Decimal Classification: 813
Subject Heading: WESTERN FICTION

Library of Congress Cataloging-in-Publication Data
Bly, Stephen A., 1944–
    Shadow of legends / Stephen A. Bly.
       p.   cm. -- (Fortunes of the Black Hills ; bk. 2)
    ISBN 0–8054–2174–2 (alk. paper)
    I. Title. II. Series: Bly, Stephen A., 1944- Fortunes of the
    Black Hills ; bk. 2.
    PS3552.L93S52   2000
    813'.54—dc21
                                                    99-16673
                                                    CIP

2 3 4 5 04 03 02 01 00

For
Russ
our firstborn

AUTHOR'S NOTES

Deadwood, D. T. (Dakota Territory), carries an image of a wild and reckless gold mining camp, even a hundred years past its prime. In that regard, it does not stand alone. Bodie, California . . . Tombstone, Arizona . . . Creede, Colorado . . . and Goldfield, Nevada . . . to name a few, likewise conjure up impressions of bad men, wicked women, and violent daily life.

The portrait of Deadwood lingers still because of the longevity of its golden veins and the length of its childhood. Gold ore is still being pried out of the stubborn earth from the fabled Homestake Mine just up the gulch in Lead, South Dakota. One hundred and twenty-five years of production is an incredible testimony to the wealth of the northern Black Hills.

No other boomtown in the late nineteenth century remained isolated for so long. The railroad first punched, prodded, and pleaded its way across the West in 1869. But Deadwood remained a stagecoach and freight wagon town until 1890. That meant for its first fifteen years, only the dauntless would make the journey. And only the courageous, and the lucky, would survive its rigors.

Deadwood was built in the bottom of a gulch so steep there can only be two streets parallel to the creek. Respectable homesites had to be carved into the mountainside to the east called Forest Hill or up the creek at the gradually sloping bend called Ingleside.

From the front porches of Forest Hill children gazed at the rooftops of their neighbors and the activities of Main Street. Below the unmarked but clearly defined "deadline" of Wall Street lay the part of town known as the badlands. It was filled with saloons, dance halls, casinos, and gunshots in the night. Deadwood society was divided by the deadline.

One thing all the people of Deadwood held in common, no matter what part of town they called home, was that they lived life in the shadows. The gulch is deep. The mountains steep. The winter sun stayed out on the Dakota plains until late morning. Finally it exploded above White Rocks and cleansed the city of shadows. Rapid City, east of the mountains, could enjoy long, beautiful sunrises . . . not Deadwood.

Some time in the middle of the afternoon, the sun stole behind the ponderosa pines of Forest Hill. Cheyenne, to the southwest, could take time to contemplate the profusion of oranges and yellows of a sunset. In Deadwood, the sun left the scene quicker than a gambler caught with an extra ace up his sleeve.

Life in the shadows. It happens to all of us. We stand so close to a dominant personality that our reflection can hardly be noticed. Someone more famous. More skilled. More powerful. Sometimes they are people we hardly know. Sometimes they are members of our own family.

But does God call us all to the bright light of day, or does He destine some of us to live in the shadows? The answer is not always easy.

Perhaps that's why Todd Fortune's struggle is not too much different from many of ours.

Stephen Bly
Broken Arrow Crossing, Idaho
Winter of '99

Be merciful unto me, O God,
be merciful unto me: for my soul trusteth in thee:
yea, in the shadow of thy wings
will I make my refuge,
until these calamities be overpast.
Psalm 57:1

CHAPTER ONE

Deadwood, Dakota Territory, June 1880

The man who stood across the counter from Todd Fortune brandished his dirt-baked and leathery brown face like a badge of honor. He flapped his greasy, tobacco-stained, drooping, thick dark beard like a flag that should garner respect.

Todd squinted his eyes slightly to keep the man's astringent odor from causing him to gag. *It must take years of disciplined effort to stay that repulsive.*

When the man opened his mouth, his two front teeth stuck slanted out a good half inch lower from the rest, which gave him a rabbit-like look—a big, hairy, dirty, skunk-smelling rabbit.

"I came to the Gulch with your daddy in '76 and I reckon that gives me a little credit, Boy," he boomed as if shouting across a canyon.

Todd rubbed his neatly trimmed, light-brown goatee and glanced around at the hardware store, which teemed with boomtown customers. His voice was soft, yet firm. "You say you're a friend of my father's?"

"Yep, me and him was what you might call partners!" He rapped thick, stubby fingers on the counter. The pine pitch and grime camouflaged any trace of fingernails.

A lady with a black silk scarf tied around the neck of her white blouse promenaded into the store. Todd glanced more than once. A flat, mountain leghorn, black straw hat turned up in the front perched smartly atop her carefully pinned long brown hair. A wreath of tiny artificial French white daisies served as a hat band. She caught the attention of every male customer and clerk, except the foul-smelling man. "Eh, what did you say your name was?" Todd asked.

"Tidy Dumont."

Todd still scrutinized the woman. "Tiny?" he mumbled.

"Tidy. The name is Tidy Dumont. Your pap told you about me, didn't he?"

The woman stopped by a barrel of used steel drilling points. Her narrow chin coyly tilted, she glanced at Todd Fortune and batted her eyelashes.

I do believe that woman is flirting with me. Todd quickly studied the crowded store to see if any others had noticed. He forced himself to concentrate on the man.

Meanwhile, the lady strolled up to the counter. She carried a three-pound steel drilling point about the diameter and length of a fat stick of dynamite. The black patent leather tip of her gray French kid boots glistened like polished obsidian as the heels danced on the hard wooden floor. "I'm sorry, Mr. Dumont, I really have never heard of you. We have to operate on cash for new folks in town."

The lady held a black-gloved hand to her nose as she caught a whiff of the big man and quickly scooted to the opposite end of the counter, still clutching the drill point. Her wide set brown eyes rollicked. Her soft, smooth voice had a giggle. "Young man, would you put this on my account?"

Todd forgot the ill-smelling man across from him. "A drilling point, Ma'am? Are you going to do some blasting?"

She chewed her tongue and rocked back on her heels, trying to suppress an outburst. "Yes, I am. But that is not what I want this for."

"Listen . . . ," Tidy Dumont interrupted. "Are you going to dispense me some credit or not?"

"Just a moment . . ." Fortune said. "Let me take care of the lady." He stepped toward the woman and noticed the bright reflection of her single-stud diamond earrings. "Now, ma'am, just exactly what are you going to do with that drilling point?"

Tidy Dumont moved down the counter like an avalanche of filth. "All I need is ten dollars credit. I need the cash."

Todd Fortune turned back to the man. "You need cash? I thought you wanted credit to purchase something in the store."

"A man cain't eat hardware."

"Nor can you drink it. Just a minute," he turned back to the woman. "You were saying?"

She banged the heavy drilling point on the counter in such a way that all conversation in the store ceased. "I intend to drop this in my husband's soup if he's late for lunch again."

Fortune folded his arms across his gray wool vest. "Your husband sounds like a very tardy man."

"He works too hard and acts as if the business could not survive without him." She laced together her thin, gloved fingers. "Perhaps I should purchase some blasting powder as well."

Fortune straightened his tie, then tugged the rumpled cuffs of his white cotton shirt. "My, you are serious."

"We have some very important things to discuss, and he promised we would do that today," she divulged.

Tidy Dumont lunged across the counter and grabbed Fortune's shoulder. "Mister, are you ignoring me?"

Fortune seized the man's wrist and shoved him straight back so quickly that the man staggered. Todd could feel his neck flush, his shoulders stiffen. He released the man's arm, opened his mouth, then glanced at the women's scowl. He let out a long sigh. "Dumont, I am talking with my wife. Would you please let me finish?"

The man wiped the back of his hairy hand across his lips. "Your wife?"

She turned to the big man and smiled. "Mr. Fortune has a habit of working through the lunch hour, which leaves me to eat alone. Don't you think that is a sad commentary?"

"Eh . . . yes, Ma'am. I didn't know you was his wife."

She turned back to Todd. "You will be home around twelve o'clock?"

"What's the bill of fare?" he asked.

"Drill point soup and a serious discussion." Then she cracked such a deep, easy smile that it made Todd's heart jump. "I'm teasing," she added.

"About which?" he prodded.

She spun around and strutted toward the door. The bustle of her imported challies skirt seemed to wave good-bye. "About the soup," she said.

"I'm glad to see you out and about," he called.

Todd Fortune watched her pause and flutter near the front door. "I only came down here to beguile you, my dear."

Tidy Dumont clenched his big fist around the steel drilling point and raised it in front of Todd Fortune as if it were a club. "I said, give me ten dollars cash credit in memory of your daddy and me."

Todd rubbed the back of his neck. "Dumont, the only thing I'll give you on credit is a bar of lye soap, and then you have to promise to use it before you ever come back inside this store."

The man laid the drilling point on the counter. "I had a run-in with a skunk," he admitted. "You ever skin a skunk?"

"No."

"Well, don't try it, no matter how hungry you are. Yep, me and your pappy was mighty hungry when we first got to the gulch in '76."

"My father arrived in the fall of '75," Fortune said.

"That's what I meant. He and I rode in from Sundance Mountain."

"He came up from French Creek in the south."

"I knowed that . . . I was just testin' you. How do I know for sure you're his boy?"

"Well, you don't. But I know one thing. You didn't ride into the Gulch with my father."

"How do you know?"

"Because he rode up here with four men. Big River Frank is buried up on Mount Moriah. Grass Edwards is lecturing at a college in California. And the other two are sitting in the back room of the Merchant's Hotel right now playing whist."

"I cain't believe your daddy never mentioned my name when he was alive!"

Todd Fortune ambled around the counter and prodded the man toward the door. "Dumont, unless you just murdered my father, he's still alive and well and sitting over at the Merchant's in that whist game right now. If you want to go over there and talk to him about grubstaking your drinking, you go right ahead."

Tidy Dumont lurched backwards. "Alive? They told me at the Piedmont Saloon that he was dead!"

"He's alive, alright. And don't come back in here lying to me about knowing my father."

Suddenly, a double-sided, foot-long blade flashed out of Tidy's battered stovetop boot and began waving at Fortune. "Are you callin' me a liar?" he hollered.

Todd's assistant manager, Dub Montgomery, corralled the customers and herded them to the far wall.

"Do you see that open door?" Todd pointed toward the front of the store.

The man shot a quick glance back, and Todd yanked a nickel-plated snaffle bit off a wooden peg and hammered it into the man's wrist. The huge knife tumbled to the wooden floor. The man cursed his way back down the aisle.

"You done busted my wrist!" he thundered.

Todd scooped the knife off the floor and backed the man out of the store. Clutching his wrist, the man staggered into the street. "You cain't kick me out!" he screamed.

"I just did."

"That's my knife!"

"I'll give it to Sheriff Bullock. You can retrieve it from him."

"Where is the sheriff?"

"He's the fourth man in the whist game over at the hotel."

The man meandered down the middle of the wagon-lined dirt street, staggering and shouting curses.

Carty Toluca scooted to the doorway, wiping his crisply ironed white canvas apron. "Sorry, Todd, I never know what to do with those who say they're friends of Daddy Brazos."

"Carty, you did good. Just send that type to me. They aren't your problem."

"So he didn't know your father at all?"

"He didn't come into the gulch with him in '75, that's for sure. If Daddy Brazos was here, he probably would have threatened to shoot the man, then given him a stake anyway."

"Your father's a generous man."

"But I'm a slave driver," Todd laughed. "Let's get back to work."

Carty followed Todd Fortune down the hardware store aisle. "This is the best place in town to work and everyone knows it. Everyone treats me nice . . . Well, almost everyone," the young man added.

"You and Dacee June still going at it?"

"Todd, why is your little sister so mean to me?"

"Well now, Carty, you're the one that wrote all over the boardwalk that 'Dacee June Fortune is a blockhead.'"

"That was three years ago."

"And then there's the time you put a dead rat in her flower basket."

"But . . . but . . . we was jist kids then."

"How about last year at the sack races on the Fourth of July when she beat you and you poured a gallon of lemonade on her head?"

"You don't reckon she still holds that against me, do ya?"

"Women don't forget things that easy, Carty. It might be good to remember that."

"She ain't no woman. She's only sixteen, like me."

"Now, Carty, you have never seen anger in your life until you tell Dacee June she isn't a woman. If you treasure a long life, it would be best you avoided telling her that."

"A man surely has to be watchful how he talks to a girl, don't he?"

"If you've got that figured out, you're a jump ahead of most men."

Right before noon Carty Toluca trotted into the storeroom in the back of the hardware. Todd glanced up from the stack of crates.

"Carty, I can't find any pick heads."

"Mr. Montgomery said we sold the last one this mornin'," Toluca reported. "That man is back."

"We've got to get that freight train in here from Sidney. There's nothing slower that an ox team, unless it's the wit of the bullwhackers." Fortune rolled up his sleeves. "What man?"

"Mr. Skunk. You know, the bummer tryin' to get credit."

"His name is Tidy. Can you believe that? Has he taken a bath?"

ONE

"No, sir." Carty Toluca led the way back into the store. "You want me to get the sheriff and Daddy Brazos?"

"I'll handle it. No reason to bother them."

"He's got an old pistol this time."

"Is he holding it in his right hand?"

"Eh, yeah, why?"

"He's got a bum wrist. If he pulls the trigger, the backfire will probably make his hand fall off."

Todd approached the man. An aisle of hinges and gate latches separated them. "Unless you have cash, you'll need to leave the store," he demanded.

"I ain't never been kicked out of no store twice."

"You have now."

"I got me a big gun!" He waved the revolver. They were still twenty feet apart.

Dub Montgomery signaled from the doorway. "I'll go get Daddy Brazos."

"Nope," Todd called back. "I'll take care of this." *Why do all my clerks think I can't get along without my father?*

"Just leave the store and I won't have you arrested."

"I ain't leavin' without money."

"You pull that trigger and you'll miss me, injure your wrist even worse than it is, and get thrown in jail for attempted murder. That's not what you want."

Perspiration dirt streaked down the man's flushed face. "Well, I cain't back up. I told 'em at the Piedmont that I wouldn't get shoved out again." He lifted the gun and pointed it at Todd.

"Did you know that Walker Colt has mud in the barrel?"

Tidy Dumont turned the barrel around and peered in. "Well, I'll be."

"Did you steal it? Or do you own it?"

"It's mine."

"I'll buy it from you for three cash dollars," Todd offered.

"It's worth five."

"I can get a brand new centerfire Colt revolver for seven. Why would anyone pay five for an outdated cap and ball?" Todd reached in his pocket and pulled out three silver dollars. He held them out. "You can hike back down to the badlands, buy a round for your

friends, and brag about how you made a good trade on an old worth-
less pistol. That's a whole lot better than hurting yourself or getting
arrested."

The man didn't lower his pistol, but Todd could tell by the man's
eyes the confrontation was over.

"Do I get my knife back?"

"Yep. Do you promise not to come in here unless you have a bath
and cash?"

"Yep, I guess I do."

Todd handed the coins over the shelves to the man and retrieved
the heavy pistol, barrel first. "Mr. Toluca, get this man his knife,
please."

When the big man ambled out of the store, Carty mumbled,
"That ain't the way Daddy Brazos would've done it."

Todd opened his mouth to reply, then shrugged. "Tell Mr.
Montgomery I've gone to lunch."

Rebekah Fortune tilted her head to the right and folded her arms
across her chest. "Do you mean after being threatened with knife and
gun on the same day you still won't even consider the offer?" she
seethed. Curls from her light brown bangs drooped across the corners
of her forehead like an inverted V. Her long hair was carefully pinned
and stacked neatly on the back of her head. Her thin lips drew tight
into a straight line.

Her brown eyes narrowed. They hid nothing.

Disappointment.

Frustration.

Boredom.

Todd Fortune had seen it all before.

Often.

Too often.

The black silk scarf ribbon tied around the high, white-lace collar of her blouse gave her a schoolteacher's scolding look. "Father
says one day Rapid City will be the most prominent city in all the
territory. Sure, there are only three hundred people there now, but
the railroad is coming. He says it's essential to open a bank there
now."

ONE

His stiff white, four-ply linen Garcia collar unfastened, his black tie hung loose, his suit coat neatly on the back of a chair, and his polished black boots by the door, Todd leaned back on the flower-print, cretonne-covered, hair-stuffed settee.

He closed his pale blue eyes and ran his fingers through his light- brown hair. In the background he could hear a familiar rumble, one that every seasoned citizen in Deadwood could sense and feel above the dull thunder of the stamp mills echoing down from Lead, four miles away. "I thought you hated the Black Hills because of the sparsity of population," he countered. "At least up here in Deadwood, Lead, and Central City we have six or seven thousand folks. This is home. I built this house with my own hands when no one lived on Forest Hill but Ol' Rocker Dan. This is where we belong."

"This is your home, Todd." Rebekah's voice softened. "Even with my father's furniture, it has never felt like mine. And now with him moving back to Chicago, I feel rather abandoned."

"It's that time of the month when everything looks bitter to you, Darlin'," he suggested, without glancing at what he knew would be an exasperated glare. "Give it more time." He listened to the reverberation on Main Street. In his mind he could see Handsome Harry Hansen holding the ribbons of a six-up team of nickel-plated harnessed white horses as they thundered up the dusty street through China Town, through the badlands district, past the Gem Theater, and roar up to the front of the Merchant's Hotel.

"More time?" Rebekah fumed as she strutted across the oval Turkish carpet. "We have been married four years. And, if you remember, I have felt like this most every day."

How could I ever forget it? Todd let his breath out slowly, trying to relax his face. He rubbed his thick mustache and goatee. "Perhaps we should go for a ride next Sunday. Get out of town. Find some fresh air," he suggested. Todd thought he heard Handsome Harry's "Yip-yip-yip-yip-yi-yi-yi-yi!" as he brought the northeast stage to a halt. *Handsome Harry. Big blue eyes. Thick drooping mustache. Rosy cheeks. Leather-tough skin. Deep booming voice. Hands as wide as a shovel.*

Rebekah stopped by the head of the settee. Todd squinted his eyes open just enough to a spot a glimmer of hope in his wife's eyes.

Rebekah Jacobson, you have captured my heart with those dancing eyes from the first day we met.

She stooped over and began rubbing his vest-covered shoulders. "Why don't we ride down to Rapid City? Just for fun. I want to look at it once more. Perhaps you're right. Maybe it will never amount to anything more than a hay camp. But I want to see it again."

"I'll take you, but I'm not going to move there. And I do not want to manage a bank," he asserted.

She bent over and placed her soft lips on his. "Thank you, Mr. Fortune."

"Junior," he added. "Folks seem to need to remind me that I'm not my father."

She stood up and stepped back. "You aren't Junior to me, Todd Fortune. Daddy Brazos has never been as captivating as his oldest son."

"You lean down here and kiss me that way again, and I'll definitely be captivating!" he chuckled.

"Do you want your pie now?"

"You know what I want now."

"Your grouchy old wife?"

"In that case, I'll have the pie."

"I thought so. Lunch hour is about over. 'Fortune and Son Hardware' will be missing its co-owner."

"They can get by without me."

"That's exactly what I've been saying!" she called back from the kitchen.

"But only for a few hours. You know that. Dad doesn't want a business to run and Dacee June is only sixteen." He could hear dishes rattle in the cupboard and didn't know if she had heard him.

He closed his eyes again. His thoughts slipped down the steep stairs to Wall Street and down to Main Street where the stagecoach would be sitting. *Fearless Handsome Harry. His white Stetson cocked to the side. Leather reins in one hand, swirling whip in the other. White horses prancing to catch their breath, and passengers doing the same.*

"Would you like me to warm it up?" she asked.

Todd tilted his head back to the kitchen's open doorway. "One look at sweet Rebekah's smile ought to melt the cheese, the apple pie, and the china plate."

"Oh, you are one smooth talker for a Texican," she laughed. "I'll warm it in the oven."

Todd laced his fingers and slid them behind his head. *She wants me to be a banker. I should have taken Mr. Lander's offer and become a Wells Fargo stagecoach driver. They must be the most fearless men in the territory. No fear of wild animals. Nor of outlaws. Nor of Indians. No worry of narrow, rutted roads.*

And no fear of a strong-willed wife with her mind made up. "In the shadow of thy wings will I make my refuge, until these calamities be overpast," he muttered as he sat up.

"What did you say?" Rebekah asked. She entered the parlor toting a slice of apple pie in one hand and a fork in the other.

"I was just mumbling a Bible verse I'm trying to memorize."

"I trust it wasn't about a nagging wife being like dripping water . . ." She handed him the pie.

"Aren't you going to have any?"

"No," she insisted. "I need to lose some weight."

Todd stared at her and shook his head. "You? You don't weigh a hundred pounds now."

"Dacee June and I stopped at the meat market today and weighed ourselves. I weigh 112 pounds. That's four pounds more than I did when we married."

"You worry about your weight too much."

"And you worry about our future too little."

"Our future is fairly well taken care of. We are partners in a successful business, own mining interests, and have one of the nicest homes on Forest Hill. What should I be worried about?"

"Me. Todd, I really do need to move," she reasserted. "I am tired of being cooped up in this house every day."

The pie tasted sweet in his mouth but hit his stomach like a lump. "Rebekah, tell me one advantage that Rapid City would have over Deadwood."

"I'll tell you two." She folded her arms again as she paced the long, narrow room. "Sunrises and sunsets."

"What?"

"There are no sunrises in Deadwood. We live in a hole in the ground. There is never a golden sunrise or a glowing sunset." She paused by the front window and glanced down at Main Street. "I

11

want to look out my window and see something besides Deadwood Gulch, pine trees, dirt, and the top of every building in the badlands." She leaned closer to the window. "And your sister running up the steps."

Todd stood and walked to the window, carrying his pie. "Is she going home, or coming here?"

"Here, apparently."

He set his pie down and began pulling on his boots. "They must need me at the store."

"She's carrying a revolver in her belt. I really don't know why Daddy Brazos doesn't insist that she be more ladylike."

"He figures she can't compete with the likes of you and Jamie Sue . . . so why not let her be herself."

"When she carries that revolver, she intimidates every teenage boy in town."

"When she carries that gun, she intimidates all the men in town. Maybe that's Daddy's point."

"Well, whatever the point, we have company."

Dacee June burst through the front door without knocking, her tall, black lace-up boots banging out a sense of urgency. "They tried to hold up the stage, and Handsome Harry's been shot!" Dacee gasped. She bent over at the waist to catch her breath.

Todd pulled his wool trouser leg over his boot and stood, fastening his starched white collar. "How's Harry?"

"He's not fumed, if that's what you mean," Dacee reported.

Todd buttoned his thin black tie and pulled on his suit coat. "Did they steal anything?"

"The treasure coach doesn't go out until next week." Dacee June was still gulping for air. "Besides, there isn't anyone who could stop Handsome Harry's stage."

Rebekah stood at the window and looked down toward Main Street, fifty feet lower than their front door. "I trust Harry will recover."

"Doc said he'd be okay. Harry worked the bullet out of his shoulder with his fingers as he drove into town!"

Rebekah's face instantly lost all color. "He what?"

"Sit down, Darlin'," Todd urged her. "I'll go check it out. Dacee June, you sit with Rebekah for a spell. She might need some smelling salts."

ONE

Rebekah plopped down on the settee and leaned over, putting her head between her knees.

"Did you see that freight train from Sidney pull up to the store?" Dacee June announced.

Todd peered down at Main Street but could only see what was revealed in front of Wall Street's narrow opening. "He finally made it?"

"Daddy thinks we ought to inventory everything as it's unloaded. You know how we had trouble with them last time."

"Yes, well, that is my job."

"I'll come down and help you as soon as Rebekah can sit up."

Her head still between her knees, Rebekah mumbled, "I'll be alright. You two go on and help Daddy Brazos."

"Daddy left with Sheriff Bullock and the others to go find the hold-up men."

Todd jammed on his broad-billed hat and scooted toward the open door. "They have a posse already?"

"Daddy got mad about them shootin' Handsome Harry, and figured the robbers ought to give account before Judge Bennett . . . or God Almighty."

"I'll go with them," he announced.

"They already left."

"I'll catch up. Where was the hold-up attempt?"

"The other side of Montana City," Dacee June reported. She pulled the revolver from her belt and waved it toward the east. "I'll bet it was out there where that mudslide was last spring. If I was a hold-up man, that's where I'd stop the stage."

Todd tugged the Colt single-action .45 from her hand. "I'll borrow this and go catch up with them."

"What about the freight wagon?"

"He can wait. We waited for two months for him to get here from Sidney . . . he can wait two hours to get unloaded."

"Todd, be careful," Rebekah called out as she cautiously sat up.

"With Daddy Brazos and gang already on their trail, the only ones that are going to get hurt are those would-be robbers."

Todd started down the steep steps that led to Wall Street. He called back to Dacee June standing on the wooden front porch by the open doorway. "How many were there?"

"Four, but there's only three left," Dacee June reported. "Handsome Harry said one was fool enough to stand out in the road and try to stop the stage."

"What happened?"

"Harry ran six white horses right over the top of the man. He said that he didn't think there was enough left of him to scrape up and bury. I sure wish I could go see that!"

Even twenty steps down, Todd could hear Rebekah's groan.

"Hey, Big Brother!" Dacee June called out. "Where did you say those smelling salts are?"

Todd Fortune rode northeast on Sherman Street to China Town, then along Whitewood Creek toward Elizabethtown. He kept the tall white horse at a canter. The stiff saddle leather slammed into his back side.

You been off the range too long, Todd Fortune. You're getting soft. I'm not a businessman. Especially not a banker. I'm a rancher. That's all I ever wanted to be. That's all Daddy ever wanted to be. But we're too successful to quit. That's the one good thing about failure; you always get to try something new.

When Todd arrived at the base of Splittail Gulch, he found a Mexican boy sitting cross-legged alongside the road on a rolled-up, green canvas tarp.

"Timateo, did Sheriff Bullock and Daddy Brazos come by here?"

"They just left, Fortuna-hijo."

Fortune Junior? Is that how I'm known? Thanks, Daddy. "Which direction did they go?"

The young boy waved his hand to the east. "Up the road, past the mudslide. Are you going to help them?"

"I thought I owed that much to Handsome Harry."

"I volunteered to help them, too," the boy reported. "But the sheriff wanted me to stay here with the dead bandit until they return."

"Where's the bandit?"

The boy pointed to the rolled-up tarp he was sitting on. "In here . . . most of him, anyway."

"Is there a shortcut I can take to catch up with them?"

"You could ride over the mountain."

ONE

"It looks kind of steep."

"Mi hermana can do it."

"How old is your sister?"

"Doce años."

"I'm a little older than twelve, but I'll give it a try. If they ride back this way without me, tell Fortuna Padre where I've gone."

A wide smile broke across the boy's face and he nodded.

The main road swung to the north, but Todd cut east through the brush and soon found himself at the base of a steep mountainside. The draws were thick with small pine trees. Most of the rest of the mountain was littered with yellow pine stumps and abandoned test holes of long gone zealous gold seekers.

Todd zig-zagged the white gelding up the loose soil and rock of the mountain. He leaned forward and slid back against the five-inch dished candle of the Texas saddle. The horse responded with each touch of the spurs by lunging on up the embankment.

I trust the west slope is not quite so severe. Must be gradual enough for a twelve-year-old. 'Course, he didn't say if she broke her neck or not. Anyway, it feels good to be riding the hills. Maybe Rebekah's right. Maybe it's time for a change. But not until Robert retires from the cavalry. He and Jamie Sue and little Frank can move to town and help Daddy and Dacee June with the store. Maybe then Rebekah and I will go to Texas and buy a ranch.

Todd reined up. "Take a breather, Boy . . ." *A ranch in Texas? Talk about isolated. She's a city girl, Lord. I knew that when I married her. I don't know if she will ever feel comfortable anywhere west of Chicago.*

He laid his large roweled spurs to the horse's flanks and started back up the mountain.

I reckon it doesn't matter. Especially when she throws those arms around me and holds me tight. Lord, I told you this before . . . but when you built Rebekah Jacobson Fortune, you did a fine job. A real fine job.

When he reached the crest of the mountain, he was surprised to find the west slope blanketed with ten- to twelve-foot pines and cottonwoods. The slope was not nearly as severe, but finding a trail through the limbs, downed trees, and six-foot sagebrush proved tedious. He surveyed the mountain ridge on the far side of the gulch and spotted a lightning-scarred pine with a blackened forked trunk.

"We'll aim for that old wishbone tree," he mumbled to the lathered pony. "The road is someplace between here and there." *I hope. I surely don't want to turn around and go back down that mountain.*

As he descended the mountain slope, the Dakota sun played peek-a-boo with the pines behind him, providing a little shade but not much relief from the heat. He paused by a thicket of cottonwoods, none much larger than a fence post. The water in the leather-clad canteen was lukewarm and stale-tasting. He swished his mouth out, then spat it out on the dry soil.

The white horse pinned his ears back.

Todd leaned forward and patted the horse's neck. "Sorry, Boy . . . didn't mean to . . ."

The horse pawed at the loose dirt and kept its ears pinned.

Todd stood in the stirrups. *What is it, Boy? Are we getting close to the road? Do you hear them coming? At least, you hear someone coming.*

Todd sat back down and pulled Dacee June's Colt revolver from his belt. He cocked the hammer back to the safety position. When he spurred the gelding this time, the horse took a slow, reluctant step.

You're mighty worried, Boy. Must be a bear . . . or a wolf. Talk about a wasted afternoon. I should have stayed at the store and got that shipment inventoried. Then I could have sat around tonight and listened to another of Daddy's "me and the boys done whupped 'em" stories. Lord, I have spent my life listening to those. The worst part is . . . . He spurred the horse around a line of short aspen as thick as a brush corral—*they're all true!*

The horse jerked his head back, and Todd found himself at the top of a sheer twenty-foot bluff staring straight down at the rutted trail of Boulder Creek Road.

He patted the horse's neck. *Well, I'm glad you didn't want to go barreling through the sage, but empty roads don't pin ears back. Is there someone down there?*

Todd surveyed the road for a mile in each direction and spotted no signs of movement. He was examining the embankment in front of him for a more likely descent when he observed dust rising up to the north.

Well, someone's barreling down the road. It's the chasers or the chased. Either way, I don't aim to be sitting up here like a moose in a meadow.

He turned the horse south and worked his way along the rim of the bluff, fighting his way through sage as tall as the horse. The rim of the gulch never dipped.

There was a flash of reflection from the boulders across the road. The horse pinned his ears back. Todd slid out of the saddle, pistol in hand, landing in a scrawny sage.

Someone's over there. Someone with a '66 Winchester glistening in the sun.

On the western slope where he stood, shadows from the mountain behind him wrapped him in a cloak of concealment, but the boulders on the far side of the road basked in direct sunlight. With the reins dropped straight from the horse's curb bit, Todd hunkered down on his haunches. He waddled forward to find a peek hole through the sage.

Somebody's waiting for someone. Either Daddy and the boys stationed a trap for the outlaws . . . or . . . the other way around.

Daddy's packing his .50-caliber Sharp's carbine, and it's so tarnished it couldn't reflect the glory of the Lord on judgment day. Sheriff Bullock still totes that iron frame Winchester. And the Jims? They don't like rimfires, so they wouldn't have a '66. Unless the posse expanded, it must be the stagecoach bandits in the boulders.

Of course, there's a possibility it's just a nervous hardware manager spying a broken beer bottle reflecting in the sun.

Todd strained his eyes across the road. For a moment the scene was as flat and still as a painted stage curtain. Then, between distant boulders he witnessed a black horse's tail swish into sight and then disappear.

Back and forth.

Hide-and-seek.

That-a-boy. Thanks for the signal. Lord, maybe there is some purpose for horseflies. Someone's cached in the rocks, but I still don't know who.

Hoofbeats rumbled and raced the cloud of dust down the road from the north.

If I spotted them, they surely could have observed me. Maybe not. They didn't shoot at me. 'Course, if they were waiting in ambush they couldn't shoot or they'd give away their position.

I've got to coyote around behind them and keep them from retreating down the road. But if I mount up, they'll spy me and open fire. 'Course, if they do that, the riders on the trail will be warned. But I'd like to be more than just bait.

Todd steered his long-legged horse through the brush to the south. He reached a grove of scrub pines that bordered the road south of the boulders, six feet above the roadway. He spied a saddled bay horse tied off at a tree but didn't see any others.

I surmise it's the posse plowing that dust. I surmise it's the stagecoach hold-up men in the boulders. I surmise I can cut off their retreat without getting myself shot. Lord, that surely is a lot of surmising. And it's about time to let the party begin.

The moment the galloping horses crested the rise in the road that led to the boulders, Todd fired a .45-caliber ball of lead into the tree trunk where the horse was tied. Splinters flew as the horse jerked free and bolted down the hillside.

The horsemen from the north reined. Several shots exploded in Todd's direction from gunmen cloaked in the boulders. He crouched in the safety of the trees and studied the horsemen up the road as they scrambled to safe positions. The first man off his horse wore a round, floppy black felt hat, a thick gray drooping mustache and chin almost as pointed as his long hawklike nose. An iron gray, bulky carbine was in his right hand.

Alright, Daddy Brazos, you're leading the posse. Now, let's pin these boys down without any of us getting hurt.

Todd emptied a couple more shots in the direction of the boulders. *I can't hit you back here, Boys, but I can keep the back door closed.*

Gunshots blasted from up the trail, and the outlaws in the boulders returned fire, ignoring Todd. He scooped several cartridges from his suit coat pocket and reloaded the cylinder as he waited for the gunman to flee up the trail.

Black powder explosions.

Puffs of gunsmoke.

Muffled shouts.

Whinnies of horses.

They won't come out of those boulders until they run out of bullets. You've got them pinned, Daddy Brazos, but you don't have them captured.

Sweat rolled down Todd's face and melted into the starch of his stiff shirt collar. His right wrist cramped as he trained the gunsights on the back of the boulders.

Then the gunshots stopped.

Someone shouted from the protection of the trees up the trail.

It was a familiar voice.

"Boys, toss out those guns and come walkin' out slow. I've got a stick of dynamite here, and I reckon I'll just toss it in those boulders if you don't come out real quick."

Todd allowed his revolver to slump in front of him. *Not the old dynamite trick, Daddy Brazos.*

"You ain't got no dynamite," someone from the rock screamed.

Todd yanked the revolver up and took aim at the boulders. *You're right about that, Mister. I presume you'll try to make your break this way.*

"Look out here. What do you see?" Todd heard his father shout.

More than likely they see a straight stick and a string. Daddy, that old bluff won't work again.

Two shots blasted from the rocks.

They aren't buyin' it, Daddy.

"You boys intend on being buried in the same grave, I take it. Won't be enough attached to tell which parts belongs to who. We'll jist pile you all up together in a common hole."

"You cain't bluff us!" a voice screamed, and a couple more shots were fired.

This time a deeper voice hollered back. "Boys, this is Sheriff Seth Bullock. I trust you know that it's Brazos Fortune holdin' the dynamite."

"Ol' Man Fortune?"

"It ain't Junior!" Bullock shouted.

"We thought the old man was dead!"

"You thought wrong, Boys," the sheriff yelled. "And I can't help you now."

An object flew through the air toward the huge boulders.

"Run fer it, Boys, he done tossed it!" the sheriff screamed.

Two men dove into the dirt of the roadway, throwing their guns out in front of them. Hands wrapped around their heads, they waited for an explosion.

Todd gazed up the trail. His father, Sheriff Bullock, and the Jims emerged from behind the trees.

The dark-headed, small unshaven man in the road sat up and screamed. "I told you he didn't have any dynamite!"

"Boys, Boys, Boys . . ." Brazos shouted as he approached with his Sharp's carbine. "You are just too gullible to be hold-up men."

The big, blond-headed man sat up and brushed off his shirt. "You're supposed to be a church-goin' man, Fortune. How come you was to lie to us like that?"

"Just to save your lives, Boys. With the Lord as my witness, I didn't want you to get yourself all shot up," Brazos said. "You don't want to go to prison wounded."

"We ain't goin' to prison at all," the dark-haired man sneered.

Todd stood and revealed his position.

Brazos showed no sign of surprise. "Glad to see you blocked the trail, Son," he shouted. "Where's that third one?"

"He's either in the rocks or dead. He didn't come this way," Todd hollered.

Brazos Fortune threw his .50-caliber carbine to his shoulder and pointed it straight at Todd.

Todd dove off the embankment head first. The dirt ground into his wool suit as the single-shot Sharp's roared. The five-hundred-grain lead bullet tore through his recently vacated position.

His face slapped into the dirt of the roadway, Todd heard a scream from the cliff behind him. He struggled to his feet, picking dry pine needles and pebbles out of his hands and hair.

"There's the third one," Brazos announced.

"You done killed Patrick!" the blond outlaw screamed. "I'll get even with you for that, Brazos Fortune!"

"There's plenty of room in Hades, if you're in a hurry to get there," Sheriff Bullock said. He and Yapper Jim snapped wrist irons on the two men sprawled in the roadway.

Todd Fortune glanced down at the nearly ruined suit. *The third one did sneak by. One more minute and he would have shot me in the back!*

Brazos and Quiet Jim sauntered toward Todd.

"I thought you was aimin' at your own boy," Quiet Jim mumbled.

"I knew he would drop when the gun was pointed. I taught them all that when they were young," Brazos said.

ONE

Todd brushed some of the dirt off his slightly ripped coat. "It would have been nice to know what was goin' on."

"Didn't have time," Brazos reported. "He had his gun drawn and was pointin' it at the back of your head."

"I don't know where he came from. I never saw him slip out of the boulders."

"Sage ain't all that good a cover."

"Well, it stopped two of them from retreating, and kept you from riding into a trap."

"That it did," Quiet Jim nodded. "And we're mighty grateful for that. How did you flank us?"

"I came straight over that mountain."

"Plumb over the top? On a horse?"

"Yes."

"What made you think to do that?" Quiet Jim pressed.

"A twelve-year-old girl."

Brazos threw his arm around Todd's shoulder. "You're a dirty mess, Boy."

"I didn't plan on diving down that bluff until you pointed that Sharp's at me."

"Rebekah will pitch a fit to see you that dirty and that new suit she bought you all tattered."

"I reckon she will."

"Who's watchin' the store?"

"What?" Todd said.

"Well, if you and me are gallivantin' around the countryside, who's takin' inventory on that bull-whacker's freight?"

"I figured it would wait. This was more important."

"This band of geezers could've taken care of this. You didn't need to come out here and get yourself tore up," Brazos insisted.

Todd grabbed up Dacee June's revolver. *No word of thanks. No congratulations. No acknowledgment. Just worried that I'm letting down on the job.*

"Well, I'm one dumb old geezer that's mighty glad you showed up," Quiet Jim added.

"This one up here is as dead as a buffalo chip in Kansas," Yapper Jim hollered.

"Let's load 'em up and get back to town, Boys," Sheriff Bullock called out. "I aim to finish that hand of whist."

"There ain't no way you are ever goin' to beat three Texans," Yapper Jim chided.

"It's sad to see how quickly old men lose their memory, ain't it?" the sheriff winked at Todd.

The laughter and upbraiding continued as Todd hiked back up the bluff to his waiting horse. Loose dirt trickled down between his skin and his long underwear as he pulled himself up into the saddle.

Brazos Fortune, did you ever think what could have happened if your oldest boy hadn't plunged off this bluff? The possibility never crossed your mind, did it?

Todd rode his horse slowly down to the road where the Jims tied the dead man to his horse.

He studied the posse.

You old men are a different breed. I can't even think the way you think. You smell danger five minutes before it happens. You make a lifetime of decisions in a split second of terror that would freeze most men. Then you put it all behind you with a joke. You go on back to living as if you haven't just teetered on the brink of eternity.

It takes me six months to think something through. You four never thought about anything for six months. Maybe Daddy's right. Maybe I should have stayed at the store. Maybe Rebekah's right. Maybe I am a hay camp banker.

I don't know what troubles me more . . . goin' to run a bank and finding out that I hate it . . . or going to run a bank and finding out that I don't.

That woman's right.

We do live in the shadows.

Not just the shadow of a shady gulch.

The shadow of Deadwood legends.

CHAPTER TWO

"You don't have that morning sickness, do you?" Dacee June blurted out as she strolled back into the parlor. She left the front door wide open.

Rebekah sat up, then slumped against the back of the sofa. She unfastened the top button of her Pride Muslin, double-ruffle, hidden-embroidery collar. "Heavens no. Why do you say that?"

"You seem to have an awfully weak stomach. Jamie Sue maintained that during the first few months that she carried little Frank, she got sick to her stomach a lot." Dacee June chewed on her fingernails as she talked. "And everyone knows how sick Columbia's been."

With thoughts of stagecoaches and strewn bodies still in her mind, Rebekah could feel her neck as well as her forehead perspire. "I'm not pregnant, if that's what you're asking."

Dacee June's sweeping, thick brown eyebrows sagged. "I guess I was, sort of."

"That's quite alright. We are sisters-in-law." Rebekah pulled a linen handkerchief from the sleeve of her blouse and dabbed her forehead.

Dacee June's voice was soft, almost sad. "I'm sorry I solicit such personal things. I suppose it's the kind of question I know I should ask my mother. Even though it's been eight years since she died, I still pine for her."

Rebekah stood and walked to the open door. Even though the drift was warm, it felt cooler than the stale air of the parlor. "I know what you mean. I miss my mother dearly as well. I regret I never met your mother. Todd speaks of her often."

Dacee June strolled up beside her. "You know what's scary? Some days I forget what she looked like. Does that ever happen to you?"

"Well, no, not really. I was much older than you when my mother died. So I have years and years of memories. Of course, she never gets older in my mind. At this rate, I'll be older than her in another dozen years."

"I don't know what I'd do if I ever lost this little locket. I don't want to ever forget her." Dacee June opened the small silver locket that hung around her neck on a thin silver chain, took a quick glance, then snapped it shut. "You would have liked her, Rebekah. Daddy says she was a lot like you."

Although ten years younger, Dacee June was several inches taller. Rebekah slipped her arm into her sister-in-law's. "Oh, how's that?"

"Daddy says you're both very beautiful and very stubborn." Rebekah flinched at the description. "He meant that in a good way. He says that's the only kind that Fortune men marry."

Rebekah relaxed and gave Dacee June's arm a squeeze. "If Daddy Brazos compares me to his Sarah Ruth, I am honored. I've never known a widower who still loved his wife as much as your father."

Dacee June rocked back on the heels of her tall riding boots. "Yeah, Daddy says love is something you choose, and he gets up every day still choosing to love her."

Rebekah gazed over the top of Deadwood at the pines on the far side of the gulch. "I suppose that's one way to put it."

"Did you ever choose to love someone before you met Todd?"

The cheesy grin of Adolphus Conners came to Rebekah's mind. "Don't you think that's a personal question? How about you, Dacee June? Did you ever choose to love someone?"

The sixteen-year-old dropped her arm and looked up with wide blue eyes. "Yes, but I broke myself of the habit."

"Oh? It wouldn't happen to be Mr. Carty Toluca, would it?"

TWO

Dacee June paced the covered front porch of the stylish house. "Heavens no! I choose to hate him every day. This was years ago. I was just a kid. Did I ever tell you about the time I rode the steamer up to Fort Pierre by myself in '75? Well, I really wasn't completely by myself at that time. The March sisters joined up with me in Kansas City. Anyway, I perched on a coil of big thick rope at the front of the boat with no one else around, and it was so cold my face was turning red. But I didn't want to go inside the cabin because I was afraid I'd miss Daddy standing along by the shore of the Missouri River. Well, this boy who worked on the boat came up and put his heavy wool coat around me and sort of hugged my shoulder. His arms were really, really strong. He looked in my eyes, and he had the softest blue eyes that made my heart start beating faster and faster and faster. I was really glad my face was already red."

Dacee June sucked in a deep gulp of air and rolled her eyes. "He said I could keep the coat until we got to Fort Pierre. He said I reminded him of a girlfriend he used to have. His voice was smooth as the river, and I got this tingly feeling way down deep at the bottom of my stomach. I thought for sure he was going to kiss me."

"Good heavens, what happened next?" Rebekah asked.

"The whistle blew," Dacee June shrugged.

"The what?"

"The steam whistle on the stern-wheeler blasted a signal and he said he had to go. And I knew at that very minute if he had kissed me and asked me to marry him, I would have said yes."

"Just how old were you?"

"Twelve," Dacee June said.

"And how old was he?"

"He said he was twenty, but I think he was about eighteen."

"Well, I'm glad you could control yourself."

"Control myself? I still wonder what would have happened if that ol' whistle didn't blow. I cried and cried that night and thought about him for at least a year after that. Every day I'd get up and say to myself, 'I am in love with Garreth.' "

"His name was Garreth?"

"I don't have any idea. But I just couldn't pine so over a boy with no name. I named him my dear, precious Garreth."

"Did you see him again?" Rebekah asked. "You know, to give him back his coat?"

"No, Mrs. Edwards . . . well, she was Mrs. Driver then . . . she insisted that his coat be returned immediately when I showed it to them. Mrs. Speaker took it back and said she had spoken to the captain and the young man would not pester me again."

"My goodness, I've never heard that story before," Rebekah chuckled.

"That's because I never, ever told it to anyone."

"Not even your father?"

"Especially not my father! I made the March sisters promise under penalty of death never to mention it. My father would have chased the boy down and shot him dead. He still thinks I'm a little girl. Look at this outfit he bought me. What other sixteen-year-old would wear a leather-fringed blouse, leather riding skirt, boots, and bandanna?"

"I thought it was your favorite outfit?"

"Some days it is. Some days I hate it."

"How about today?"

"Both. I loved the feel of it this morning when I put it on, but when I stand next to you, I hate it."

"Why is that?"

"Because you are so beautiful. And I'm so plain. When I'm around you or Jamie Sue, I just want to go hide."

"Dacee June, what are you talking about? You are a very handsome young lady. And you're the most well-known girl in all the Black Hills."

"They don't really know me," Dacee June insisted. "Nobody knows what's inside of me. They think they know me because of my father. 'Oh, aren't you Daddy Brazos's little girl?' I hear that every day of my life."

"That will change soon enough." Rebekah stepped over to the edge of the porch next to the railing. Both women gazed down the Wall Street opening to Main Street. "I bet there will be plenty of young men asking you to the balls, come winter."

Dacee June shoved her hand into the pocket of her leather skirt. "How much you want to bet?"

"That was a figure of speech," Rebekah said.

TWO

Dacee June glanced at Rebekah, then stood up straight and threw her shoulders back. "I bet Carty Toluca two bits that four freight teams would roll up Main Street before noon today."

"You shouldn't wager away your money."

"Yeah, but I won. And then that crummy Carty Toluca wouldn't pay off. If he asks me to one of the winter balls, I think I'll ask him for that quarter. Or maybe I'll punch him in the nose." Dacee June's voice softened and deepened. "Do you know why I really dress so out-landish sometimes?"

"Why is that?"

Dacee June's voice was barely audible. "To get people to turn their heads and notice me."

"It's that important?"

Dacee June's shoulders slumped, and she stared down at the porch railing. "I see the way people stare at you and Jamie Sue when you walk into a room."

"You're exaggerating."

"No, I'm not. The men stare at you like you were a gold bar in the bank window . . . and the women . . . they hold onto their men like they were about to drop over a cliff."

"That's ridiculous. Very few people even know that I'm in town," Rebekah insisted.

"That's because you hide up here at the house too much. You're the mystery woman on the Forest Hill porch."

Rebekah felt her shoulders stiffen. "I am not a recluse. Why, I was just downtown this morning."

"Are you going to the Raspberry Festival at the church on Friday night?"

"Of course I am."

"Oh, good. Todd said he didn't think you were going."

"I changed my mind," Rebekah said. *Just this minute.*

Dacee June slipped her arm into Rebekah's. "Forgive me for say-ing those things. I really do think I have the most wonderful and beautiful sisters-in-law in the world."

Rebekah hugged her. "Don't grow up too fast, Young Lady. You are a joy and a delight to have around."

"Are you feeling better, now?" Dacee June asked.

"Yes, thank you."

"Maybe I should go down to the store and tell them to wait to unload those freight wagons until after Todd and Daddy get back. Besides, I have more work to do. Todd's letting me assemble the new bolt bins."

"I'm sure Mr. Montgomery and the clerks would appreciate having one Fortune there."

"I know one clerk that won't appreciate it." Dacee June pointed at the house next door. "I think I'll go home and change my blouse. This one is too childish. You know what I mean?"

"I suppose it's warm also."

"Do you know what I'm going to do at 4:00 P.M.?"

Rebekah tried to suppress a grin. *This is one girl who enjoys life to the fullest!* "No, I can't imagine."

"Don't tell Daddy, but me and Irene Seltzmann are going down to China Town," Dacee June whispered.

"Good heavens, what for?"

"To take Mr. Gee his new washboards."

"You make deliveries to China Town?"

"I heard Mr. Gee say that he needed them quickly because Lola Paul and Franette brought a dozen of their dresses for him to clean. We thought if we happen to bring the washboards, he would let us see the dresses. They work at the Gem Theater, you know."

"So I've heard." Rebekah glanced across the flat roof of the Gem Theater before them. It was laid out like a barren cube.

"They aren't the main actresses, but they are almost the main actresses. I once saw one of Lola Paul's dresses. It had cattle brands and little roses embroidered all over it. It was red and had a full skirt and little basque, short sleeves, and everything! It was the most marvelous dress I ever saw in my life."

"It sounds quite unique."

Dacee June stepped closer and lowered her voice. "Do you want to come with us?"

"Eh, no . . . I think I'll rest here at home."

"You won't tell Daddy that I went to see the dresses, will you?"

"No, I won't tell him."

Dacee June strolled toward the top of the steps. "Rebekah, don't be mad at me, but I pray every night that you and Todd won't move away."

"You do?"

"With you here, it's like I have an older sister. It allows me to be just a kid. If you weren't here, I'd be the only Fortune woman, and I'd have to be grown up and respectable all the time, and wear boring clothes and funny hats. I'm glad I don't have to do that. Did you enjoy being sixteen?"

"I hated it."

"Did you have trouble with a boy?"

"Sort of," Rebekah admitted.

"Well, I like being sixteen."

"Good."

"Should I come back and check on you later?"

"Dacee June, you can check on me any time you want."

"Except when the shade to your bedroom is drawn."

"What?"

"Daddy says I can never come over and visit you and Todd when you have the shade drawn in your bedroom. And I won't, either. I'm not completely dumb, you know. Are you sure you don't want to go see the Gem girls' dresses?"

"I'm sure."

Rebekah watched Dacee June scurry across Williams Street and down all the Wall Street stairs.

She stared across to the far side of the gulch at Mount Moriah and the White Rocks on top. Scattered summer clouds blocked the sunlight and darkened Deadwood. *This is no place to raise children. It's like a human zoo. We're all caged in by these dreary hills. And every type of specimen is wandering up and down the street.*

Rebekah closed the door behind her and meandered back into the parlor. She slumped down into the worn Austrian bentwood rocker.

Father, you left all your furniture . . . and me! You moved us to a then-illegal settlement in the heart of Indian country . . . started a bank, married off your daughter . . . and went to Chicago to find a new wife. Look at me. What do I have to do today? Now I have to sew a dress to wear at the church's Raspberry Festival that I don't even want to attend. And what do I have to do tomorrow? Something equally tiresome.

Rebekah stood and waltzed across the room. "And Mrs. Fortune, what would you like to do?"

"Well, thank you for asking . . . I think I'll rent a hack and ride out on the north side by Lake Michigan . . . Perhaps I'll stop at Lincoln Park for a concert . . . then maybe meet Sylvia and Daphne at Mayberrie's across from the Water Tower and we'll discuss the latest English novel we're reading over flat salt crackers and Chinese tea."

"Those days are forever gone, Mrs. Fortune."

"Thank you for being so pessimistic."

"You're welcome."

She folded her arms and stared down at the rooftop of the Gem Theater. *At least the girls who work at the Gem have interesting diversions each day. The reviews say they have a very talented cast this summer. I trust that means their acting.*

Through the narrow glimpse of Main Street that the Wall Street portal offered, she spotted Mert Hart's hack trot by. *There you go, Rebekah dear. Just take a little jaunt on Mr. Hart's three-seater. Why you can ride up to Central City, over to Lead, and back again for less than a dollar. Of course, the round trip is only seven miles, and we'll halt sixteen times to pick up and let off other passengers.*

At Lead I can stop and listen to Mr. Hearst's mind-numbing stamp mill. Why, if I'm just going to complain, I might as well just stay home and sew.

She scooped up a well-worn mail-order catalog off the open desktop of the fall-front oak secretary. She scanned the pages as she wandered through the parlor.

All right, "Jordan, Marsh and Company, Boston, Mass." . . . just exactly what should I sew? "English mohairs and brilliantines will be very popular this season. For durability these goods are unexcelled. All the new and plain colors, gray and brown mixtures. Also brocades, stripes, checks, and fancy weaves."

That's what I want . . . a fancy weave brilliantine!

She tossed the catalog back onto the oak secretary.

"And here on Forest Hill, in Deadwood, Dakota Territory, used zephyr ginghams are making a handsome revival . . . and here we have the latest . . . green and white checks. Anyway, it will be good enough for the Raspberry Festival."

Raspberry! That's what I want . . . six yards of raspberry-colored silk lansdown . . . and six miles of black lace!

She snatched her sewing basket off the glass ball and claw feet parlor table, then instantly set it back down.

I am not going to sew. I'm going to read and wait for Todd to get back to town. He had no reason to dash off after the others. It's the sheriff's responsibility. We hire lawmen to take care of such problems. The rest should stay home. Especially those who were not even asked. They chase after robbers like a hero in a melodrama with fake fights and rubber knives. I did not marry a marshal, Todd Fortune. I do not want to spend my nights and days wondering about your safety. I want you to be right down there at the store, where I know where you are at every minute of the day, just like my mother knew where father was. At least . . . she thought she knew.

Rebekah towed the Austrian bentwood rocker out to the covered front porch, then returned to the house. The volume in her hand had a pressed violet bookmark.

A breeze skimmed down Whitewood Gulch and conveyed an aroma of dust, pine, and the mercury that was used to separate gold from dirt. Dry, but not hot, the wind drove Rebekah back inside for a glass of lemonade before she even sat down. The sun had now popped out from behind the clouds.

When she did finally relax in the chair, she unbuttoned the cuffs of her white blouse. *Do not worry, Mother, I will not expose the fleshy part of my arms, but at least I can loosen my sleeves.*

The book flipped open to the violet bookmark abandoned on a page next to a quote marked "so true" in pencil in the margin.

Mrs. Speaker, I am grateful for the lending library you run out of your home, but I wish you wouldn't write little notes in the borders of your books.

Well, Mr. Longfellow, just what enamored Mrs. Speaker?

Her eyes scanned the verse.

*"The holiest of all holidays are those
Kept by ourselves in silence and apart,
The secret anniversaries of the heart."*

Oh? And just what anniversaries of the heart did you have in mind, Mrs. Speaker?

Secret anniversaries of the heart sound delightful. Somehow these depressing Black Hills have drummed all the confidential jubilees out of me.

Sunlight reflected on a deep, jewel-tone, burgundy-colored dress on a woman far below who bustled out of the back door of the Gem Theater. Rebekah laid her book on her lap and watched. *There's my Raspberry Festival dress! I'll order the material from Paris and have one whipped up by Friday night!*

Rebekah plucked up her lemonade from the deck of the porch and sipped it as the woman in the radiant dress far below stared up at Forest Hill.

Are you gaping at me? Do you expect me to wave? I don't even know your name. Of course, I don't want to be rude, either.

Rebekah cautiously raised her hand to her shoulder and waved it back and forth twice, then let it drop in her lap. The black-haired woman dashed for the base of the Wall Street stairs up to Williams Street.

No, no . . . I didn't want anything. I was just trying to be civil. I hope she didn't think I was signaling her.

Rebekah crept over to the front of the porch and waited for the woman.

Long black hair pinned upon her head.

Rustling silk dress.

Considerable makeup.

Strong, attractive features.

Troubled eyes.

"Mrs. Fortune?" the woman called out as she reached Williams Street.

"Yes? I trust you didn't come clear up here because you thought I signaled you."

"Oh no, I understand. Rather awkward, I know. I hesitated coming up here. But I very much need to speak with you."

Rebekah brushed a wisp of hair from her eye. "Yes?"

"May we sit on your porch?"

"Yes, of course," Rebekah motioned. "Come on up. May I get you some lemonade?"

"That would be very nice."

When Rebekah Fortune returned from the kitchen with another glass of lemonade, the woman rested on a rough wooden bench next to the rocker.

"Would you rather sit in the rocker?" Rebekah offered.

TWO

"Really? You wouldn't mind? Just for a minute."

"Please help yourself."

The woman in the beautiful burgundy dress rocked back in the chair and closed her eyes. "It brings back some pleasant memories."

"You had a rocker as a child?"

The woman opened her eyes and surveyed the tops of the Main Street buildings. "It hasn't been that long," she murmured. She had a wide mouth and full, dark lips. "I've seen you up here lots of days and wondered what it would be like to sit on the throne."

Rebekah sat down on the bench, a lemonade in her hand. "On the throne?"

"Oh, some of the girls at the Gem see you as the queen of the gulch."

"Why on earth do they do that?"

"Because most of the time we only see you when you sit up here in Forest Hill. And when you walk downtown, you carry yourself like royalty, at least the way I imagine royalty would walk."

"I was unaware I walked differently."

"It's a compliment. Really."

Rebekah took a sip of very sweet, lukewarm lemonade. "I'm ashamed to admit I don't even know your name. Here you know all about me."

"I go by Abby O'Neill."

"I've seen the handbills! You're the star of the current show, aren't you?"

"At least one of them. Have you seen any of our productions?"

"Oh, no. I'm afraid I don't often go into the badlands. But I read a quite splendid review of it in the *Courier.*"

"Yes, well, I am a professional actress and singer. But that's all. The Gem has a reputation I'm not always proud of. I didn't know that when I contracted to perform here until September. I have nothing to do with what happens in the private boxes. Do you believe me?"

"Yes, I do."

Abby continued to rock and stare at the roofs along Main Street below them. "You have an incredible view up here. No wonder you like this house. You can see all of Deadwood from your porch, can't you?"

Rebekah stood up and gazed around. "Yes, but my one regret is that I can't see the front of our hardware store from here."

Miss Abby O'Neill took a sip of lemonade. "I suppose you'd like to sit up and keep an eye on your husband."

"That's not what I said," Rebekah stiffened, then shrugged. "But I guess that's what I meant."

"Don't worry about your Todd . . ."

My Todd . . . is that how he's known in the badlands?

". . . he's a treasure. All the girls think so."

"I trust they aren't prospecting."

"No, ma'am. Not for your Todd, anyway. He's the strong, serious type. Does he ever laugh and have a good time?"

Rebekah stared at the woman.

"Forgive me," the actress blurted out. "That was personal and uncalled for. I retract the question."

"Well, Miss Abby O'Neill, what can I do for you?"

"I have a desperate kind of favor to ask. Let me air it out before you turn me down. It's kind of complicated."

"I hope you don't need me to do something illegal or unbiblical," Rebekah said, a bit startled at the slight tease in her own voice.

Miss O'Neill's eyes tightened, then relaxed. "Oh, no . . . well, not illegal, anyway. I'm not a very good judge on what might be biblical. Here's the predicament. I have a daughter who's five years old . . ."

"Does she live here in town with you?"

Abby's eyes dropped to her lap. "Oh, no. At the moment, she lives with my mother in Omaha."

The well-dressed woman in the rocker no longer looked like an actress, but more like a worried mother. "I imagine you miss her," Rebekah probed.

"Yes, I do. I only contracted for the summer. It didn't seem right to move her out to the frontier. This is not exactly the kind of place to raise children, if you know what I mean."

Rebekah rested her hands on the wooden bench beside her. "I couldn't agree with you more."

"Oh, I don't mean up here on Forest Hill, Mrs. Fortune. This is a picturesque place to raise a family, I would imagine. You're up here away from the dust of the street, the shouts of drunks, and the unsavory elements."

TWO

"It can be a little cramped and confining," Rebekah added. *I suppose it all depends upon what you compare it to.* She reached over and patted Abby on the shoulder, "Now, what is this favor you need from me?" *Why did I do that? I don't even know this woman. This is the most relaxed conversation I've had with a stranger since moving to Dakota.*

"My mother and my daughter are coming out to visit me. They'll be here Thursday."

Rebekah leaned against the railing of the porch. "I imagine you're looking forward to that."

"Yes and no. I want to see my mother, and I certainly want to be with my little girl . . . but . . ."

"Do they know you work at the Gem?"

"They know I act and sing at a theater called the Gem. But they don't have any idea what goes on inside a theater like that. A theater in the East is not nearly as rough and . . ."

"Risqué?"

"Yes."

"And you'd like for them to never find out?"

"Exactly."

"That does present a problem."

"I've rented myself a nice room at the Merchant's Hotel. They'll stay with me there. We'll have a good time. They're only going to be here a few days."

"Well, it sounds like you have everything nicely arranged."

"All but one thing."

"Oh?" Rebekah questioned.

Abby stood and strolled to the edge of the porch, her back toward the house. Rebekah noticed they were both about the same height. "One thing I wanted to do was to rent a carriage and drive up to that French restaurant in Central City."

Rebekah nodded. "It's a very nice place to eat if you have several hours to finish a meal."

"Yes, but here's the real problem. Amber is only five, and it wouldn't be good to take her along. The only people I really know in Deadwood live and work at the theater, but that's not the type of place . . ."

A wide smile broke across Rebekah's face. "And you want me to recommend a baby-sitter?"

Abby swung around, her fingers laced together and pressed to her raspberry-colored lips. "It's even more impertinent than that. I wanted to ask you, personally, to baby-sit."

"Me?"

"I told you it was rather brazen. Could you, please? I'd pay you." Abby held her breath and pleaded with her eyes.

"Nonsense. I will not take pay. Yes, I'll baby-sit one evening for you."

A flood of relief broke across the woman's firm face, and she threw her arms around a reluctant Rebekah and hugged her. "I somehow knew I could count on a Fortune. Your whole family treats people square."

Abby stepped back and dropped her embrace. "Sorry about the hug. I'm kind of a demonstrative person."

"That's alright," Rebekah said. "Now, which night do I need to keep your daughter?"

"Friday."

"Oh, dear . . ."

"Is there something wrong?"

"Well, that's the night of the church Raspberry Festival and Auction."

Miss O'Neill bit her lip and clenched her fists. "Perhaps I could change and . . ."

"No . . . no . . ." Rebekah insisted, "that's quite alright. You don't mind if I take your daughter with us to the church social, do you?"

"Oh, heavens no! That would be wonderful. You really don't mind?"

"Of course not. Just let me know what time you need to drop her off."

"I'll leave word with Dacee June at the store," Miss O'Neill suggested.

"You know Dacee June?"

"I don't think there's a man, woman, or coyote in the Black Hills that doesn't know Miss Dacee June Fortune. And she certainly knows everyone. She knows when they arrive, when they depart, and who they saw while in town."

"I didn't realize she was that notorious."

TWO

"Most of the girls at the theater agree that if we could live our teenage years over, we'd all like to be Dacee June."

"She does seem to enjoy life . . ."

"Without sinning." Abby turned back to gaze across the gulch. "Having fun without sinning. That's not an easy combination to sustain, especially in Deadwood."

Rebekah fidgeted with her fingers. "I believe that's our challenge wherever we live. Some have trouble with one element more than the other, I believe."

"And that's where we're different, aren't we?" Abby laughed. "I have trouble not sinning . . . and you have trouble having fun."

Rebekah bit her lip. *I hardly know this woman and she's judging my life? I certainly know how to have fun!* She felt her shoulders slump. *At least, I think I remember.*

"I talk too much. It's the actress in me. I'm always trying to get in another line. I'm a little nervous and I ramble on when I'm nervous."

"You're nervous about your mother and daughter coming to visit you."

"Yes, and I've got one more favor to ask you. I write to my mother twice a week and tell her about things in Deadwood. Well, sometimes there isn't much I want to report on in my world, so I take some item out of the newspaper and tell her those things as if I had overheard it at the café. She has this idea that I know most of the folks up here on Forest Hill."

"There's nothing wrong with reporting the news."

Abby puffed out her cheeks and released her breath slowly. "Would you have lunch with me, my mother, and my daughter at the Grand Central Hotel? I'll pay of course, and could you, sort of, pretend that we're friends? I don't want to have to admit to them how lonely this kind of life really is."

"Only if you'll let me pay for my own meal," Rebekah insisted. *Lonely? This woman and I have a lot more in common than I ever imagined.*

"Why?"

"Because when friends go out to eat they usually pay for their own meal."

"Oh . . . yes! I don't know which is more audacious . . . my demands . . . or your generosity. You are a very gracious lady." Abby's green eyes bounced in such a way that the makeup-covered creases next to them seemed to melt. "When I first came to town, a girl named Sawnah told me that not all the fortunes of Deadwood were hidden in the ground. Now I know what she meant."

"This is a very small, isolated town. I believe we should all help each other out if we can."

"Yes, I know what you mean, and if there's anything I can ever do for you . . . ?"

"I can think of one thing," Rebekah replied.

"You can? What is it? I'll do it."

"It's just as presumptuous as your requests."

"Really? How delightful. That way I won't feel so guilty at my demands."

"You haven't heard the request."

"It's not illegal or unbiblical, is it?" Abby grinned.

Rebekah joined in the laughter. "We're beginning to sound like good friends. Abby, do you have a shawl or a wrap that goes with that beautiful dress?"

"Oh yes, and a hat, too."

"May I . . . may I borrow them for the Raspberry Festival at the church?"

The actress reached over and clutched both of Rebekah's hands. "Yes, of course! Would you like the golden-heeled slippers, too?"

"I think the dress, shawl, and hat will be wonderful."

"Oh, this is so grand . . . I'll just say, 'Mother, my friend, Mrs. Fortune, needs to borrow my dress.' That sounds like we're good friends, doesn't it?"

"Not if you call me Mrs. Fortune. You'll have to call me Rebekah. Shall I call you Abby?"

The actress wrinkled her nose. "Could you call me Abigail? Until I came to Deadwood, I was always called Abigail. My mother is not too fond of Abby. She says it reminds her of a convent."

"You'll be Abigail. I'll be Rebekah. What's your daughter's name?"

"Amber. She's a very bright girl. She can read and she's only five."

TWO

"Abigail, I think I need to ask you a personal question. If we are to be old friends, I need to know something about Amber's father."

The smile dropped from Abigail's face. "What do you need to know?"

"Is he alive? Where does he live? Those kinds of things."

"As far as I know, he's alive. I have no contact with him, but I imagine he still lives in Chattanooga."

"Were the two of you . . . ?"

"Married? Oh, yes. Dr. and Mrs. Philip Gordon Jr."

"Doctor?" Rebekah couldn't keep her hand from flying to cover her mouth. "Your husband was a doctor?"

"Rebekah Fortune, you do look shocked. He's a doctor. But he's not my husband anymore. He divorced me when I ran off with Amber."

"You ran off? Did he mistreat you?"

Abigail looked away. "This is getting personal, isn't it?"

"How good a friend do you want me to be?"

"He didn't hit me, if that's what you mean." This time she stared Rebekah in the eyes. "After the first few months, he just ignored me completely. In a big house full of servants I was consumed with lone-liness and boredom. I'm an actress. He knew that when he married me. He wouldn't even let me go to a theater."

"So you just left him?"

"I cried, begged, pleaded, prayed, and threatened to try to get him to change. He would call me immature, unreasonable. About a year after Amber was born, we left."

"There was no way to reconcile?"

"When he started bringing women into our home for 'consulta-tions' and locking the study door behind them, I decided we should leave."

"Have you seen him since?"

"No."

"Has Amber?"

"No. He doesn't even write to her or anything."

"What do you tell her about her father?"

"What can I tell her? If she asks, I lie. I say he is a kind man who has many important things to do, but we're not one of them."

"You'll have to tell her the truth someday."

"I know, and God help me when I do."

"He'll help you, Abigail."

"I know that. God has never run away from me, no matter how many times I've run away from Him."

"I do believe you and I can be friends."

"When do you want me to send up this dress?"

"Whenever it's convenient," Rebekah said.

"You might want to stitch it in a place or two," Abigail offered.

"Would you mind?"

"A good friend like you?" the actress grinned. "Of course not."

On some days the seventy-two stair steps from the end of Wall Street straight up the gulch to Williams Street seemed hardly a challenge at all to Todd Fortune.

This was not one of those days.

A sharp sting blazed up his right leg. It originated at his ankle and concluded with a knotted muscle in the back of his thigh. Each step began the cycle again, and by the time he reached the front door of his Forest Hill home, he was ready to collapse. The sun had long since dropped behind the hill. It was hot, but scattered clouds stacked up in the west and teased of a lightning storm. Kerosene lamps flickered up and down the gulch as he glanced back down the steps and caught his breath.

Rebekah's right about one thing. Rapid City is a lot flatter. I've almost forgotten what it would be like to walk home on level ground. 'Course, a ranch in Texas would be fairly flat, and I wouldn't have to do much walking.

Rebekah swung open the front door. "Are you going to just stand at my door, waiting like a teenage boy who doesn't have nerve to knock?"

"Evenin', Darlin'." Todd pulled off his hat and ran his fingers through his light-brown hair. "Guess I was catching my breath."

"My goodness!" she gasped. "What happened to you? Your coat is torn! You're covered with dirt! You didn't get run over by a stagecoach, did you?"

He jammed his boot heel into the black iron bootjack shaped like a giant beetle and pulled off one boot, then the other. "I took a tumble when we captured those stagecoach outlaws. Then I strained my leg when we unloaded those freight wagons."

Rebekah tried brushing off his coat sleeve with her hand. "Dacee June came up and provided a full report of the arrest. I understand Daddy Brazos shot one of the men."

"That he did." Todd followed his wife into the house.

"Todd, that's part of what I tried to explain at lunch. This is a dangerous place to live. You could have been hurt! What if you had been caught in the crossfire?"

"That was a real possibility," he recounted.

She walked into the kitchen. "How did you get so dirty? I'll try to brush your suit out and mend it, but it will never be the same. Just place it there in the pantry."

Todd hung the coat on a peg above a burlap sack of potatoes, pulled off his tie, then unfastened the top button on his soiled white shirt. *I don't think she'd understand that I had to dive off an embankment to avoid getting shot by my father.* "Well, we had them penned down, and as I went down to the road, I stumbled off an embankment."

"You had no business going out there. They could have taken care of it on their own, I'm sure."

Todd sighed. "I keep having people tell me that. They seem to insinuate that I'm not of much value other than running a store. The truth is, those old men would still be chasing the outlaws if I hadn't cut off their retreat."

Rebekah stared into his eyes, then finally spoke, her voice much softer. "I didn't mean to sound so crabby. I worry, that's all. An attempted stagecoach robbery is not worth getting yourself killed over." She hugged his shoulders, then reached up on tiptoes to kiss his cheek. He held her face in his rough hands and pressed his lips to hers.

"Well," she laughed after the kiss, "I'm glad to see you are making a speedy recovery. I hope you're hungry for onion soup."

"Sounds fine, as long as I don't have to hike up a hill to get it."

"Do you need some rubbing alcohol on that bum leg?" she asked.

"That would be nice."

"Perhaps we should eat first. While I finish up, tell me how it came about that Daddy Brazos had to shoot one of the men."

"They were shooting at us, and one of them snuck around behind. Daddy was the first to spot him."

"So a man gets killed for sneaking?"

"No, he was shot because he held a gun to one of our heads and was about to pull the trigger."

"I don't want to know anymore. I feel faint even thinking about it. Let's change the subject." She poured him a cup of coffee from a fluted, nickel-plated, long-necked coffeepot.

Todd flexed his shoulders to keep his back from cramping. "I heard you and Dacee June had quite a discussion." His large porcelain cup was decorated by a single navy blue border around the rim.

Rebekah carved the pan of cornbread into three-inch wedges. The steam from the cornbread warmed her fingers. "I believe that girl needs a mother to teach her a few things."

"You had one of those girl-to-girl talks?"

"It was more like a woman-to-woman talk."

"She used to talk a lot with Louise Driver, but since she and Mr. Edwards married, I think their conversations have ended."

"I don't suppose Mrs. Speaker is of much help?"

"Thelma keeps handing her books, but she is much too embarrassed to discuss things with Dacee June. I'm glad she has you to talk to," Todd added.

The kitchen was filled with the aroma of sweet onions and spices. She could hear the soup percolate. "Yes, but I'm not her mother. All I can do is tell her what I think I'd tell my own daughter. But that's not the same."

"By the way, how old is *your* daughter now?" he challenged.

"Todd Fortune, that is not funny," she snapped.

"No ma'am, I reckon it wasn't."

"We will have children someday, and you know it. But I will not raise a child where they can tumble off their front porch and end up fifty feet below on Main Street, or where a stagecoach might drive over the top of them, or they have to be a mountain goat to go see a sunset."

He unbuttoned the sleeves of his white shirt and rolled them up two turns. "I think you made your point at lunch."

"Are we going to ride down to Rapid City on Sunday?"

TWO

"Yes, Ma'am. Raspberry Festival on Friday, ride on Sunday. You have a busy week. That reminds me, Thelma Speaker stopped by the store and bought fifty steel washers."

"Washers?"

"You know, for bolts. They're about the size of a two-bit piece. Here's the funny thing. She said they were for the new dress she's making for the Raspberry Festival."

"For a dress? She's going to have steel washers on her dress?"

"Apparently. I told her you were going to spend the afternoon working on yours."

"Actually, I have mine done. I decided to borrow one." Rebekah scurried off to the bedroom.

Todd buttered a wedge of steaming hot cornbread. *I need to make a poultice out of this and apply it to the back of my leg. A camphor rag . . . I'll have Rebekah warm a camphor rag.*

She waltzed out of the back room carrying the silk dress on a thick, wooden hanger. "Isn't this the most absolutely beautiful, raspberry-colored dress you've ever seen?"

"It is beautiful. I presume that wrap is permanently attached to the shoulders?"

"Yes, it is," she nodded. *At least it will be by Friday night.*

"Who did you borrow it from?"

"Mrs. Abigail Gordon," she said.

"Mrs. Gordon? I don't believe I know them. What's her husband do?"

"He's a doctor, but it's a rather sad story. They're divorced."

"How long have you known her? I don't recall you mentioning her name. Where does she live? Is she new in town?"

"We just met. I commented on how lovely this dress would look at the church Raspberry Festival."

"You invited her, I trust?"

"She had a previous engagement but insisted I wear the dress."

"That was quite generous of her."

"Yes, that's what I thought."

"Sounds like you had quite a visit."

"Well, I did have her up for tea this afternoon."

"That's good. There are new people moving to town all the time. There might be others you'd enjoy getting to meet."

"I hope you don't mind, but I agreed to baby-sit for her five-year-old daughter."

"You'd better watch out, Mrs. Fortune. You start playing with little girls like that and you'll want one for your own," he chided.

"That thought did occur to me."

"When is she coming over?" he asked.

"Friday. I thought we'd take her to the festival with us."

"Being divorced and all, what does Mrs. Gordon do for income? I would imagine she's a seamstress, with a gown like that one."

"Actually, she's an actress and singer."

"Oh . . . the Opera House! She's with that new troupe from Philadelphia, no doubt. I hear their Gilbert and Sullivan is quite impressive. Let's invite Dad and Dacee June to go with us."

"I agree . . ." Rebekah tugged at her diamond earring, then laced her fingers in front of her. "Todd, Mrs. Gordon does not sing at the Opera House. She sings, and acts, at the Gem Theater."

His eyes locked on hers. "You're baby-sitting for one of the girls at the Gem?"

"What difference does that make? Are their children not worthy of good care?"

"That's not what I meant!" he fumed. "How did you say you met this woman?"

"I was outside on the porch reading, and she stopped by to visit."

"Stopped by? She had to hike up seventy-two stairs to get here. You're going to wear a theater dress to a church meeting?"

"You said it was a beautiful dress."

"Of course, it's beautiful . . . it's just . . ."

"Do you assume that all the girls at the Gem are immoral and unworthy of kindness?"

Todd pushed his soup bowl toward the middle of the table. "Which one is she?"

"Abby O'Neill."

"The star of the show?"

"So I understand. Her real name is Mrs. Gordon, and her former husband is a doctor in Chattanooga. She assured me, her only performances were on the stage, and she did not work the boxes at the Gem."

"But . . . but . . . when I encouraged you to get more involved in the community I didn't mean with . . ."

"I see. You want me to get involved with activities and people of your choosing only. While you, on the other hand, do business with any reprobate or sneakthief who has a dollar to spend, and see nothing wrong with trading shots with outlaws and stagecoach robbers." She stood up and marched toward the bedroom.

"Aren't you going to eat supper?" he called out.

"I'm not hungry."

"Come back in here and sit down."

She paused at the doorway. "Is that an order?"

Todd Fortune let out a deep sigh. "You're right. It sounded like an order. Please, come on back in here. I'm tired, I don't mean to sound so . . . so . . ."

"Contemptuous?" Rebekah finished. She returned to the kitchen and stood behind her chair.

"Sit down . . . please . . . let's have supper and try this again," he insisted.

She seated herself, but refused to pick up her spoon.

"Todd, it really is Deadwood. I love you dearly, and here I am getting angry with you. I don't even understand it myself."

"Listen, you can baby-sit for anyone you choose, and borrow any dress . . . providing it's not risqué . . ." A sly grin spread across his face. "Actually, you can borrow the risqué ones too, but you can't wear them out of the house."

"There are some dresses I would not even wear for my husband, Todd Fortune. I have no intention of shocking the heavenly hosts. But, I really do like Abigail. I need to find my own place in Deadwood, Todd. I know that's hard to understand, but maybe there are things for me to do that will be different than you."

"Actually, it's not that difficult to fathom."

"Really?"

"You are Rebekah Fortune, not Todd Fortune. And I am Todd Fortune, not Henry 'Brazos' Fortune."

Rebekah snatched up both soup bowls.

"What are you doing?" he asked.

"I'll reheat this soup. I like my French onion soup to be steaming." She poured the rich brown broth soup back into the pan on the woodstove.

"And what shall we do while we wait?"

"Let's keep it peaceful," she suggested.

"I agree, let's don't say anything at all."

"Oh?"

"Come here."

"And what do you have in mind, Todd Fortune?"

"You could sit on my lap and we could practice kissing."

"I've kissed you before, Mr. Fortune, and I can assure you, you don't need any practice."

"Come here!"

"Is that an order?"

"More like a beg from a needy man."

"Oh well, in that case," Rebekah grinned. "It is my Christian duty to help the needy."

Rebekah perched on his knees and wrapped her arm around his neck. As their lips touched, the back door banged open.

"Oh! I'm sorry," Dacee June blurted out. "I didn't . . . I mean, I didn't see the shades drawn or anything!"

Rebekah stood up and brushed her skirt down. "That's alright, Dacee June, we were just waiting for the soup to warm up."

"Is that what you call it?"

Rebekah pointed to the pan on the stove. "The French onion soup. I have some cornbread for you and Daddy Brazos."

"That's wonderful! I made some biscuits, but I think I used too much salt. They taste sort of like the water in Galveston Bay."

Rebekah divided the pan of cornbread in two, and placed half on a china plate with tiny violet flowers.

Dacee June grabbed the plate and scooted toward the still open back door. "Now you two can go back to . . . warming the soup."

"Thank you, Lil' Sis," Todd grinned.

Dacee June stopped at the doorway. "Don't you two ever do anything but kiss?"

"We argue and fight a lot," Todd said.

Dacee June whooped, "Oh, sure, and I'm a shy and bashful girl who likes to sit in the house all day and knit doilies."

CHAPTER THREE

Three men with graying hair under wide-brimmed felt hats and suits, slightly rumpled, sat around the black iron stove at the back of the hardware store when Todd Fortune unlocked the front door. The scene was a Deadwood tradition. Each of the men had their own keys to the store. Each held a tin coffee cup in his hand. And each tipped a hat in Todd's direction.

"Mornin', Son," Brazos called out from his perch on a wooden packing crate with an upside-down label marked: *Warsaw, Indiana, this side up*. "Did you hear about Carl McRoberts?"

Todd hung his narrow-brimmed, crisp brown hat on a peg and walked toward the men. "Which one is Carl?"

"He came here in November of '75, right after eighteen inches of snow. He and a short little Italian took claim on #23 below Discovery." Brazos rubbed his drooping gray mustache. "Remember? He was the one with only one thumb."

Quiet Jim scratched the back of his thin, long neck, then took a slow sip of steaming coffee. "He's missin' a whole lot more than a thumb now." There was no smile on his face.

Todd adopted a thick blue porcelain mug and approached the coffeepot. The steaming coal-black liquid reflected the lantern light as it bubbled into the mug. He took a sip and felt it singe the tip of his tongue. "What are we drinking today?"

"Your daddy calls it Panama Black." Yapper Jim swirled a mouthful, then gulped down the swallow. "But I've been to Panama and the only thing that is black is the swamp. It looks like India ink, but my, it does have eye-opening taste."

Brazos splashed his tin cup full. "Fer years now, I've tried to educate this bunch on coffees of the world, but what do I have to show? They cain't even tell the difference between this and boiled bark."

"Ever'one knows Brazos makes the best coffee in Dakota," Quiet Jim offered. "He thinks we show up for gossip and jollification, but it's the coffee that does it."

"It's a cinch you don't show up for gossip," Brazos asserted. "Why, there's no gossip around this stove. Nothin' but pure truth, right boys?"

Quiet Jim leaned forward and rested his elbows on his knees. The wool suit trousers couldn't hide the thinness of his legs. "That's a fact. We leave the gossip for the *Daily Times* and the *Pioneer*."

"Speakin' of which . . ." Yapper Jim strolled over to the coffeepot. "Did you boys read about the knifin' down at the Gem Theater?"

Todd took another swig of coffee. This time the heat of the swallow trickled a blazing trail down his throat and assaulted his tonsils. "Wait a minute . . . before you get into gossip about a knifing at the Gem, tell me the truth about one-thumbed Carl McRoberts."

"He's dead," Yapper Jim reported.

Quiet Jim strolled over to the coffeepot and poured out another dollop. "He was down below in the Esmeralda mine in Blacktail Gulch chargin' a hole. He must of figured the black powder was spoiled or damp, so he was drying it off between his finger when some of it flipped up on his candle. Set off quite an explosion."

"Yep. They said he might of come out of it only losin' his hearin' and an arm if it weren't fer them steel drilling bits flyin' through the air like Goliath's spear," Yapper Jim added. "Lived long enough to say his prayers, though. Hate to lose any of the boys of '75."

Quiet Jim turned his head and wiped an eye. "Ain't many of us left."

"Most of 'em dead or gone," Brazos added. "Don't blame some for leavin'. Ever' gulch in the Black Hills is swarming with miners."

"Most of 'em ain't got an idea in the world what they're doin'," Yapper Jim offered.

"Which is a whole lot like us when we snuck into the hills in '75." Brazos gazed across the room . . . and the years. "Remember that riffle box we built along French Creek that first day? The whole thing washed four miles below by morning!"

"We didn't do that," Yapper protested. "That was you, Grass, Big River, and them."

"We did some dumb things," Quiet Jim admitted, "like that one time we . . ."

"Wait a minute," Todd protested. "I'm still worried about McRoberts. Did he have a family here in town?"

"Not in Dakota. But I know he had a daughter down in New Mexico somewhere." Quiet Jim stared at his coffee as if gazing into the past. "Years ago, when we was all down near Custer City, I wrote letters to her for him. I believe her name was Cynthia. That's a mighty purdy name, ain't it?"

The men at the iron potbellied woodstove all nodded.

Todd tugged on his shirt collar as the coffee flushed his face. "Getting blown up is a mighty rough way to go."

"You think that's tough?" Yapper Jim leaned back, bracing his arms against the rough wooden bench. "How about when that hundred-ton block of rock fell on that miner at Terraville? By the time they got it moved, they couldn't even identify the victim. Two different women claimed it was her husband that was crushed. The mine settled with both of them, even though only one man died. The other jist disappeared. Never showed up. I reckon he's running around like a soul set free."

"I never did like bein' underground," Quiet Jim added. "If I can't wash it in a pan, a tom, a rocker, or a sluice, I ain't interested."

"Ownin' shares is a lot safer than diggin' it out, that's for sure," Yapper Jim added.

All four twisted around to gaze at the glass and oak front door when a young woman sauntered into the store.

"Whee—ee, Miss Dacee June, don't you look beautiful?" Yapper Jim called out. "If I was twenty years younger I'd ask you to marry me today."

"If you were twenty years younger, you'd still be twenty years too old, Uncle Yapper," Dacee June chided. Her long brown hair was partially contained under her hat.

"That's a fact," Yapper Jim mumbled. "But it's a mighty fancy dress."

"Oh, this attire?" She waltzed up to the stove and did a slow pirouette. "It's just a silk lace, with surah lining, profusely trimmed with ribbon and a four-inch black lace gimp."

"Is this the same lil' sis that was packing a pistol and wearing leathers yesterday?" Todd teased.

"You must have confused me with some other sister of yours," Dacee June glowered.

"I only have one sis . . . eh, this side of heaven." Todd refused to glance over at his father. *No, Daddy, I have not forgotten Veronica and Patricia, bless their souls.*

"I just felt more mature today," Dacee June explained. "I will be seventeen in the fall."

"Well, you certainly look more mature," Quiet Jim added. "You'll have to pack more than one pistol today."

Dacee June fiddled with the emerald-colored paste earrings that brushed against her cheeks. "However, I certainly enjoy the discerning eyes of older men." She stood next to Quiet Jim and rested her hand on the shoulder of his brown leather vest. "How's Columbia?"

Quiet Jim's voice almost became assertive. "Little Sarah kept her up all night with a fever. I hope they're both sleepin' now. She needs to be strong. Doc says that new baby could be along any week now."

Yapper Jim rubbed coffee drops from fleshy lips that hid behind his full beard. "I keep tellin' him his quiver's about full. You know, for a man of his advanced years."

"We want one more after this," Quiet Jim added. "Five is a nice number, don't you think?"

Dacee June strolled by her brother, allowing her elbow to poke him in the ribs. "Yes, I think it's a nice size family. What do you think, Todd?"

He turned his back toward the woodstove, coffee mug in hand. "I think I'm going to get to running a store while you parade around town looking like some Paris fashion model."

THREE

Dacee June put her right hand behind her head and strutted a lap around the stove. Then she traipsed after Todd, catching up with him halfway across the store. "When is Carty coming to work?"

"I told him to wait until ten. He worked late helping me inventory that new freight." Todd continued toward the wide empty wooden counter at the back. "Why do you want to know?"

Dacee June propped a boot up on a nail keg and rubbed her ankle. "Because these shoes are grieving my feet something horrible. But I don't want to change them until he sees me."

Todd stooped and yanked a ledger from under the counter. "So, you dressed up in order to impress Carty?" He dipped his pen in the vile of black India ink, then wrote in the ledger without looking up.

"I am not interested in Carty Toluca! There's a young man working at the International Hotel who has a quite fetching smile. Perhaps I dressed this way for him. But I wouldn't mind making Carty regret all those mean things he did to me." Dacee June glanced down at the ceramic mug on the counter. "Do you need a refill?"

"Might as well, my tongue's calloused now."

Dacee June carried Todd's mug over to the stove as the conversations continued.

"Hey, what do you hear from 'Professor' Edwards?" Yapper Jim was asking.

"He wrote to say the *Ambrosia trifida* was abundant this year," Brazos answered.

"The what?" Dacee June queried.

"Ragweed. Said they'd be home . . ."

Todd squatted down and spun the dial on the safe. *Dad has his pals. Every morning of the year they are here . . . to laugh, tease, plot, plan, dream, and reminisce. Maybe that's what's missing in Deadwood for me. I'm not one of the old-timers. I'm not one of the newcomers. I'm somewhere in the cracks in between. I'm always in the corner of the room, watching the action.*

Maybe Rebekah's right. A new town. A new start. Where we'll be the old-timers some day.

Dacee June found Todd in the back storeroom. White shirtsleeves rolled up to his elbows, gray wool vest unbuttoned, and black tie loosened, Todd Fortune finished cutting the last of twenty-four eight-by-ten-inch replacement glass panes for the International Hotel.

"I don't suppose you'd consider firing Carty Toluca," Dacee June quizzed, resting her hands on the ruffled folds of her dress waist.

Todd rubbed his light brown goatee. "Did he steal money from the cashbox?"

"No, of course not," she frowned.

"Did he cheat a customer?"

"No." Her scowl almost brought her dark brown eyebrows together above her nose.

"Did he talk back to Dub Montgomery?"

"No."

"Well, I reckon I'll just keep him on." Todd grinned as he began to crate the small pieces of glass. "He didn't pull your hair or slip a chink of ice down your dress, did he?"

"He hasn't done those things for years!"

"Well, what did he do?"

"Nothing. Absolutely nothing!"

Todd layered each slice of glass with a piece of heavy brown paper. "You want him fired for doing nothing?"

"Oh, I don't really want him fired. I just wish he'd find a job some other place. He aggravates me every time I come into the store."

"Aggravates you? I thought you said he did nothing."

"And he said nothing. Not one word. Look at me, Todd Fortune. Am I ugly? I mean, I know I'm not beautiful like your Rebekah or Robert's Jamie Sue, but I'm not ugly, am I?"

"Dacee June, don't beg for compliments. You know that I think you're the cutest girl in the Black Hills."

"Perhaps he has poor eyesight," she blurted out. "Do you think there's anything wrong with his eyes?"

"I take it he didn't say anything about your dress?"

"Not my dress, my hair style, my shoes, my perfume, my lip rouge . . . he said absolutely nothing."

"Some boys are embarrassed by beautiful girls."

"They are?"

"Sure. The prettier the girl, the more nervous they get trying to talk to her. The extremely attractive are so striking, some fellas just get tongue-tied."

THREE

Dacee June's eyes widened. "I bet that's it. He's used to my, well, my average daily beauty, but when I'm polished up like this, he's speechless."

"Could be."

"Thanks, Todd. It sure is good to have at least one brother around." Dacee June seemed to float toward the storeroom door, then turned back. "It's going to be fun next week, staying with you and Rebekah. She promised to teach me to . . ."

Todd straightened up. "Staying with us?"

"She's going to teach me to draw people and animals. She sure is good at drawing. Yes, isn't it fun? I get to stay for at least two weeks. Of course, I only live next door, and I'll go home and sleep in my own bed, but I get to eat with you two."

Todd tacked a wooden lid on the crate of glass panes. "I think I missed something. Why are you staying with us? Where's Daddy going to be?"

"Oh, you know . . ." Dacee June squinted at a cloudy mirror fastened to a post next to the workbench. "He's going on that hunting trip with the Jims."

Todd laid down the tack hammer. "What hunting trip?"

"Over in the Bighorns." She stood on her tiptoes and sucked in her stomach.

"The Bighorns? That's a hundred-and-eighty miles. When did they decide on that?"

"This morning. Didn't Daddy tell you?" Dacee June threw her shoulders back and her chest forward as she continued to look in the mirror.

"It must have slipped his mind," Todd mumbled. "When are they leaving?"

Dacee June made a face at the image in the mirror. "After lunch."

"Today?" Todd rolled down his sleeves and refastened them. "Did he talk to Rebekah about you staying with us?"

"No, but I did. Daddy said I could go with them, but I think he needs to get along without me once in a while. After all, one of these days he'll be on his own, you know, when I have my own family to tend to, and then . . ."

"You going to have that family soon?" Todd chided.

"No, not soon!" she snapped. "Frankly, I think those old men just want an excuse to check out the gold discovery over in Devil's Canyon."

"That's Crow land. No one's allowed to prospect in there," Todd cautioned.

"That didn't keep them out of the Black Hills, either. They said it sounded like the early days of Deadwood. But they don't intend to prospect. They just want to hunt and look around."

"Where's Daddy now?"

"He went to the livery to rent a pack string."

"Is he coming back to the store?"

"I don't think so. I think he's just going to gather his gear and leave. I already told him good-bye."

Todd pulled out his pocket watch. "It's almost noon. Think I'll take a break and find him. Would you have Carty pack this crate of glass over to the International?"

"I could take it."

"It's too heavy."

"I could go over to the International and have one of their clerks come pick it up."

"The one with the fetching smile?"

"Oh!" she beamed. "I never thought of that!"

"Have Carty do it."

"Perhaps you could write down your instructions for him."

"Why?"

"Because I have no intention of talking to him until he gives me a compliment about how I look."

"Does he know that?"

Nebraska Livery stretched along Whitewood Creek, between Sherman Street and the east side of the gulch. Brazos Fortune reclined on the split rail corral fence when Todd ambled up and rested his elbows on the top rail. "There's a rumor flying around Deadwood that you're pulling up stakes and drifting west."

Brazos's eyes were aimed at the animals in the corral, but his gaze seemed to drift across some memories. "Figured I was due for a huntin' trip with the boys."

Todd stared down at the corral dirt. "Who are you talking to? Is there anyone within shouting distance that believes that line? You aren't tracking a couple hundred miles just to go hunting."

"Them Bighorn Mountains is full of game."

"What do you intend to hunt with a gold pan, shovel, pick, and a jar of mercury?" Todd challenged.

"Yapper Jim thought we ought to pack those along. But I'm not a prospector, you know that." Brazos shot a quick glare at Todd, then returned to his scrutiny of the animals. "Never have been."

"You claim you aren't a businessman, either. But you own a few buildings and a store."

"You can run the store without me a few days. Shoot, you can run the whole thing without me for a year. Ever'one knows you're the businessman of the family."

Todd noticed his father was wearing his revolver under his suit coat. "It just seems strange for you to make plans about leaving without checking with me first."

"I'm checking with you now. Do I have your permission to leave town for a couple weeks, Son?"

"You don't need my permission."

"Then what's this conversation about?"

"Dad, look . . . I'd just like to know what your plans are ahead of time, so I can make arrangements."

"Shoot, Son . . . I don't even know what my plans are ahead of time. That's the joy of havin' you here in Deadwood with me. It's mighty comfortin' to have a partner in the store and know I don't even have to show up. Say, can lil' sis board up with you and Rebekah? She doesn't want to travel with me like she did when she was young."

"We'll take care of Dacee June."

"I knew I could count on you," Brazos nodded. "Think I'll take these two brown jacks." He pointed out at the corral. "What do you think?"

"Depends on whether you plan on carrying meat or gold dust."

"I told you I'm not interested in startin' back into prospectin', if that's what you aimin' at."

"Come on, Dad, you and the boys are getting restless. I can hear it in your conversations every morning. It's crowded, almost civilized in Deadwood. Movin' on is in your blood. You know that."

Brazos pointed up toward White Rocks. "No more. Beneath that Dakota Cross . . . this is home. I've got friends up on Mount Moriah. More and more ever' year. This is where I dropped anchor, and this is where I'll stay. I'm not movin'. Not to the Bighorns. Not back to Texas. Not up to western Montana, though the Lord knows it's a wonderful country up there. But jist because a man don't dance is no reason he can't enjoy the music. I'm goin' out there to listen to a new tune. That's all." Brazos's eyes sparkled.

"Well, take care of yourself, Old Man. You've got a daughter you're not through raising and a prodigal that still needs to come home."

Brazos's shoulders slumped. He suddenly looked ten years older. "You and Rebekah haven't heard from Samuel, have you?"

"Not since Christmas. I wouldn't hold that back."

"I know, Son . . . I know." Brazos rubbed both corners of his eyes with the same hand. "He'll be back. I know he will."

"And you'd better be here waiting for him," Todd insisted.

Brazos climbed down off the corral fence. "Two weeks. We'll be back in two weeks."

"Who's going with you? Dacee June said the Jims might tag along, although I can't imagine you running off with Grass Edwards out of town."

"I'd like to have Grass, but he's tied up a lecturin'. But, it's boiled down to just me and Yapper Jim. Quiet Jim . . . well, he's got to help Columbia with the children, her bein' infirm and all."

"You leavin' this afternoon?"

"As soon as we get gathered up, I reckon," Brazos said.

"You going to say good-bye to Mrs. Speaker?"

"Why don't you tell her for me."

"Daddy . . . she's looked after us . . . including you . . . since she got to the hills. Stop and tell her good-bye. As you would say, it will satisfy her bones."

"You're right." Brazos punched his hat back with the thumb of his right hand. "Thelma's a fine lady. She'd be an even finer lady if her husband wouldn't have died."

THREE

In his office on the second floor of Fortune & Son Hardware, Todd closed the ledger. In front of him were two pages of concise, neatly written inventory to be ordered. The afternoon sun reflected through the window and revealed tiny dust particles that seemed permanently imbedded in the stuffy air. He walked over and opened a window facing Main Street. To the northeast he spied the double freight wagons of an ox team plodding up the street.

I hope it's not one of ours. That's not true. We need the inventory. It's just . . . I'm tired. I want to go home, kick off my boots, and relax. Just me and Rebekah . . . and Dacee June!

Lord, I'm almost thirty. I've got a fine wife. A business to run. Good standing in the community. When Dad's around, I whine to You about standing in his shadow. Then as soon as he leaves, I miss him. It's easier to take the center stage when I know he's in the wings. I should be over that by now.

Could I even run a business by myself?

Or a bank.

If your daddy dies young, you surely find what you're made of a lot sooner. But then, you miss all those great years together. Robert's made his mark in the cavalry. None of the boys in blue, down on the border with General Crook, call him Brazos Fortune's baby boy. And Sam . . . well . . . along that owlhoot trail in the Indian Territory, it's a cinch they don't know about his daddy.

That leaves the oldest boy, the one who is supposed to follow the old man's footsteps.

He watched the stagecoach rumble in from Cheyenne. The stage stopped at the Merchant's Hotel owned by Professor and Mrs. Grass Edwards. The cloud of dust it generated scurried down the street. Three men rode up top with the driver. At least eight passengers climbed out of the coach.

I think I'd be a whole lot more content if Rebekah was satisfied. She misses her daddy. She misses her Chicago. She misses her friends.

Get to work, Fortune. Melancholy doesn't become you. Your mother, bless her soul, told you that.

He rebuttoned his sleeves, straightened his tie, and slipped on his jacket before he descended the stairs at the back of the store. The assistant store manager, Dub Montgomery, met him at the counter, twisting his rakishly curled waxed mustache.

"The man with the bowler is looking for you." Montgomery, as tall as Todd, but weaker in the shoulders, pointed toward a man near the front door.

Todd glanced across the room at the gray haired man with hat in hand, the suit layered with a tinge of red road dust. "Is he a drummer?"

"Didn't say," Montgomery added, finally releasing his mustache. "I've never seen him before, but if he's got boiler plating we'll take every section he can ship."

Todd surveyed the busy store. "It's getting desperate for plating, isn't it?"

"The DeSmet and the Evergreen Mines will shut down if they don't get their steam engines repaired soon," Dub announced.

"I'll go talk to him."

The man was about four inches shorter than Todd and looked as old as his father. His bushy sideburns seemed to get wider and wider until they reached his chin . . . which was clean shaven. His hair reflected an equal mixture of black, gray, and red.

"Are you Mr. Fortune?" he asked.

"I'm Todd Fortune, the son in 'Fortune & Son'."

"I'd like to speak with your father, please."

"He's gone. What can I do for you?"

"Probably nothing until your father returns." He pulled a tiny ledger from his vest pocket and studied one of the pages. "May I set up an appointment with him for tomorrow?"

Todd could smell the man's shaving tonic. "He won't be around for a couple weeks . . . or more."

"No! What a disappointment! I came all the way from Cleveland and he's gone for that long. Is it possible to telegraph him someplace?"

"He's on a . . . eh, hunting trip to the Bighorn Mountains of Wyoming. I run the store. Perhaps I might be able to help you."

"Well, it's certainly store business. But I have to talk to the owner."

"I'm a co-owner. Are you a drummer? What's your product line?"

"I hardly look like a salesman. My name is Tobias Olene."

"Olene Steel and Assembly of Cleveland, Cincinnati, and St. Louis?" Todd asked.

"Yes, that's us."

"We really need all the boiler plating you can ship in here. We can pay extra shipping if you'll send it up the river to Fort Pierre, then down by mule train rather than ox. We need quarter-inch, three-eighths, and half-inch, plus . . ."

"Wait, wait, wait . . ." The man waved his hands. "I told you I'm not a salesman. I don't take orders from customers."

"Well, what do you want?"

The man rocked back on the heels of his polished brown boots. "I want to make you an offer on buying the store."

Todd tilted his head to the right and stared deep into the man's brown eyes. "Buy the hardware?"

"We are interested in owning a retail outlet in the Black Hills, and a friend I know in Chicago suggested I check into Fortune and Son."

"Who's your friend in Chicago?"

"DeWitt Jacobson."

"He's my father-in-law," Todd said.

"Yes, and how is Rebekah?"

"You know my wife?"

"We've met on several occasions, but that was a few years ago."

"She's fine, thank you. Mr. Olene, I'm sorry you traveled all this way to look into buying our store. It's just not for sale."

"But you haven't heard my offer."

"It doesn't matter."

"Of course it does. There is one thing I know for sure." Olene rubbed his sideburns. "Every business is for sale if the price is right."

"Well, you just met the exception to the rule," Todd insisted.

"If I remember right, Mr. Jacobson said you and Rebekah would be moving to Rapid City soon, and . . ."

Todd's shirt collar suddenly seemed extremely tight. "If Mr. Jacobson said that, he was wrong. We aren't moving."

"Well . . . perhaps I did come out here foolishly," Olene snapped.

"Perhaps you did." Todd felt like shouting, but worked to keep his voice muted. "You should have written us ahead of time and we could have saved you the effort."

"If you're not interested, I understand there are a couple of other hardware stores in the area. I'll be checking to see which would make the best buy. I aim to pay top dollar. Of course, I could always just build a store of my own, but I'd rather have good community relations by purchasing the good name of an existing store. When we eliminate the wholesalers, we'll be able to sell for much less. I thought, perhaps, this would be a good time for you to sell. You know, before our competition drives all the other stores out of business. It was strictly out of friendship with DeWitt Jacobson that I came to you first."

"Mr. Olene, up until this moment, I've been partial to your company's products. But you seem intent to browbeat me, trying to pressure me into doing something I do not want to do."

Olene jammed his hat back on his head. "Well, I've never heard of a businessman who refused to even hear what the offer is."

"You have now," Todd replied.

"Perhaps I should wait until your father comes back."

"That's your prerogative. You are not going to wait in the doorway to my store."

"Well, Deadwood's a fine town!" Olene sneered. "I've been here five minutes and already been rudely treated."

"Mr. Olene, I apologize for the rudeness, but we're not interested in selling the store. Your tactics probably fit the East better than the frontier. If you do not have a place to stay, I would recommend the Merchant's Hotel across the street. Good day, sir."

Todd Fortune left the man standing in the doorway. With a fifty-pound keg of sixteen penny nails on his shoulder, Dub Montgomery scooted up beside him. "What'd that old boy want?"

"Wanted to buy the store."

"No foolin'? What did you tell him?"

"No."

"You're right about that. You couldn't sell," Dub banged the nail keg to the floor. "It wouldn't be Deadwood without Fortune and Son."

When Dacee June buzzed into the store right before quitting time, she wore a completely different outfit. A long black denim skirt hung to the floor, and a long-sleeve white lacy blouse was buttoned right under the chin. She strolled quickly past several male customers and right up to Todd. "Rebekah wants to know if you'll be home for dinner by six."

"You changin' clothes ever' hour?" Todd pressed.

"You did not answer my question," she huffed.

"Yes, I'll be home on time tonight. There's no freight train, no stage robbery . . . and no long-winded stories around the stove."

"Pretty boring day, huh?" she laughed.

"Well, I did have one interesting visit. I'll tell you over supper." Dacee June pushed her face into his. "What was that?"

"Let's save it for tonight, then I will only have to tell it once."

She didn't back away. "Did someone get killed? Is it someone we know? Did they strike a new vein of ore? Are they going to build a railroad to Deadwood? Did Columbia have her baby? Is there some cute new boy in town? Did he ask about me?"

Todd laughed and shook his head. "You're wrong on all accounts. Now, what about my question? Why the change of clothes?"

"A woman has the prerogative to change clothes as often as she deems necessary," she lectured.

"You didn't learn that line from a sister-in-law of yours, did you?"

"Perhaps I did. Anyway, my dress didn't impress too many."

"Well, it impressed me, Sis." He put his arm around her shoulder and gave her a hug. "I think you should wear it more often."

"You don't count. You're just a brother. Anyway, it didn't work."

They strolled to the back of the store. "What, exactly, was it supposed to accomplish?"

"I certainly thought I would . . . you know, get a little more attention. People that I talk to all the time suddenly got shy, and I'm not inferring only a certain store clerk. A young man over at the International is just as backward. It's like people didn't even know me. Of course, there were some who liked the dress."

"Oh?"

"A couple of the girls at the Gem Theater said it was . . ."

"The Gem? What were you doing in the badlands?"

"I was on an errand for a friend."

"Picking up the gold-heeled shoes to go with that burgundy dress for Rebekah?" he quizzed.

"She told you?"

"Yes, we do talk, you know."

"I thought all you two did was sit around and . . . hold hands." Dacee June spun around. "Bye, see you at supper."

"Leaving so soon?"

"I have no intention of talking to a certain one of your clerks."
Todd heard footsteps behind him, but he didn't turn around.

"Was that Dacee June?" Carty Toluca quizzed.

"Yes, it was."

"What happened to her clothes? I mean, those fancy ones?"

"She decided to change."

"I was jist gettin' used to the other ones. They surely made her
look all grown up, didn't they?"

Todd gazed at the wispy beard that barely covered the skin blem-
ishes of the teenage boy. "Carty, perhaps you should tell her that next
time you see her."

"Are you kiddin'? Dacee June would hit me alongside the head
with a shovel handle if I said something like that."

*You're probably right, Mr. Toluca. But she'll cry herself to sleep
tonight because you didn't say it.* "Well, once in a while you should take
a chance. Most women do enjoy a compliment on their clothing."

As Todd Fortune locked the front door of the hardware, dust
hung across Main Street like airborne mosquito netting.

Only it didn't filter out the bugs . . . or the heat.

"Excuse me!" a man's voice called out from the corner. "Are you
closed?"

"Happy to open back up for a paying customer," Todd offered.

"I don't need to buy anything." The man glanced down at a small
piece of paper in his hand, then looked up. "I just need to see a
Mr. Brazos Fortune."

"I'm afraid Dad's out of town for a couple weeks. I'm his son. Can
I help?"

"Perhaps so. Perhaps so. I'm looking for a woman, and I'm told
Mr. Fortune knew everyone in town."

"Just a woman . . . or a particular woman?" Todd gibed.

"What? Oh my, no, I'm looking for a Mrs. Abigail Gordon. No
one in this town seems to have heard of her."

Todd stared at the slightly nervous but strong-shouldered man.
*Lord, I don't know if you meant this to be a coincidence, but this makes for
a fascinating saga.* "Would you happen to be Dr. Gordon?" he asked.

The man's eyes lit up. "No . . . no . . . I'm Watson Dover, from
Chattanooga. I'm from the law office of Woodson, Goldberg &

THREE

Dover. I see you know Mrs. Gordon. I haven't had any luck until now. I was beginning to think I had come to the wrong Deadwood."

"I didn't say I know her."

"Well, you certainly know the name of her former husband. If you'll just tell me where she abides, I have an important matter to discuss with her."

Todd folded his arms across his chest. "Just what is the nature of your business with Mrs. Gordon?"

The man pulled a white linen handkerchief from his pocket and wiped his forehead. "That's none of your concern."

"No, it isn't. But it is her concern. And when I ask her if she wants to see you, she will ask what it is about. It is highly unlikely she'll agree to such an anonymous meeting."

The lawyer studied Todd from boots to hat. "All I can say at this time is that I represent her former husband, and it has to do with a legal matter concerning their daughter. As you can see, she will obviously want to meet with me."

"It's not obvious to me, but I will see if she's in town and transfer the message. Where can she reach you?"

The man looked up and down the street. "I suppose I'll be staying over there at the Merchant's Hotel. When can I expect to hear from you?"

"I have no idea. If she's in the area, if I can find her . . . and if she wants to see you . . . I suppose I'll let you know in an hour or two."

The man turned to cross the street and Todd headed for the corner of Main and Wall Streets. Even as he began the ascent up the steps to Forest Hill, he could see Dacee June wave at him from the porch in front of the house. When he glanced back, he thought he saw the lawyer still peeking around the corner at him.

"What's the news you're going to tell me about?" Dacee June shouted as he reached the top of the Wall Street stairs that ran perpendicular to one-sided Williams Street.

"Actually, I have a couple of things to discuss. I can't believe I know some things that you don't. That must be a first."

"I didn't get to visit much today . . . I was . . . you know, too busy changing clothes," she admitted.

"Well I'm not saying a word about them until we're sitting down at the supper table."

"Todd!"

"That reminded me of Texas."

"What did?"

"That whiny voice of yours."

"I did not whine."

"Of course you did." He threw his arm around her shoulders as they walked into the house. "But that's alright. I have fond memories of when we were all on the ranch in Coryell County."

"Yes, and I only have shadowy, vague memories of those days," she admitted.

Prayer was said.

Pot roast was passed.

Biscuits were buttered.

"Dacee June tells me you have important news," Rebekah remarked.

"Yes, well first of all, we had a visit from Tobias Olene. He's president of the company in Cleveland that we purchase a lot of merchandise from."

"Mr. Olene?" Rebekah quizzed. "He's a friend of my father's."

"That's what he said."

"Well, where is he? Why didn't you invite him for supper?" Rebekah hopped to her feet and grabbed Todd's plate before he could cut into his meat.

He waved his fork in the air. "What are you doing?"

"I'll put your plate into the warming oven while you go downtown and invite Mr. Olene to eat with us. Why, my father would be insulted if we didn't invite his friends to supper," she fussed.

Todd grabbed her plate-clutching arm. "Just wait a minute. There was a reason I didn't invite him."

"He had other commitments?" she pressed.

"No . . . he wants to buy the store."

"What?" Dacee June's face paled. "It's . . . it's not for sale."

"That's what I told him, but he's sort of a pushy fellow."

"How much did he offer us?" Rebekah questioned as she lowered Todd's plate to the table and returned to her chair.

THREE

"I didn't get that far." Todd ran a bite of roast beef through a flood of dark brown gravy. "I told him we weren't interested, no matter what the price."

"What does a rich manufacturer from Cleveland want with a hardware store out here?" Dacee June probed.

Todd popped the bite of meat into his mouth and chewed slowly before he answered. "He wants to cut out the middleman and sell direct to the mines from a Deadwood store."

"Would the prices be lower?" Rebekah probed.

Todd cracked open a biscuit and felt the steam float up. "At least at first."

"What do you mean?" Dacee June questioned.

"Well, he'd undersell the other hardware stores until everyone goes out of business . . . but then . . . well, I suppose they could raise the prices back up to where they were and make himself a very nice profit."

"If he doesn't buy Fortune's, then he'll buy some other store," Rebekah concluded.

"That's what he said. Either that or just build a new store."

"So we either sell to them or get underpriced and eventually run out of business?" Dacee June moaned.

"That's all speculation," Todd cautioned. "That might be just his sales technique. He might up and decide tomorrow that Deadwood just isn't the right place and go someplace else. There are a lot of things that could happen."

Rebekah pushed her chair back and stared at an empty silver fork in her hand. "You should have at least let him make an offer."

"Why?"

She laid the fork down and drummed her fingers on the edge of the oak table. "Because he's father's friend, and who knows, maybe it's the right time to sell."

"What do you mean, right time?" Dacee June asked.

"What if . . . Daddy Brazos finds a claim over in the Bighorns and wants to move?" Rebekah suggested.

"He went on a hunting trip. He doesn't want to move," Dacee June insisted.

"He's not going to bring meat one hundred eighty miles through Wyoming summer heat, is he?" Rebekah questioned. "He has other things on his mind."

"She could be right, Lil' Sis," Todd added, then stuffed half a biscuit in his mouth.

"And . . ." Rebekah continued, "what if Daddy Brazos wants to move, and the big mines . . . the Homestake, the DeSmet, and some of those, begin to decline? Then this just might be the right time to make a nice profit and build a business elsewhere."

Todd wiped crumbs off his mustache. "Like a bank in Rapid City?"

"That's one possibility."

Todd glanced at Dacee June's troubled eyes. "No, I think we'll want to ride out this wave. Fortunes were here when gold was discovered in this gulch. I figure we ought to be here when it dies off."

"Well, I say it was impolite not to invite Mr. Olene to supper and at least hear what he had to say. The Bible says we should practice hospitality." Rebekah's neck reddened as she spoke.

"And we should live at peace with all men as much as we are able. Having him for supper wasn't going to be peaceful for me. He struck me as arrogant and insensitive. Did you know him well back East?"

"No, I really didn't. But I believe we should respect my father's friends."

Todd laid his fork down. "I agree with you on that. Why don't you invite Mr. Olene to lunch tomorrow?"

"Can I come, too?" Dacee June asked.

"Of course," Rebekah said, then turned to Todd. "Will you allow him to present his offer?"

Todd folded his arms and stared across the food-filled table.

"Todd?"

"Out of my love for you and respect for your father, I'll let him make his offer. However, we will, of course, reject it."

"Don't you think you need to talk to Daddy Brazos before you reject anything?" Rebekah cautioned.

"Nope. I'd have to talk to him if I was convinced to sell. That's a decision for the whole family. But the decision not to sell is a decision either of us can make on our own. And it's my decision we're not selling."

"I still think it wouldn't hurt you to go downtown right now and invite him up for supper," she reiterated.

"I can't do that, because we have another item to discuss." Todd took a sip of coffee and surveyed both ladies' eyes.

"What else do you have to address?" Dacee June blurted out.

"Mrs. Gordon."

Rebekah dropped her fork in her plate.

"Who?" Dacee June quizzed.

"Miss Abby O'Neill at the Gem. Her real name is Mrs. Abigail Gordon," Todd explained.

"It is? She never told me that," Dacee June murmured.

"What about Abigail?" Rebekah inquired.

"A lawyer from Chattanooga showed up today looking all over town for a Mrs. Gordon. No one knew her, of course."

"What did he want?" Rebekah asked.

"He is Dr. Gordon's attorney and has some legal matters to discuss with Abigail concerning their daughter."

Rebekah leaned across the table toward Todd. "Did you send the lawyer down to the Gem?"

"No. I didn't want him to bust upon her like that. I figured she should deal with this on her own time and at a place of her choosing," Todd explained.

"I'm glad," Rebekah nodded. "Did you send word to the Gem?"

"No, this attorney was watching me as I left. So, I just hiked up here."

"We've got to go tell Abigail," Rebekah insisted.

"I'll go," Dacee June offered. "Todd can't go or that lawyer guy, might still be watching him. And I know Rebekah won't go into the badlands. Besides, Mr. Swearengen lets me go in the back door of the Gem for free."

"Why does he do that?" Todd asked.

"Because I run errands for the girls sometimes. Daddy knows all about it. Now, what am I supposed to tell Abby?"

Todd pulled out his pocket watch. "I don't think her show begins for an hour. Tell her that her husband's attorney is in town looking for her, and I wouldn't reveal her position until she tells me to do so.

Ask her if she can come up before the show, and I'll explain what I know."

Todd held the door open for a breathless Abigail Gordon and talkative Dacee June.

"There was this man with a silk top hat, waiting for the first performance, and he asked me if I would like to attend the theater with him," Dacee June gushed. "He had on a really nice black suit, didn't he Abby?"

"He was old enough to be your father," the actress added.

"But the point is, he noticed me and treated me like a lady."

Abigail wore a blue and brown plaid suit with bias skirt, plain waist, and leg-of-mutton sleeves. Her simple brown straw hat held three blue French silk roses. "He treated you like a woman. Whether he would treat you like a lady is yet to be determined," she said.

"This is one of Abby's costumes," Dacee June explained. "She wears this when she sings 'Douglas, Douglas, Tender and True.' It is a very wonderful song that I'm trying to learn to play on my pump organ."

"What is this about Dr. Gordon sending an attorney? How did he know I was here? What did he want? Did he have a court order?" Abigail queried.

Rebekah motioned toward the parlor. "Would you like to sit down?"

Abigail shook her head intensely. "I just want this man to go back to Chattanooga and leave me alone. It can't be good news."

"How do you know that?" Rebekah questioned.

"No woman ever got good news from her former husband's attorney. He hasn't contacted us in over three years; why would he do that now?"

"Perhaps you should ask the lawyer," Rebekah suggested.

Abigail stared at Todd and held her breath. "Why don't you meet with him and ask him?"

"He won't talk with me," Todd explained.

"Well, I'm not meeting with some attorney in my dressing room at the Gem."

"How much time do you have between shows?" Todd asked.

"Forty-five minutes. The orchestra only has a thirty-minute break, but we get a little more."

"Why don't I arrange a meeting here at our house for 9:15 P.M.," Todd advised.

"Yes," Rebekah added. "That way he won't know where you live and can't pester you."

"What should I wear?"

"What you have will do nicely."

"It's boring, isn't it?"

"Well, it's nontheatrical. That might be the right thing to wear when meeting an attorney."

"Will you sit in on the meeting with me?"

"If you'd like," Todd agreed.

Abigail took a deep breath. "I'd like that," she muttered between clenched teeth.

Todd was on a second helping of sliced, boiled potatoes and thick, dark-brown gravy when Dacee June returned from walking Abigail back to the Gem Theater.

"Boy, she sure is nervous," Dacee June reported.

"She loves her daughter and is threatened by an attorney showing up," Rebekah reasoned.

Dacee June brushed her long hair behind her ears. "If she loves her daughter so much, how come she has her stay with her mother in Omaha?"

"She just wants to make enough money this summer to start a business in Nebraska."

"You can't make that kind of money working at the Gem," Todd added.

"Some of the girls make a lot of money. You should see the dresses they buy straight from Paris," Dacee June reported. "But I don't guess they make it all from acting."

Todd glared at his sister, then said to Rebekah, "Perhaps he just needs to finalize some legal documents with Abigail's signature," Todd counseled.

The banging on the front door brought all three to their feet.

Todd swung open the solid oak front door. There with hat in hand stood Sheriff Seth Bullock. "Todd, I got word from Yankton that those two old boys from that botched stagecoach job escaped and might be headed this way. You and me are the only ones in town that they would recognize."

"And Quiet Jim. Did you tell Quiet Jim?"

"Didn't he go huntin' with your daddy?"

"No, he changed his mind and stayed in town."

"I'll go tell him," the sheriff said.

Rebekah's face revealed more concern than her soft voice. "Are they looking for revenge?"

Todd rubbed his hand slowly across his chin whiskers. "If they had any sense they wouldn't come within a hundred miles of the Black Hills."

Rebekah slipped her arm into his. "This region seems to attract those with little sense."

CHAPTER FOUR

"It's a lot of money," Dacee June demurred. She toyed with the small locket on a gold chain hung around her neck and placed it, like a truffle, between her full, dark lips.

Todd's black tie hung loose around his neck like a miniature scarf. "And it's almost midnight, Lil' Sis. You want me to walk you home?"

She rolled her eyes and puffed in such a way that it fluttered her curly bangs. "I live in the house next door. Why do you need to walk me home? You never asked that before."

"The house is dark, and your daddy is not waiting for you this time." Todd brushed his goatee with his fingers. "Family just seems awfully valuable all of a sudden."

"You're beginning to act like Irene Seltzmann's father. Sometimes on a Saturday night, he actually walks her out to the privy, then stands guard." Dacee June looked straight at Rebekah, who was crocheting a red, white, and blue doily. "Do I really have to leave? No decision has been made yet," she whined. "As soon as I leave, you'll decide something. Then I won't know until tomorrow."

"This might be one of those decisions that waits until morning," Rebekah cautioned, never losing a stitch.

"Your sister-in-law is right, Dacee June," Abigail Gordon concurred. "I've got a lot of thinking to do. It's time I get some sleep, too." She turned to Todd and Rebekah. "You will never know what an important place you've played in my life. I felt like I had an upper hand on Mr. Dover and Amber's father tonight. I don't think that has ever been the case before. I doubt I would have felt that way if he had accosted me in my dressing room at the Gem."

"Abigail," Rebekah said, "now that you have found the stairway to Forest Hill, I will expect you to visit me again."

"I'd like that." Abigail plucked up her small brown straw hat from the coffee table and tied the ribbon under her chin. "In fact, could I come and talk this over with you two again tomorrow?"

"Which two?" Dacee June chimed in.

"Lil' Sis isn't bashful," Todd explained.

Abigail grinned. "Yes, I've told her repeatedly that she'd make an excellent actress."

Dacee June cupped her hands under her chin and flashed a phony, toothy smile. "Yes, I could play the tomboy. Every melodrama has a tomboy."

"Don't let her daddy hear you say that," Todd added.

The pose dropped off Dacee June's face. "I still didn't get an answer. Which two do you want to visit with?"

Abigail brushed down her dress, then looked at Dacee June. "Why, all three of you, of course."

"You don't live next door," Todd added as he accompanied her to the door, "so, let me walk you home. It is quite late."

Abigail raised her eyebrows and glanced back at Rebekah.

"I insist," Rebekah said, then broke into a smile, "and I insist that Dacee June go with you also."

"I couldn't agree more," Todd said.

"I've got to chaperon my thirty-year-old brother?" Dacee June groaned.

"No," he laughed. "You are going to chaperon the rumors."

Dacee June scooted over next to him. "What rumors? I haven't heard any rumors."

"See what a good job you're already doing?" He tossed his arm around her shoulder and led Dacee June out the door.

FOUR

Rebekah was laying on her back in bed when Todd returned from the stroll down to the Gem and the hike back up the hill. He yanked his boots off with the bootjack at the door, then pulled off his tie and vest.

The lace collar of her flannel gown tickled her neck. She tried to tuck it under the cotton sheet that was pulled up to her chin. "Did you get your ladies safely home?"

"I reckon they are safe. One of them sleeps with a revolver."

"The sixteen-year-old?"

"Yes," Todd reported. "Do you think she totes that gun too much?"

"Yes, I do."

"I suppose Abigail has learned how to take care of herself, too."

"She's a determined woman." Rebekah could feel the cold sheets as she wiggled her bare toes. "It's a tough situation she's in, Todd."

He rubbed at the back of his neck. "I know."

"She did get a generous offer. With a five-thousand dollar nest egg, Abigail could move to Omaha and open that business she wants." Rebekah raised the sheet and fanned her suddenly flushed face.

Todd carefully hung the white shirt on the back of the wooden chair. "But, I certainly understand her hesitation. It's a dramatic step to sign a legal document that neither she nor Amber will ever visit nor contest the will and/or estate of Dr. Gordon. It's like saying that Amber has no father at all." The polished wooden floor felt cold and good on his bare feet.

"He's trying to totally disinherit his daughter for $5,000. How can a man do that?" Rebekah plopped both arms above the covers and pushed the sleeves of her gown up to her elbows. "How can he marry a woman, have a child, commit adultery, ignore the child . . . then buy them permanently out of his life? What kind of man is that?"

"You're asking me?" Todd folded his light wool trousers across the chair.

"Not exactly the way Fortune men act, is it?"

Even in the shadows of a flickering lantern, he thought he saw her brown eyes sparkle.

"It would be a permanent disgrace for any Fortune to act such." Todd flipped back the white cotton sheet and crawled next to

Rebekah. A lone kerosene lamp on the nightstand illuminated the room. "But Abigail is right. If she doesn't take this, Amber might well get absolutely nothing from the man. He must have a lot of assets to protect."

Rebekah rolled her head toward him. Her hair made the pillow feel like silk against her cheek. "I hear he owns a lot of race horses."

Todd reached over and stroked the bangs out of her eyes. "He doesn't want little Amber to show up some day wanting one of his precious ponies, I guess."

Rebekah pulled his hand to her lips and kissed it. It felt strong, calloused. "I suppose he wants to save them for his stepchildren and any more he and his new wife have."

"If she takes the money she gets to live with her daughter and do something besides acting," Todd noted.

"I understand she's a very good actress."

"But traveling from theater to theater is a difficult way to raise a daughter." Todd let his hand slip down lower than her face. "And she must eternally keep her daughter away from the girl's father."

"Or, Abigail could refuse the offer, and pray that father and daughter could maybe, just maybe, be reconciled in the future." His hand felt warm and Rebekah closed her eyes. Her thoughts wandered.

Todd slipped his hand into Rebekah's. "How do you feel about Abigail's dilemma?"

"Guilty." Rebekah reached back with her free hand and turned the lantern off. "I'm relieved that it's not me who has to decide, and that makes me feel very guilty . . . very happy with my situation, and very guilty."

"Sort of like the song, 'It's your misfortune and none of my own,' " he said as he tugged her closer in the darkened bedroom.

"Exactly," she whispered. Without seeing him, she knew his face was only inches away. Rebekah slipped an arm around his waist and laid her head on his chest. "I'm sure we'll have our own misfortunes, but I'm glad that isn't one of them."

In the dark of the room, Todd ran his hands gently through her hair. Like gentle strands of silk, it tickled the soft flesh between his fingers. "It seems strange to have Olene show up on the same day that the Chattanooga lawyer arrives. For us, this deal about selling the hardware store might be just as crucial a decision as Mrs. Abigail Gordon's."

She held him tight and listened to his heartbeat, a sound of which she never tired. "But our decision is much more academic. It doesn't involve our children."

Todd stopped stroking her hair and laid his hands on the sheet behind her head. "Doesn't it?" he probed. "Of course it involves our children."

Rebekah pulled back a little, but left her arms at his waist. "What do you mean?"

Todd flopped his arm back on his side of the bed. "I mean, you don't want to have children in Deadwood. You've made that quite clear. So the number and ages of our children, if we have any, is directly affected by selling the store, isn't it?"

She pulled away from Todd. The back of her head pinned his other arm beneath her.

Todd took a deep breath and let it out slowly. *Now she's angry . . . and I don't know what to say next. But it's the logical conclusion. Why doesn't she think these things through?*

Finally, she spoke softly. "Are you going to invite Mr. Olene to lunch?"

His reply was curt. "I told you I would. I presume the other subject is concluded."

She turned her back to him but held onto his arm beneath her head.

He could hear her start to sniffle. *Todd Fortune, you have no idea in the world how my heart aches to have children, and how terrified I am of raising them.* "Todd, I've tried to like Deadwood. Really, I have. I just don't know how to live in a town like this."

She rubbed her eyes on his arm. He could feel the hot tears. *Lord, sometimes I just don't know how to talk to this woman.* "I reckon Deadwood isn't much unlike any other place," he murmured.

Rebekah rolled over on her back. "See, that's the problem. It is different to me. You and I are so dissimilar. This evening the sheriff came to the door to warn you that two gun-toting, violent, lawless men have escaped and perhaps headed to Deadwood. If they do, they could try to take revenge against you. You and the sheriff shrug that off as if it's an everyday occurrence. Well, it's not an everyday occurrence to me, Todd Fortune. The thought of men in this town looking for a way to gun down my husband absolutely terrifies me. It makes me want to hide under the covers of my bed and never, ever come out!" she sobbed.

He rolled over, almost on top of her. "I'm not too fond of the idea myself, Mrs. Fortune. You reckon I could just hide under the covers with you?"

She reached up in the dark of the room and rubbed his cheek with the palm of her hand. "You can hide under my covers any time you want, Mr. Fortune," she sniffled. "But, what do you intend to do about those gunmen?"

He leaned down and brushed a soft kiss across her lips. For a split second every worry in her mind melted. "I suppose I'll pray a lot," he whispered.

Her voice was much, much more relaxed. "Are you going to pray right now?"

Todd lowered himself down until their noses touched in the darkness. "No," he whispered. "I'm not going to pray right now."

It was almost noon the following day before Todd had a break in store business and stepped out on the wooden sidewalk to gaze down Main Street.

The crack of a bullwhacker's whip and the adjoining shout caught his attention as dual freight wagons plodded their way up Main Street. There were also loaded farm wagons, buckboards, and horsemen crowded in the streets. They were all going somewhere. Doing something. The sidewalks, too, seemed crowded with busy people.

Only the white puffy clouds in the sky sauntered along.

It's a hard-working town.

The perfect spot for a hardware store.

But Rebekah hates this gulch. I know that. I wonder why you bury earth's treasures, Lord, in such desolate locations. I love this town, probably for the very reasons she hates it. It's rough, coarse, independent, and sometimes violent. But it's a town that produces. Using the genius of engineers and mining geologists and the backs of a thousand strong men, gold is dug out of the ground and shared with the entire world. No one has to remain poor in Deadwood. There are no frills. No pretense. No protocol

FOUR

from the past. Nobody cares what you used to be. You get a new chance to prove yourself.

Everyone gets a second chance in Deadwood. Even sinners.

I know you've promised to go with us wherever we go, Lord. But Rapid City is a step down. After that she'd want me to be a banker in Des Moines . . . then Molene . . . and somehow we'd end up in Chicago. I couldn't do it. It would kill my soul . . . which is probably a lot the way Rebekah feels right now.

Lord, my heart and my soul can't agree and my mind refuses to take sides. How about You deciding this one?

"I say, Mr. Fortune? I was just going to find your house."

Todd glanced east, toward Shine Street. A nobby-dressed man headed his way wearing patent leather shoes and a neatly pressed light wool suit. "Mr. Olene, I was on my way home. Our place is not difficult to find, but you'll have to climb the stairs on your own."

"It's a steep ravine."

"I carried most of the cut boards for our house up this hillside on my shoulders," Todd informed the man.

The two men strolled past the Stebbins and Post Bank, then waited for a freight wagon to pass before they crossed Lee Street.

"I'm delighted you decided to reconsider my offer," Olene explained. "Your invitation to lunch was a very pleasant surprise, indeed."

Todd pulled his watch out of his vest, glanced at it, then let it drop back into the pocket. "Mr. Olene, I don't want you to get up any false hopes. I do this out of respect for my wife's father, and his friendship with you. I really haven't changed my mind about a thing."

"Well, yes, young man," Olene challenged, "but just as soon as I tell you what I'm prepared to offer, I do believe you'll be impressed. Yes, indeed. Good money most often changes good intentions, I always say."

Todd struggled to stay silent. *Lord, I don't even want to hear the offer. I don't understand why I should even have to go through this. Olene is exactly the type I don't like doing business with. I could never be a banker. It would be dealing with men like that all day long. Alright, Daddy Brazos . . . if you didn't up and shoot the man, what would you say?* Todd studied the man as they walked. "Mr. Olene, what town did you grow up in?"

Tobias Olene's gray head jerked around. "I say, what?"

"Where's your hometown?" Todd prodded. "Were you born and raised in Cleveland?"

"Oh, no. I grew up in Wellington, Ohio."

"A little place?"

"Yes, quite small. Southwest of Cleveland."

Todd stared the puzzled man in the eyes. "Well, that's sad, isn't it?"

Olene took long strides to keep up with the younger man. "What do you mean, sad?"

"Sad that a town that close to a big city never grew much," Todd explained.

"No one there is complaining." Olene's hands dropped to his sides, swaying in time with his steps. "People there like it small. It's exactly the way they want it to be."

Todd tugged the brim of his hat lower in the front. "And that, Mr. Olene, is true of Deadwood. It is just as we want it to be."

Olene's face blushed. "Are you telling me to keep my nose out of Deadwood?"

"I have a feeling there is no one on earth that could tell Mr. Tobias Olene to keep his nose out of anywhere." Todd stopped to give the older man a break. "Don't take that as an insult. The same thing could be said of my father, and I love him dearly."

A slight smile broke across the businessman's face, and he nodded slightly. "I look forward to meeting Brazos Fortune."

"Well," Todd grinned. "The first thing you want to do is pronounce his name Braazis . . . Anything else will produce a definite rile."

"Just in case . . ." Olene pulled several folded papers from the inside pocket of his suit coat, then replaced them. "We can discuss this part later. I mean, I know the odds are slim . . . but just in case my offer happens to be acceptable, there would be a certain amount of paperwork to take care of. Since I need to return east in a couple of days, would there be a chance you or your father will be in Cleveland in the next month or so? We could finalize things there."

Todd leaned his head back until he could see the Dakota blue sky. "Mr. Olene, you'd have a better chance carving Mr. Lincoln's bust in a limestone cliff in the Black Hills than you would of having my father go to Cleveland," he laughed. "If sufficiently bribed, you might get him to go to Cheyenne . . . but don't press your luck on Denver. And Cleveland? You might as well ask him to meet you in Hades. He won't go."

"Yes, well, I suppose I won't have to return west. I can send a team of lawyers to . . ."

Todd put his hand lightly on the man's shoulder. Mr. Olene flinched. "That would ruin the deal for sure. My father would think of it as an insult to have to talk to lawyers. I can guarantee that he won't sell the business without a personal handshake from you. And neither would I. Out here some things are just more important than lawyers and papers."

"Well, I'm certainly learning a lot about your father before I ever meet him. He sounds like a real character."

"He's a Deadwood legend, Mr. Olene. A hundred years from now enthusiastic novelists will still be writing mostly true stories about him. But he is extremely predictable in some respects. He won't sell the store."

"My, you are a persistent and pessimistic young man." Todd thought he could see a slight smile in Olene's lingering expression. "Don't take that personal. In my business, I find that a very commendable trait. But I don't understand your resistance to progress."

"Mr. Olene, Deadwood has a very unique, distinct personality. It's an isolated island of frontier in a quickly settling West. Some folks like it. Some don't. But those of us who call it home are here because of that fresh, exciting unpredictability. Some of us are kind of afraid of making it progress too quickly. I guess we have a fear of waking up some morning like Jacob in the Bible and finding out we married the wrong sister. We don't want a little Cleveland, or a little Chicago . . . We don't even want a little Denver."

"My word, you're quite a philosopher."

Todd began to laugh. "I've hung around the potbellied stove too much."

"Sentimentality often stands in the way of progress. But I must warn you, it seldom, if ever, succeeds."

A short man in a crisp bowler and slightly crinkled brown-striped suit waited for them at the corner of Main and Wall Streets.

Todd pushed his narrow-brimmed felt hat back and rubbed his sweaty forehead. "Mr. Dover, are you waiting for me?"

"Mrs. Gordon sent word for me to meet with her at your house for lunch, so I thought I'd walk up with you."

Todd rubbed his light-brown mustache in an effort to cover his surprise. *Dover's coming to lunch, too? I wonder if Rebekah knows about this?* He turned to the older man. "Mr. Tobias Olene of Cleveland, this is Mr. Watson Dover, of Woodrow, Goldstein and Dover, of Chattanooga."

As the men shook hands, Dover corrected, "That's Woodson, Goldberg and Dover."

All signs of civility dropped from Olene's face. "Is that the law firm that defended that scamp John Casebolt?" he blurted out.

"I don't remember Mr. Casebolt as being a scamp," Dover bristled. "You aren't Olene Steel Company, are you?"

"The same," Olene growled.

Dover's reply was almost a shout. "You should have gone to jail for the way you treated Casebolt."

Olene yanked off his hat. Veins bulged on his forehead. "That is a slanderous remark!"

"Whoa . . . whoa . . ." Todd stepped between them. "May I suggest that is old business? If you want to pitch a fit over it, you'll need to do that before or after lunch. Rebekah will not accept that tone at her table."

"Quite so . . . ," Olene admitted, letting out a deep breath. "I'm not sure why you need a Chattanooga attorney at this meeting, but . . ."

"Mr. Dover is meeting with a friend of ours on a separate matter. It just so happens that we will all sit down at my wife's table."

"Yes . . . well," Dover cleared his throat. "I apologize to you, Mr. Fortune, for getting carried away over past dealings. I appreciate greatly the use of your home for this meeting."

The three had just silently reached the base of the Wall Street steps up to Williams Street when a girl's voice rang out. "Todd, wait up. Could you help us?"

Dacee June strolled toward them with two small children, one at each hand, toddling along beside her.

FOUR

"You're baby-sitting for Quiet Jim and Columbia?" There were moments when his sister actually looked mature. This was one of those times.

"She's not feeling well. Quiet Jim has his hands full with the baby, so I agreed to take Quintin and Fern."

A curly headed boy wearing short pants tucked into long socks grinned. "Hi, Uncle Todd."

He plucked up the lad. "Well, Quint, have you trapped any bears today?"

The round brown eyes of the boy widened. "No. I'm all out of bait," he squealed.

They started up the steps. Dacee June carried Fern. Todd packed Quintin. Olene and Dover followed.

"Young Man, what do you use for bear bait?" Olene asked, as he puffed his way up the steps.

"Bobcat meat," Quintin replied.

"And what kind of trap do you have?" Olene quizzed.

"Quint has a nice big packing crate propped up and a stick tied to a string," Todd replied.

Olene stopped hiking the steps and caught his breath. "Oh, my . . . I sincerely trust you haven't caught one."

"Nope," Quint replied. "I told you I didn't have the right bait."

"Mr. Olene, excuse me for forgetting to introduce her, but this young lady ahead of me is my sister, Dacee June."

Olene tipped his hat. "Just how many Fortunes are in Deadwood?"

Todd began to laugh. When he did, young Quintin and his sister laughed as well. "How many fortunes in Deadwood? That, Mr. Olene, is what every man, woman, and child in the Black Hills is trying to find out."

Olene and Dover stood awkwardly in the parlor as Dacee June, Quintin, and Fern scrambled around them.

Todd was busy in the kitchen.

"I didn't know we were having a banquet," he mumbled as he tugged an oak table leaf out of the pantry.

"Nor did I." Rebekah buzzed past him and strained on her tiptoes to retrieve an airtight tin from the top shelf. "When we told Abigail she could meet the lawyer at our house, I didn't know that was an invitation to lunch."

Todd followed her back into the kitchen, the thirty-six-by-eighteen-inch slice of polished oak under his arm. "We aren't going to get any business done with this whole gang here."

"We have to try," she insisted as she opened a large can of stewed tomatoes. "After we eat we can send Dacee June next door with the children and . . ."

Todd stopped in the middle of the room. "Lil' Sis won't like that."

"She's the one who brought the children home." Rebekah tugged at the tight, high-necked velvet collar of her fancy green checked blouse.

"She didn't have a choice."

"I know . . . I know . . . I'm not complaining, really. I'm just a little frazzled." Rebekah stirred the tomatoes into the large pot of white beans, but stopped when she heard someone knock at the door. "Oh, no! Who is it now?"

"Relax, Mrs. Fortune," Todd chided. "It's probably only Mrs. Gordon."

"Who?"

"Abigail . . . Miss Abby O'Neill, remember?"

Rebekah tried brushing her bangs back off her forehead, but they flopped right back in the same place. "You set up the table and entertain. I'll have things ready in just a minute. This turned out to be quite a crowd. I'm not used to cooking for this many."

"You mean you never had crowds at your big home on the north side of Chicago?" He heard Dacee June speak to someone at the front door.

"Yes, often." Rebekah reflected on her parents' house crammed with well-dressed people. "But they all presented their printed invitations to one of the servants at the door. And our cook took on extra help."

Todd sat at one end of the heavy oak table with thick spiral legs. The dining room felt crowded, the conversation shallow, expectant of things to come. He passed the ham-stacked china platter to Tobias Olene at his right. Next to him, in the middle of the table sat Abigail

Gordon, once again wearing her "Douglas, Douglas, Tender & True" plain dress. On the other side of her, Watson Dover sulked like a lawyer with an unpopular defendant. He buttered a roll as if he were trying to mash it to death. At the far end of the table was Rebekah's place. She, however, spent most of the meal scurrying between the kitchen and the dining room. On the far side of the table, next to the north window that provided a view of the steep, treeless backyard, sat Quintin, Dacee June, and young Fern, who delighted almost everyone by mashing a stewed tomato on top of her head.

"I'm certainly glad to find out these are not your children," Olene blurted out over a fork full of beans. "I mean to say, I would have been quite lax if you had children, Rebekah, and I hadn't known it. I believe your father would keep me informed of such important information." His awkward smile made his thick, brushy sideburns look clownlike.

Rebekah buzzed around the table refilling coffee cups. She was surprised to find herself enjoying the mealtime. "Quintin and Fern are very special. Their father, Quiet Jim, is a dear, dear friend of Daddy Brazos. They are like family to us."

"You're a very gracious hostess," Watson Dover added as she poured his cup. "I'm afraid my wife would be quite flustered with such a sudden assembly."

"Living on the frontier means having plenty of unexpected opportunities to practice hospitality." Rebekah set the silver coffee-pot on the serving cart and slipped into the chair at the end of the table, not bothering to remove her dress-length apron.

"Frontier?" Olene's voice thundered like a company president addressing a roomful of subordinates. "Deadwood is a booming town. Hardly seems like the frontier."

Abigail's voice was soft, melodic, and beautifully controlled. "Obviously, Mr. Olene has never spent a night in the badlands." She took a delicate sip of coffee with her small finger properly arched.

"The badlands? I heard someone at the hotel mention the 'bad-lands district.' Is that in Deadwood?" Watson Dover quizzed.

When the light caught Watson Dover right, Todd thought he looked a little like a thin-chested Ulysses Grant. "The badlands is any part of town lower than the dead line," Todd informed as he ran a bite of ham through a puddle of molasses.

A startled look flashed across Tobias Olene's pinkish face. "The dead line?"

Todd leaned back in his chair and savored the bittersweet taste inside his mouth. "Wall Street separates town. On the lower side you have saloons, gambling parlors, theaters, and other accompanying businesses," he explained.

Dover's beard-covered chin seemed to bob up and down as he talked. "Why do they call it the dead line?"

Dacee June's wide grin revealed a mouthful of large, straight white teeth. "Because past that line, you're liable to find yourself dead."

"It's not all that bad. But it is definitely the frontier." Abigail's eyes sparkled with an I-know-more-than-I'm-saying dance.

"I presume you all stay out of that section." Dover held his coffee cup in front of him as he spoke, and Rebekah noticed his manicured fingernails.

Dacee June reached down and scooped Quintin's buttered biscuit off the floor. She gave it a quick glance, then popped it back into his eager hands. "Oh, it's fine in the daytime. But at night we usually just sit up here on Forest Hill and watch. Even the sheriff doesn't patrol past the dead line."

"My, it sounds like a difficult place to raise children," Olene said.

Todd refused to look across the table at Rebekah. *Thanks, Olene. I do trust you'll go back through Chicago and tell Rebekah's father how dangerous Deadwood is. Perhaps Mr. Jacobson sent you here to chide us to move to Rapid City. Or did his daughter arrange this?*

"Actually . . ." Dacee June blurted out as she tried to wipe stewed tomatoes out of Fern's ear, "all of Deadwood is safe for kids. Everyone in the whole town looks out for you. A kid can roam from China Town to Ingleside clear up to Central City and never worry about anything. It's sort of like being adopted by the whole town."

"Dacee June is right about that," Abigail added.

Watson Dover wiped his mouth with the blue cotton napkin, then turned to Abigail Gordon. "Speaking of children, I thought perhaps you would bring young Amber to this luncheon."

Rebekah watched her response closely.

FOUR

Abigail cleared her throat. "If we have business to discuss, I thought this was not a place for her to attend." It was the reply of a mother, not an actress.

Dover tapped his fingers on the rim of his coffee cup and glanced down. "I do trust you have good baby-sitting."

"What kind of baby-sitting I have, or don't have, does not concern you, Mr. Dover." The controlled voice came out with such authority that everyone at the table froze in place.

The attorney looked as if the opposition had just introduced new evidence. "Well, not me personally. It's just that I wanted to bring some kind of report to Dr. Gordon."

When Abigail turned to the man next to her, her eyes flashed like a mama bear protecting her cub. "Dr. Gordon has not seen fit to contact his daughter or me for over three years. I doubt seriously if he cares who is her baby-sitter. Your presence here confirms that. If he is concerned about her, I expect he will come to visit her."

Rebekah hid her grin behind her coffee cup.

Dover responded like a man vainly trying to placate a lynch mob. "Oh no, he's remarried now. It wouldn't be appropriate."

Abigail's words slammed down like a gavel. "Nor is this conversation appropriate!"

"Well, I agree," Olene blurted out. "Certain attorneys seemed locked on caustic comments. I'm curious about the support and care offered to the children by the whole community you mentioned. I would have thought everyone was so concerned with getting rich, they might tend to neglect the children. How do you account for this widespread compassion and generosity?"

Most at the table resumed their eating. Except Watson Dover. He sat stunned.

"Some of it has to do with all the babies dying," Rebekah's voice was soft.

"Oh my," Olene pressed. "What happened?"

"For a couple of years we had an outbreak of diphtheria, smallpox, and scarlet fever," Rebekah reported. "It hit the children the hardest. It was horrid. I believe over two hundred infants and children died in two years." In her mind, Rebekah could see an endless procession of tiny wooden caskets. She could still hear the sobs of grieving mothers.

"My word," Olene nervously tugged at his gold cuff links. "I had no idea of the primitive conditions out here."

"But all of that seems to be settled down now." Dacee June stared in horror as Fern grabbed a big handful of stewed tomatoes, then was somewhat relieved when she stuffed the whole wad into her mouth.

Tobias Olene sprinkled salt on top of his white beans. "What caused things to settle down? Did they find a cure? What made the difference?"

"The fire." Dacee June popped a bite of ham into her mouth like a person who didn't know when she would have another opportunity to eat.

Watson Dover broke his self-inflicted paralysis and took a sip of coffee.

"What fire?" Olene quizzed.

Dacee June mumbled something, pointed to the bulge in her mouth, then nodded at her brother.

"We just about lost the entire town last fall," Todd explained. "Three hundred buildings were destroyed."

Dacee June swallowed hard, then took a deep breath. "But only one man died. The deaf Englishman called Casino Jack. I guess he was drunk and passed out. He must not have smelled the smoke. It's a cinch he didn't hear anyone yell," she reported.

Dover stared at his plate and pecked away at his food. He seemed to ignore the conversation around him.

"Three hundred buildings?" Olene waved a silver fork across his plate. "But there is no trace of that fire now."

Todd surveyed those at the table. "Folks in Deadwood don't sit around and mope much. We just jumped in and rebuilt. As you can see, we used a lot more brick this time around."

Olene seemed to be calculating replacements costs. "Did the hardware burn?"

"Nope. The fire started in the Empire Bakery on Lee Street and swept east," Todd reported. "We built our brick store building a few years ago. A brick company over in Spearfish went under and owed Dad quite a sum. So he took it in bricks and we rebuilt then. Of course, we did a lot of business after the fire."

Olene rubbed his clean-shaven chin with his fingers. "It sounds like a quite profitable venture."

FOUR

Todd ground his teeth, then glanced down the table to Rebekah.

"Actually, Mr. Olene," Rebekah replied, "Fortune's Hardware sold most everything at wholesale to any who wanted to rebuild. We didn't think it right to make a profit from others' tribulation."

Todd laid down his fork and turned to the Cleveland businessman. He forced himself to talk slowly. "Tell me, Mr. Olene . . . if you had a monopoly on the hardware business in Deadwood and half the town burned down, would you sell to them at your cost?"

"I, eh . . . I've never heard of anything like that. I, eh . . . well, I, of course, don't work in our sales division so I really couldn't predict what . . ."

"Mr. Olene, I believe it is a very good question," Dacee June piped up as she cut a ham slice for a biscuit-chewing Quintin. "What would you do?"

Todd could see Watson Dover visibly relax as Tobias Olene took the witness chair.

"I, eh . . . well, as I . . . this is, conjectural, of course . . . I don't see how this . . ."

Todd watched Olene squirm. *Feed them and grill them. Not a bad strategy.*

Olene pushed his chair back. Its legs squeaked across the polished floor. "What does this have to do with selling me your hardware?"

Rebekah glanced at Todd. He liked the way her eyes flashed. *Go to it, Mrs. Fortune. You've got the fight in your eyes now!*

"I believe all of us Fortunes will need to know the answer before we consider any sales," Rebekah insisted. "If Deadwood burns . . . and it surely will again someday . . . will you sell at wholesale to any who want to rebuild? You see, Mr. Olene, this is the way business is done here in the West."

By his fidgeting Todd surmised that Olene was ready to bolt to the front door.

"Do I understand that you are forcing this to be a condition of the sale?" Olene blustered.

"Not at all. We aren't obliging you to do anything. You came to Dakota and made an offer to purchase our store," Todd corrected. "The answer to this question will help us to appraise what kind of company we're dealing with. What's your answer? Are you the kind of a company that sells wholesale when neighbors get burned out?"

Olene cleared his throat. "I will give you an honest answer. I doubt very much if we could maintain a profit margin and afford to sell wholesale under such circumstances."

"We didn't ask if you could afford it," Todd persisted. "We asked if you would do it."

"That's all very hypothetical. With so many buildings rebuilt in brick, I don't know if there is a very real problem. We would, of course, be very supportive of the volunteer fire department." Olene tugged on his shirt collar in an unsuccessful attempt to loosen his tie. "That's as much of an answer as I can give at this time."

"I reckon it's obvious where you stand," Todd said.

"Would anyone like some more ham?" Rebekah stood and retrieved the large platter from the two-wheeled serving cart. Todd knew it was her signal that the matter had been pressed hard enough, for the time.

The conversation trailed off. Todd finished his coffee, then helped young Fern remove her hand that was stuck fast in the cream pitcher. He then glanced down the table at the determined look on his wife's face. *Mr. Tobias Olene, you have made a capital offensive blunder. Under no circumstance should you have aggravated Mrs. Rebekah Fortune. On the other hand . . . thank you, Lord. His insensitivity and arrogance was more convincing than six months of my best logic. If she gets aggravated enough, she'll insist we stay here and run the store the rest of our lives. 'Course, I could just be getting cocky and optimistic!*

By the time the peach cobbler was served, Dacee June had taken the children out to play on the front porch. The front parlor window was open wide as Todd helped Rebekah clear the table.

"What now?" he whispered as they entered the kitchen. "Which one of these charming men should we deal with first?"

Rebekah stacked dishes on the counter and scraped the scraps into a tin bucket on the floor. "How about Mr. Olene?"

"But you said Abigail's business is much more important," he cautioned.

"Most certainly . . . that's why we'll get the other out of the way first."

"You are riled over him, aren't you?" he grinned.

FOUR

"Yes."

"I'm glad."

"I know you're glad, Todd Fortune. But the matter is not resolved just because he peeved me."

"What shall I tell him?"

"Nothing." She blinked her long, dark eyelashes. "I'll take care of Mr. Tobias Olene. There's a little actress in every woman."

Todd trailed Rebekah back out to the parlor. Both Dover and Olene were standing. She scooted over to Tobias Olene and slipped her arm in his as she led him to the hat rack. "Mr. Olene, please give my fondest love to my father when you see him next. I trust he hasn't remarried without notifying me."

"Oh, no . . . I'm sure he hasn't . . . at least, I don't think he has. My word, he was with Mildred Dodge the last time I saw him." Olene unsuccessfully resisted her prodding and inched to the door.

"Oh, don't worry about Mrs. Dodge. She was dropped several months ago, according to his letters." Rebekah handed him his hat.

"Eh, we haven't discussed this proposal." He pulled several folded sheets of paper from his coat pocket.

Rebekah plucked them from his hands. "Thank you, Tobias, for making the trip to Deadwood. Todd or Daddy Brazos will contact you in a few weeks and let you know what we think."

"A few weeks?" He spoke like a man sentenced to be hung a few days before Christmas.

"Let's say a month, just to be sure. Of course, if you don't hear from them, the answer is obvious." With one hand still on his coat sleeve, she held the front door open for him.

"But, I've got to have decided something this week. I didn't get a chance to explain."

"This is a family business, and the whole family will have to discuss it. I'm sure you understand. Mr. Olene, you told us quite a lot today, actually," she insisted.

"But we have much more to discuss," he continued to protest.

"I'm sure a good businessman like yourself has everything articulately explained in these documents. I assure you we will read the details very carefully."

"But . . . but . . ."

She grabbed his shoulders as he stepped back out on the porch, then she leaned over and kissed his blushing, bushy cheek. "Take that home for my father, would you, Mr. Olene?"

"Yes, well . . . certainly, Rebekah. I'll be stopping in Chicago for a few days on my way home. Eh, thank you for dinner. I'll, eh, look forward to hearing . . ."

The door was closed before the sentence was completed.

Todd Fortune ushered his wife back into the parlor where Watson Dover and Abigail Gordon awkwardly waited. Both gazed at a painting of a neatly arranged flower garden that was signed in the corner, *Rebekah Jacobson.*

"You are a very smooth lady, Mrs. Fortune," Todd whispered.

"And sealed with a kiss," she winked.

"Do you always have your way with men?"

"Just the pushovers like you, Todd Fortune."

He turned to the Chattanooga attorney. "Now, Mr. Dover, why don't we all sit down. We'll let you and Mrs. Gordon finish discussing this proposal of yours."

Dover perched himself on the edge of the settee. Abigail Gordon chose the straight-backed side chair across the room. Todd and Rebekah remained standing at the wide doorway leading to the entry hall. The lawyer glanced back at the open window where Dacee June hovered on the porch, trying to look uninterested. He cleared his throat. "I thought perhaps Mrs. Gordon and I could have a private discussion."

Todd joined Rebekah on the sofa. His shirt collar felt damp with sweat. "Mrs. Gordon asked us to sit in with her." He leaned back and slipped his arms on the back of the couch.

Abigail folded her arms across her thin chest. "Mr. Dover, you require me to make a decision that will drastically affect my daughter for the rest of her life. I do not consider such a proposal lightly. I appreciate the counsel of such friends as the Fortunes. However, if that is unacceptable, I could arrange to have my attorney present at this discussion."

"Oh . . . no . . . ," Dover mumbled, "it's not that I don't . . ."

"Perhaps Judge Bennett is home." Rebekah patted her husband's knee. "Todd, would you step down and ask the judge to sit in on this?"

FOUR

Dover wiped perspiration from his forehead with a white linen handkerchief and shook his head. "No, no . . . that won't be necessary. I just want to keep everything confidential, out of respect for all involved."

Todd stretched out his legs in front of him. The more he relaxed, the stiffer Dover became. "I assure you, my wife and I can be trusted to keep things private," he said.

"Me, too . . ." Dacee June echoed from the porch. Her words caused Dover to twitch all the more.

"Perhaps I can make all of this easier," Abigail announced. She stood, then laced her fingers together in front of her narrow waist. "I have considered Dr. Gordon's proposal and find it unacceptable, Mr. Dover. So, there is really nothing to discuss, nothing to keep secret."

"I believe that is a decision you will regret," Dover stammered.

"If it is, I will learn to live with it, as I have other decisions that I regret. However, I believe this is one that will produce no remorse."

Dover's round, bearded face flushed. "Dr. Gordon said that you might very well turn him down and, therefore, he has authorized me to offer you ten thousand dollars, instead of five thousand."

"What?" Abigail gasped.

"It is a generous offer beyond all necessity. It reflects Dr. Gordon's sincere compassion and mercy." He smiled as if in triumph.

Rebekah Fortune marched over to the grinning attorney. "Mr. Dover, your presence in our home is a disgrace! I must ask you to leave immediately, and you are not invited to return."

"What? You're throwing me out because I made a better offer?"

"I'm throwing you out, Dover." Todd joined his wife. When he did, Dover grabbed up his coat as he scurried to the door. "You came to town to barter a daughter's future with her father. You offered a cut-rate amount to see if you could save money. When there were no bargains, you upped the ante like a poker game. I believe Mr. Lincoln abolished the buying and selling of humans years ago."

"What are you talking about? This is not slavery. This is a business deal."

"Not to me, it isn't," Abigail stormed over next to Rebekah.

"What's wrong with putting into writing what is already in practice? Dr. Gordon has no contact with the child now."

"That's a fact he will have to live with. If he wants to come discuss this with me in person, he may do that."

"He doesn't have time to . . ."

"People have time to do anything they choose," Abigail snapped.

"But, if you turn this down, little Amber will never get one penny from Dr. Gordon. You are condemning her to a life of poverty."

"As long as I have breath, she will not live in poverty," Abigail corrected.

"Dover . . ." Todd nudged the man to the front door with his clenched fist jammed in the man's stomach. "If you or the good doctor thought there was absolutely no chance of Amber receiving part of the Gordon inheritance, you would never have traveled this far and made this offer. Obviously, you are worried about something."

"Ten thousand dollars is a lot of worry," Dacee June called out from the porch.

"This whole matter is preposterous! I came in good faith trying to help a young child and . . ."

"You came trying to save money, Dover. Good day. I would appreciate that while you are in Deadwood you would avoid our home, our store, and especially hassling Mrs. Gordon." Todd led the man down the steps to Williams Street and watched as he descended the steps to the end of Wall Street. "Remember, Mr. Dover, this is the frontier. Justice is swift and thorough for those who harangue women and children."

"Are you threatening me?" Dover snapped.

"You are much wiser than I've given you credit for."

When Todd returned to the house, Dacee June had led the children back into the parlor.

"What have I done?" Abigail sighed. "I'll never save up ten thousand dollars in my whole life."

"You've done the right thing," Rebekah counseled. "Amber needs to have a chance to choose whether she knows her father or not. I'm sure it is what the Lord would want you to do."

Abigail took a deep sigh and slumped her shoulders. "It's not easy. Sometimes doing the right thing is just a strain. I can't believe I just said good-bye to ten thousand dollars."

FOUR

"There are still some things money can't buy," Todd reassured her. "It is a lesson that both the doctor and the counselor at law needed to be reminded of. If this is as big a concern as it seems, I believe you have not heard the last of Dr. Gordon."

Abigail fingered her rings. Todd noticed for the first time a gold wedding band. *She still wears her wedding ring?*

"You mean, he'll make another offer?" she questioned.

"I'm not sure of that," Todd replied. "But you said you'd discuss it with him if he came in person."

"He won't come. He doesn't care two figs about Amber. He was highly insulted when she wasn't a boy. He never took any interest in her . . . or me . . . after she was born."

"He might not come for her sake," Rebekah offered. "But he might come to settle financial anxieties."

"I wish Amber was here right now," Abigail murmured. "I need a hug."

Rebekah swung around and pulled Abigail to her. "It's not like hugging your Amber . . ." Abigail Gordon threw her arms around Rebekah and held her tight.

It was after dark when Todd hiked up the stairway to his house on Forest Hill. Every bone in his body ached. Each step seemed to tug at his thighs and calves. His right shoulder was trying to cramp, and he kept swinging his arm to find a more comfortable position. Draped across his left arm were his suit coat, vest, and black tie. His white cotton shirt was unbuttoned at the top. The sleeves were rolled to the elbows.

He opened the front door slowly. Dacee June sat on the parlor floor reading a book to two children who seemed to be fast asleep on a blanket at her feet. She waved to him but kept reading in a soft, low voice. Todd walked lightly toward the kitchen where Rebekah was washing dishes.

"Evening, Mrs. Fortune," he said.

Rebekah pulled her hands out of the dishwater and began to dry them on a tea towel. "You had a long day."

"I hope Carty made it up the hill to warn you that I'd be late."

"Yes, he said the steel plating came in and you needed to deliver it to the mines." She took the clothes from his arm and laid them across the back of a kitchen chair.

"Only half the order arrived." Todd opened the lid on the coffee-pot and peeked inside. "So I split it among the three biggest customers."

"Were they happy about that?"

"Partially. They all need the remainder of the plating." He slumped into one of the kitchen table chairs. "We're a long trail from suppliers, no matter what direction you travel. Someday the railroad will finally decide that Deadwood is here to stay and they'll build a line to us. Then we can get things more quickly."

She started to say something. Instead, she turned back toward the counter and retrieved a plate. "I'll fix your supper. I hope you didn't mind if we went ahead and ate."

"Of course not. What were you going to say?" he prodded.

"About dinner?"

"About something else."

"Nothing."

"Rebekah?"

"It was a foolish thought about railroads."

"You were about to say that plans had already been made to bring a railroad into Rapid City, weren't you?" Todd challenged.

"I suppose. But then I got to thinking it would be too much like nagging. Anyway, it's been a long day for all of us. That discussion can wait for another day."

Todd looked down at a bowl of boiled cabbage, potatoes, and leftover ham chunks. "I'm surprised to see the children still here. I take it that means that Columbia is no better?"

Rebekah stepped over and rubbed the back of his neck. "I paid her a visit this afternoon and . . ."

Todd let his shoulder slump but didn't look back at her. "You went out across town by yourself?"

"Yes."

"All the way to Ingleside?"

"It's only a couple miles. I hailed Mert Hart's hack." She stopped her rubbing. "You act like I never leave my house. Do you want to hear how Columbia is or not?"

FOUR

"Most definitely," Todd replied as he reached for the pepper grinder.

"The doctor says she must stay in bed until the baby is born. He's afraid the child is in the wrong position."

"Is it . . ." he paused and glanced over his shoulder at Rebekah. "Could this be dangerous for Columbia?"

"Having a child is always life-threatening. But the doctor didn't seem alarmed."

"I suppose it puts a strain on Quiet Jim." The cabbage tasted flat, but Todd knew he was far too tired to care.

"He has that lumber mill running so smoothly, he hardly needs to supervise. So he's spending most of his day taking care of Columbia and baby Sarah. Dacee June has agreed to take Quint and Fern for now."

"That will be a large assignment."

"Yes. I told them I'd come by each day right after lunch and give Quiet Jim a break. You don't mind if I spend the afternoons in Ingleside?"

Todd reached his hand back and pulled her around to his side. "I would appreciate it greatly if you did. You know that Quiet Jim is just like family to us."

"There's no 'just like,' Todd Fortune. Quiet Jim *is* family. He misses having Yapper Jim and Daddy Brazos in town."

"I reckon those two are out there pretending to be Lewis and Clark, exploring new territory."

"I think the sheriff misses them, too," she added. "I suppose you heard about that shooting in Terraville?"

"What shooting?"

"A storekeeper and his clerk were shot by a couple of bandits."

"I was over at Central City and didn't hear anything," he said.

"The sheriff just found out late this afternoon. He wanted Quiet Jim to go with him, but he couldn't leave Columbia. He came up here looking for you."

"He did?" Todd slurped a spoon of soup broth. "He's so desperate he had to look for the reserves?"

"I told him you were out on deliveries. I suppose he rounded up some others."

Todd fished out a bite of sweet ham, then stared at it on his spoon. "Am I going to get a lecture on how dangerous life is in the Black Hills?"

It was a voice of peaceful resignation. "Life is dangerous. Anywhere. Anytime. It's the legacy of sin that we brought into this world."

"Spoken like a Baptist preacher. You're beginning to sound like a natural-born Fortune," he said.

"Yes, it's frightening, isn't it?"

"I like it."

Rebekah brought two cups of coffee to the small table and sat down next to him.

"We had quite a day. Important decisions were made," he commented.

"At least, for the time being," she corrected.

"Oh?"

"Everything is up for review from time to time. Did you ever look at Olene's proposal?"

"I didn't have time."

"Well, I did," she reported. "He is making an incredibly generous offer for the store."

"But he won't agree to help people rebuild after a fire."

"Why not write that into a counterproposal and see what happens? You never know what you will get."

The knock brought both children out of their nap with a cry. Todd scurried to the door.

A breathless Carty Toluca pranced on the porch. "Someone broke into the store, and I can't find the sheriff anywhere! The window's busted, and the front door is kicked in!"

Todd grabbed the shotgun by the front door and took the steps two at a time. Dacee June held her long denim skirt up over her ankles and clamored after him, which left Rebekah with two whimpering, sniveling children.

"Is anyone still in the store?" Todd hollered to Carty several steps ahead of him.

"I couldn't see . . . it was too dark in there. I didn't want to go in alone."

FOUR

Only the kerosene street lantern at the corner of Lee and Main Streets lit the deserted sidewalk. Behind him, Todd could hear the usual shouts and songs of the badlands. Several of the cluster of small window panes on the Main Street window were shattered.

Todd examined the busted lock on the front door.

"What if they are still in there?" Carty asked.

"Have you got a gun on you?" Todd asked the clerk.

"I have a pistol. Do you want me to go in with you?"

"You stay here at the door. Don't shoot anyone, unless they try to shoot you."

"How about me?" Dacee June asked.

"Do you have a gun?" Todd replied.

"Yes!" She reached in her pocket and retrieved the revolver. "I'll go with you."

"You'll go across the street and watch."

"I'm not afraid," she pouted.

"I am. I need you to watch. If there's gunfire, I need you to run for some help."

"Who do I fetch? The sheriff's out of town."

"Eh, go get Quiet Jim. He'll know what to do."

Todd entered the dark building and immediately turned to the wall-mounted lantern next to the front door. *Lord, if someone's in here with a gun, they are going to take a shot at the person next to the lantern. I wish I knew if someone's in here. But then, there are a lot of things I wish I knew . . .*

He put himself between the darkness of the store and the lantern, then struck the sulfur match on the rough cedar wall. He lit the lantern, turned down the wick, and stepped toward the shadows.

Well, I haven't been shot at yet . . . that's a good sign.

CHAPTER FIVE

The first sound of gunfire from Main Street brought Rebekah Fortune to the window. At the second and third shots, she scurried out to the porch. In the gulch, below the safety of Forest Hill, she could hear horse hooves thunder. Fern was in her arms. Quintin trotted out and clutched her skirt. The June evening air was still mild, but a shock of chill slid down her back. Her hands trembled as she rocked the baby back and forth.

Fern whimpered.

"It's all right, Darlin' . . . it's all right . . ." The words rolled off her lips like a chant by a scared kid walking through the cemetery.

It was not the first dark Dakota night when gunshots had been heard in Deadwood. If the ground-shaking rumble of stamp mills in Lead were the bass section of the Black Hills orchestra, gunshots in Deadwood were the trumpet section, often carrying the tune.

Rebekah had heard shouting, screams, and curses before.

That was the frontier.

Gold towns.

Sudden wealth.

Impetuous passion.

Unanticipated anger.

And instant violence.

"Fire works?" Quintin asked. His chubby hands patted his ears.

Rebekah stroked the fine, wild hair that darted in all directions from the top of his head. "Well, Darlin', I don't think anyone's celebrating the Fourth of July . . . in June. There are no fireworks tonight."

Looking down Wall Street, she could see men running southwest along the shadows of Main Street.

Men in boots don't run anywhere, unless it's a disaster. They aren't going toward the badlands. It's at the store. Oh, Lord, watch over them!

A cold sweat beaded Rebekah's forehead as she paced the porch and fixed her gaze toward Main Street. Quintin staggered to keep up.

"Moon!" Fern shouted and waved her arm to the east.

Suddenly, Rebekah felt like all the attention in the universe was focused on the hardware store . . . and she couldn't see what was going on.

I can't take this, Lord. This is not for me. I don't operate like this. I like the quiet. Peaceful, sunny days. Harmonious voices. Where people respect each other, and hatred is restrained to the heart.

Oh, Lord . . . protect Todd . . . and Dacee June.

There's no more shooting.

Is everyone dead?

I didn't hear a shotgun, did I?

Then Todd didn't get a chance to shoot.

She began to gasp, fighting to control her breathing . . . and her tears. The girl in her arms began to cry.

"It's okay, darlin' . . . it's alright . . . he's safe . . . no one got hurt . . . someone was just hurrahing town." She tried to take a deep breath and hold it. It didn't work. "Oh, God . . . oh God . . ." she sobbed, and returned to the house.

I'm so scared, Lord. I've got to go down there . . . children and all. I can't wait! . . . I have to wait. This is not good.

Rebekah marched right into the kitchen and sat Fern on the floor next to Quintin. She washed her face, then led the children into her bedroom. "It's time to go to sleep, punkins . . . come on . . . I'll get you ready, and you can sleep in our bed."

She changed both children into flannel nightshirts. She felt so removed from what was taking place in the room, it was as if she was watching herself take care of the children. Fern lay still but watched

Rebekah's every move with big round brown eyes. Quintin didn't bed down that easy.

"No, I want my bed!"

"You aren't going home tonight, darlin'. You're going to stay at our house."

"Dacee-une!" he protested.

"I know you miss your Dacee-une . . . she'll be back in a minute." Rebekah's heart pounded so severely she could only speak a word or two before running out of breath. "Now you . . . stay under the covers . . . with Fern."

"No, I want up!" Quintin pushed the covers back, and squirmed out of the tall bed.

"No you don't, Young Man. Back to bed. You are going to mind me, and you are going to mind me right now," she snapped.

She shoved his shoulders back, but he giggled and ducked under her hands. *Relax, Rebekah. Don't take it out on the children. Oh, Lord, I'm losing control. I've never lost control in my life. You promised to send Your Comforter . . . well, I need Him . . . and I need Him right now!*

Quintin squirmed under the clutch of her hand on his shoulder. "I want my own bed."

"We've gone through all that before." She scooped him up and wanted to throw him back on the bed. Instead, she let out such a deep sigh the trembling in her hands ceased. She laid him gently down. Fern watched everything intently.

"Quint, I know this isn't what you were expecting, but I'm just a little scared right now. So I need you to help me, alright? What do you do when you get scared?"

His voice was very soft. "Mommy reads to me."

Rebekah brushed his bangs off his forehead. "OK . . . I'll try. You go in the parlor and find a book."

Quintin slid down out of the thick-mattressed bed and scampered out of sight.

Fern reached out her stubby little arms. "Hug me!"

"You're right about that, young lady; we all need a hug."

Rebekah crawled on top of the covers, lay down on her back, and hugged Fern with her right arm. Soon, she had a child on both arms. Quintin held the book, but after about three pages both nodded off.

The kerosene lantern flickered shadows across the hammered copper ceiling.

Why hasn't someone returned to tell me what's going on? Maybe it wasn't at the hardware, but next door. What if they don't know anything about this and are merely sweeping up the store? What if all this worry is for nothing?

What if they're all dead?

Lord, Your will be done. There are so many things in this life that I have absolutely no control over. I can't let them terrify me and imprison me up here in this house anymore. I'll do what I can and leave the rest to You. I can hug children and read them stories. I know that much.

She heard a dog bark on Williams Street. She strained to hear footsteps that never sounded.

Lord, we can't stay in Deadwood. I'm not going through this again. There are some women who grow stronger during trials and hardships. But I'm not a pioneer woman. I did not choose to come out here. I came with father. Lord, remember how I cried when we left Chicago?

I know I'm weak. Maybe I shouldn't have married a westerner. It's not fair to Todd. He needs a stronger woman. But oh how I love that man.

There has to be a place somewhere that fits both Todd and me. But I don't know if I could handle Rapid City . . . or Cheyenne . . . or any other place any better.

How can I plan the future when I don't know what's happening down there? I wish I was strong. I wish I could grab a pistol, hike down the hill with a child at each hand, and go to the aid of my husband.

"What did you do when you heard the shots, dear?"

"Oh, I hid in the bed behind some friends' children."

Rebekah's chin started to quiver.

"Get behind me, Satan! I have the peace of Jesus!" She hugged both children and was surprised that neither woke up at her outburst.

What if these were my children? What if I was left a young widow with children? That would be so tragic.

The silence of the house stabbed at her mind.

There are worse things, Rebekah Fortune. What if I'm left a widow with no children at all?

Cold tears slid down her cheeks.

I don't have any children, Lord. We've been married almost four years and I don't have any children! I can't believe I put myself in this position. You are a selfish, presumptuous prig, Rebekah Jacobson Fortune! What if something happened to Todd? What if you never have his child? That would drive me insane. If we are going to live here, I am not going to live this way.

Lord, give me a chance to make it right. Bring him back.

Quick! . . . before I die of worry.

The footsteps on the porch caused her to sit straight up between the two sleeping children.

It's not Todd. It's Dacee June.

Her hands shivered. "Thy will be done . . ." she mumbled as she scooted to the end of the bed. She was so careful to not wake up the children that she hardly noticed when the trembling ceased.

At the first gunshot, Todd dove behind the barrel of strap hinges. There was a woman's shout and two more shots as he rose to his knees and aimed the shotgun toward the darkened street.

Horseback riders galloped toward Shine Street.

Everything was quiet.

"Carty!" Todd yelled out the broken window.

"I'm here!"

"Are you shot?"

"No. Are you?" Carty yelled.

"No. What about Dacee June?"

"She looks OK. She's coming across the street now."

"Who did the shooting?" Todd hollered.

"Two men on horseback."

"Are they still there?"

"They rode off."

Todd crept toward the door, turned out the lantern, then stepped outside carrying the shotgun in front of him. He could hear footsteps approach from the dirt street. "Lil' Sis?"

"I'm OK," she called out in the darkness. "How's Carty?"

"I'm alright. Thanks for giving me that warnin' shot," he replied.

"What warning?" Todd asked. Suddenly Dacee June appeared alongside him, carrying her pistol in her hand.

Todd looked down the street in the shadows toward the sound of footsteps running their way from the badlands.

"You need any help, Fortune?" A man called out from the front steps of the hotel, diagonally across the street.

"It's alright, now," Todd called out. "Just a couple boys hurrahin' up the place. Wish they'd stay down in the badlands."

"Ain't that the truth."

Several men gathered on the hotel porch, but none crossed the street.

"You want us to go look for the sheriff?"

"He's busy, boys . . . I'll take care of it," Todd shouted. Then he turned back to Dacee June and Carty Toluca. "What happened out in the street?"

"Two men rode out of the alley by the Merchant's Hotel," Dacee June explained. "They stopped in the middle of the street and stared into the store for a minute, as if looking for a particular person. Then, all of a sudden, they took aim at you or Carty, I couldn't tell which. So I aimed over their heads and fired a warning shot."

"One of 'em fired into the store. I guess they was shootin' at you . . . or me." Carty looped his thumbs in his suspenders. "When I heard Dacee June's shot, I dove for cover and fired at them myself."

"You hid under a bench and shot into the dirt right in front of you," Dacee June scoffed.

"I was just admonishin' them. I didn't want to kill nobody."

"Admonish?" Dacee June chided. "You're lucky you didn't shoot yourself in the foot."

"But it was my shot that chased 'em off," he asserted.

Todd lit a sulfur match and studied their youthful faces.

"I'm a little dirty," Carty admitted. "That's all."

"I should have shot them dead," Dacee June griped. Her lower lip puckered to a pout.

"You did the right thing," Todd assured. "I can't believe anyone was looking for a serious gunfight if they ran off when a couple shots were fired. Could you tell who it was?"

"It was too dark," Dacee June explained. "All I could see was shadows. One was taller than the other, but all I saw was their backs."

The match went out, and Todd chewed on it like a toothpick. "How about you, Carty? Have you seen them before?"

"I didn't even know they had rode up until I heard Dacee June's gunfire."

FIVE

"You couldn't see them because you were hiding under a bench," Dacee June said.

"It don't matter where I was, Dacee June Fortune," Carty retorted. "It was too dark to recognize them, and you know it."

"How about the horses?"

"They were dark," Dacee June admitted, "but I couldn't tell if they were black or brown or bay."

"Nothing seems to be missing from the store," Todd explained. "I don't think it's a robbery. There was no one in the store. It's like someone smashed the window, kicked in the door, then just waited to take a shot at whoever showed up."

"They seemed to hesitate about shooting. Maybe they were looking for someone who wasn't there. Who did they want?" Dacee June asked.

"If you threw a brick through Fortune's Hardware, who would you expect to show up to investigate?" Todd asked.

"Not me," Carty shrugged. "I was just going down to . . ."

"Down to where?" Dacee June demanded.

"Down to get me some supper in China Town. I just happened to notice the busted window. I reckon they was expecting you, Todd."

"And Daddy!" Dacee June added. "If they didn't know he was out of town, they would have expected to see Daddy, that's for sure."

"And maybe Sheriff Bullock," Carty added. "He always comes runnin' at gunshots . . . especially those up in this part of town."

Dacee June scooted up next to Todd. "Do you think someone was trying to ambush us?"

Todd suddenly felt the cold receiver of the shotgun in his right hand. "Maybe. Either that or put the fear of ambush in us."

"Well, that part worked." She stared out at the night as a crowd gathered in the shadows down at the corner. "What are we going to do now?"

"Carty and I will board up this window, clean up the glass, and repair the front door. The excitement seems to be over now."

Dacee June rocked back on her heels. "Do you want me to go to the livery and get some horses?"

"Why do we want horses?" Carty asked.

"So we can ride out after them. That's what Daddy would do. He'd form a posse and ride them down if it took all summer."

"That's not what we're going to do," Todd announced. "Not even the legendary Daddy Brazos can track two men through the Black Hills at night. We'll check with Sheriff Bullock when he comes back. Meanwhile, I need you to go let Rebekah know what's going on. She's bound to be a little concerned."

Several men scurried up the wooden sidewalk from the direction of the badlands. "Fortune, you need any help?"

"No thanks, Boys, it's settled down now."

"What happened?" one called out.

"Someone took potshots at the windows."

"What really happened?" A deep familiar voice sliced through the night directly behind Todd.

He spun around. Quiet Jim stood behind him. His duck coat was buttoned only at the top. His hat was pulled down over his eyes. His '73 Winchester carbine was cradled in his left arm. He had no smile, and his eyes pierced the night air.

"How's Columbia?" Dacee June asked.

In the dark shadows, Todd could see Quiet Jim tip his hat to Dacee June. "They were asleep. Thanks for askin'."

Todd put his hand on Carty's shoulder. "Walk Dacee June home, would you?"

Carty's reply was enthusiastic. "Yes sir."

"I don't need any help," she insisted. "I have a gun, you know. And I'll use it if I need to."

"We all know that," Todd assured her.

"And I won't feel one bit better having him along."

"No, but I'll feel better," Todd said.

"You goin' to tell me what really happened?" Quiet Jim repeated.

"Let's go warm up some coffee and clean up this mess, and I'll tell you what I know," Todd offered. *I don't know what these old men have, but it surely does feel good to have Quiet Jim standing alongside me, Lord. I can think of another old codger that I wish was here about now, too.*

It took nearly two hours for them to board up the big window at the hardware. Carty traipsed home. Todd locked the front door. The evening air felt cool on Todd's sweaty face.

"Thanks for fetching me those one-by-twelves, Quiet Jim."

Quiet Jim's voice sounded like striking the lowest note on a piano over and over. "I told your daddy I'd look after you."

FIVE

Todd slipped the store key into his vest pocket. "You really think it's those stage robbers looking for revenge?"

"Some old boys is funny that way," Quiet Jim explained. "They don't intend to let anyone get the upper hand on them."

"But it doesn't make sense," Todd countered. "If you just escaped, wouldn't you go someplace and lay low for a while? If I was them, I'd be halfway to Texas by now."

"But you ain't them; that's the point." Todd always figured that Quiet Jim's voice was too slow for daytime use, but it fit the darkness well. "They don't think like you and me, Todd. I reckon it's the devil's doin'. It's like their soul and mind's been bent, and it cain't be straightened. Take that Doc Kabyo, for instance. You remember how he called your daddy out to the plains when he done had all the cargo stolen? He held a gun on you and Robert just because he wanted to personally kill Brazos. Meanness, that's what it is. Inhuman meanness. Once they turn that way, there's nothin' that stops them short of a noose or a bullet. Or the judgment of God Almighty. It's like a rabid dog—there is nothin' you can do but put 'em down."

"Well, before we decide to hang these two, we'd better find out who they are. Might be just a couple of drunks looking to wear off some whiskey."

"If that's all they was, they should have stayed in the badlands where the pickin's easy."

"When's the sheriff coming back?" Todd asked.

"I thought he'd be home tonight, but maybe he's on the trail to somethin'. You want me to come up and get Quint and Fern and take 'em home?" Quiet Jim asked.

"No, go on back with Columbia."

"You sure you want to keep them up there tonight?"

"Go on," Todd insisted. "It doesn't matter if they're at your house or my house. It's all family and you know it."

"Yeah, that's the way I figure it, too," Quiet Jim replied. "I just want to be careful not to impose on Rebekah. She's a delicate thing like my Columbia. You Fortunes, you're all tough as nails, and straight as Arapaho arrows. But them ladies from the East is a different breed."

Todd hiked up a nearly deserted west end of Main Street. Quiet Jim's words bounced in his head. *Some of us are not nearly as tough as others. Two men shot at me, and I was so busy hiding I never got a shot off. Dacee June and Carty did better than that.* The lights from the bad-lands district glowed across Wall Street as he turned the corner. Someone laughed. Another shouted. A piano played. There was a moan from a losing poker hand and a shout from a winning one. The cool air drifted down Whitewood Gulch, bringing the drumbeat of the Homestake Mine stamp mills.

Just another night in Deadwood.

Maybe Rebekah's right.

Perhaps it is too-dangerous a place to raise children.

The seventy-two steps up to Williams Street were only seven inches high each. But this time each one seemed two-feet tall. Todd was puffing by the time he reached the top of the stairs and spotted a familiar silhouette that waited on the porch.

"What are you doing out here?" he asked.

Rebekah put her finger to her mouth. "Everyone's asleep inside." Her small crocheted shawl dropped to the porch when she threw her arms around him. Her thick robe was buttoned to her neck.

He held her tight, but it was too dark to look into her eyes. "Everyone?"

"I put the kids to bed with me, and Dacee June took over when she came home. You and I are going to have to spend the night upstairs in one of the guest rooms."

With his arms around her, he rubbed her back. "I suppose Dacee June filled you in on the shooting?"

"It sounded like an ambush, Todd." She laid her head on his chest. "And it scares me to death."

He rocked her back and forth and glanced out at a star-sprinkled night sky. "I'm not fond of it, myself."

She stepped back, scooped up her shawl, then led him by the hand into the house. She snatched up the one burning lantern from the hall table. Todd put his shotgun back on the rack.

"Lock the front door," she said.

"We don't need to . . ."

"Please!"

He shrugged and stepped back to the door, throwing the dead-bolt. "Everything will be more relaxed come daylight."

"I know . . ." She reached back and tugged his hand as she started up the narrow stairs.

FIVE

Even though Todd stepped lightly, he heard the stairs squeak at each step. The air in the house was warmer as they reached the platform at the top of the stairs . . . and sweeter.

"Are you wearing that new perfume?" he asked.

"Yes. I was tired of smelling like boiled cabbage." Her voice resounded like a musical whisper. "Do you mind?"

"Of course not. I would mind less, if I weren't so exhausted," he mumbled.

They strolled into the smallest of the upstairs bedrooms at the back of the house. The old feather bed that had been Rebekah's as a young girl waited with sheets turned back and pillows fluffed. She set the lantern down, then lit a fat, round, cream-colored candle.

"Candlelight?" Todd teased.

"It's that vanilla candle that Thelma Speaker gave me for my birthday," she said. "The air's kind of stale and musty up here. I think I'll leave the windows open tomorrow and air it out."

Todd plopped down on the edge of the bed and held up a foot. Rebekah tugged off his boot. "I haven't been up here in months," he admitted. "I thought it was still piled with your sewing projects."

"It was. I cleaned it up a little."

"Tonight?"

"Is that alright?"

"Sometimes I forget the two rooms we have up here."

"It's a nice house, Todd."

"Thank you, Mrs. Fortune. I enjoyed building it and wondering who it was the Lord would bring into my life to share it with. But all of this is the prelude. I'm waiting for the sermon."

Rebekah began to unfasten a double row of buttons on her robe. "You mean about how incredibly dangerous Deadwood is, and how I was terrified beyond description tonight when I thought you could have been shot. And now I've decided that we have to pack up and move some other place, like maybe the north side of Chicago? You mean that kind of sermon?"

Todd stood frozen in place, his mouth dropped open. "Sort of . . . yeah."

"Well, you're wrong, Mr. Fortune. I'm not even going to mention those things."

"That's nice of you." He slipped off his soiled and wrinkled white cotton shirt. "Is there anything else you *aren't* going to mention?"

She tossed her robe on a chair and brushed down the front of her long flannel nightshirt. Her unpinned light brown hair flowed down her back. "And I'm not going to mention a very important thought that came to me while I was lying in bed between Quintin and Little Fern wondering whether I was a widow or not."

Todd tugged off his socks. "What was that?" He thought he could see her eyes flicker.

"I said, I'm not going to mention it." Rebekah scooted under the covers.

His trousers neatly folded across the back of the chair, Todd stretched his arms and yawned. "Somehow I feel like I'm being left in the dark."

"Don't worry," she assured. "I'll leave the vanilla candle lit."

He sat on the edge of the bed with his feet on the floor. "That's not what I meant, and you know it."

"You were right. We can talk about all those things in the light of tomorrow. Would you please lock the bedroom door before you come to bed?"

He turned back and looked her in the eyes. "Aren't you letting your fears get carried away? We've got the outside doors latched, and there's no one in the house but Lil' Sis and two children. Just exactly who is it you intend to keep out of our room?"

"Lil' Sis and two children," she grinned, then pulled the sheet up over her head.

"It was all a wild goose chase," Seth Bullock reported the next morning as he stood by the stove at the back of Fortune's Hardware. "When I got to Terraville, nobody knew of anyone being shot. Said they thought there was a ruckus over at Cheyenne Crossing. But, when I got there, they reported the only excitement around there was a lot of commotion down at China Camp in Spearfish Canyon."

"Did you ride on down there?" Todd asked.

"Yeah . . . and the strange thing is, they all left."

"The Chinese?"

"Not a one of them left at China Camp. Packed up and gone."

"Daddy always said there wasn't much gold over there," Todd said.

"I rode half the night, then camped on the other side of Anchor. Half the time a sheriff's job is investigatin' things that don't happen." Bullock finished his coffee and set the tin cup next to the row of others on the back shelf. "My word, it's a pitiful sight."

"What's that?"

"Everyone's coffee cup lined up there and not one man sittin' around the stove," the sheriff sighed.

"It does seem pleasantly peaceful, doesn't it?"

"Peaceful? It's downright boring," the sheriff complained. "Think I'll wander down into the badlands and see if anyone knows something about those old boys who busted your window."

"Quiet Jim thinks it might be those two stagecoach outlaws who escaped," Todd offered.

"I reckon it could be. But no one's seen them in town. Still, they didn't seem smart enough to stay out of sight very long."

"I don't hardly remember what they looked like. I didn't pay them much mind."

The sheriff brushed back his long, curling gray mustache. "The blond one was bigger and taller, but it was the shorter, dark-haired one that did all the cussin' and threatenin'. They had the drop. I can't figure why they didn't put a bullet in you. Nothin' personal, but maybe they were lookin' for Brazos, since he's the one that shot their pard."

"That's not really too reassuring."

"Well, I hope your daddy and Yapper Jim stay away for a few more days. Might give me a chance to find where they're hidin' out." Sheriff Seth Bullock moseyed toward the front door. "Until we find 'em, I'd pack a gun if I were you."

Todd pulled open his suit coat to reveal a belt holster and a short-barreled .45 Schofield Smith and Wesson.

"That should do it. Let me know if you spot anything suspicious. I don't figure they'll show themselves in daylight. But I reckon you, me, and Quiet Jim ought to watch ourselves at night. We were all a part of bringin' 'em in."

"This evening's the Raspberry Festival at the church," Todd reminded him. "I don't think even that bunch would take potshots at a church meeting."

"I reckon we'll find out." Bullock pushed his hat back and meandered out into the street.

The lady at the door donned a smile as wide as her face. The burgundy-collar silk dress with black velvet shawl swished as she strolled into the store. Her black straw hat with French flowers was at a waggish tilt.

"Good morning, ma'am," Todd grinned.

"It's well past noon, Mr. Fortune," she lectured.

Todd pulled his pocket watch out of his vest, and glanced at it. "Yep. Did you miss me at lunch?"

"With Dacee June and two children, we hardly knew you were gone," Rebekah admitted.

"You look mighty nice for going to visit a sick friend," he grinned. "You aren't sneaking out dancing, are you?"

Rebekah laughed. "If I would have known a dress like this was so captivating, I would have sewn one up years ago."

"You didn't need a dress like this to captivate me last night," he murmured.

"You, Todd Fortune, are a pushover. I love it." She waltzed down the hardware aisle as if actually inspecting the merchandise. "This is the day Abigail's mother and daughter arrive. I might get so busy later that I won't have time to change clothing."

"I figured you just dressed that way to torment me."

"Did it work?"

"Yep."

"Good. Besides, I like the way this dress makes me feel. Like I'm someone important."

"You are important." Todd shook his head. "I still can't figure you out, Rebekah Fortune. After the shots were fired at the store last night, I thought you'd be depressed for a month. I thought you'd be in tears. Instead, I come home to find you . . ."

With gloved hands she examined a mule shoe. "Just how did you find me, Mr. Fortune?"

"You know . . . all friendly like. Sometimes you're a puzzle."

"A lady of mystery? I like that. You never know what she might do. On the other hand, some things are predictable. Have you reserved a carriage for our drive to Rapid City on Sunday?"

FIVE

"Eh, no . . . I figured that maybe . . ."

"Maybe I'd changed my mind? Mr. Fortune, when a lady of mystery changes her mind, you will be the last to know!" She turned and strutted toward the front door.

A worn-out Quiet Jim greeted Rebekah when she arrived at their Lincoln Street home in the Ingleside district. He opened the big glass and oak front door wide and ushered her into the parlor.

"Did Baby Sarah fuss last night?" she asked.

"Sarah fussed, Columbia moaned, and I stewed around after I checked out the shootin' down at the store. I reckon I didn't sleep thirty minutes all night." At five-foot six, Quiet Jim measured only a fraction taller than Rebekah. When he leaned close, they stood eye to eye. His eyes were tired and red. "Don't tell Columbia that Seth thinks those stage robbers are still on the prowl. She's got enough worries without that."

Rebekah hugged the slight-framed, mostly gray-headed man like a favorite uncle. "Don't worry about a thing. You go on and stretch your legs. Get some air. Check on the lumber mill. Stop by and have coffee at the store. That stove has been very lonesome since Daddy Brazos left."

"It ain't the only thing that's missed that old man."

"We all miss Daddy Brazos, don't we? He kind of holds the clan together."

"Yep, and if they stay away a few more days, I might even start missin' Yapper Jim, too." A sly grin crept across Quiet Jim's narrow lips.

"If you want to, go on up to the house and take a nap. You won't be able to keep this up night after night," she said.

"Some days I feel like a complete fool for marryin' a gal twenty years younger."

Rebekah laid her hand on his arm. "Columbia loves you dearly, Quiet Jim."

He looked away and wiped a tear from the furrows around his small gray eyes. He cleared his throat. His voice was barely above a whisper. "Are Quintin and Fern behavin' themselves?"

"They act their age. It's delightful. Dacee June enjoys them immensely."

"That Dacee June is golden. Ever' Fortune in the Black Hills is pure gold."

Columbia reclined in the center of the high-post red mahogany bed with ruffled white cotton sheets tucked around her. There were ruffles on the comforter, ruffles on the curtains, ruffles on the pillow slips, ruffles on her nightgown, and ruffles on little Sarah's nightshirt.

Mother and daughter were sleeping as Rebekah slipped into the wooden rocker beside the bed without a sound. She pulled off her black straw hat with burgundy French roses and laid it on the table beside her. She fussed to make sure her long hair was still neatly tucked into her ebony combs. She brushed down the skirt of her dress, then folded her hands in her lap and began to rock.

The chair squeaked and Columbia's eyes flipped open. Her face was thin and pale, but her complexion was perfectly smooth. Not one wrinkle in her face, not even around her eyes. Her black eyelashes were the longest, most dramatic that Rebekah had ever seen. On more than one occasion Columbia had batted those lashes and paralyzed every man within one hundred feet.

She smiled faintly through tightly drawn lips and studied Rebekah.

"Sorry . . ." Rebekah whispered. "I didn't know the chair was noisy."

Columbia glanced at the sleeping eighteen-month-old next to her. "Us ladies decided we needed a nap . . . again." She glanced back at Rebekah. "Did you come over here to shame me?"

Rebekah leaned toward the bed. "Shame you?"

"I'm teasing, Mrs. Fortune. You look absolutely beautiful in that dress. Suddenly, I don't mind missing the Raspberry Festival. I would feel horribly plain."

"You? Everyone knows you are the most glamorous woman who ever set a dainty foot in the Black Hills."

Columbia's smile widened. Anxiety seemed to melt from her face. "It just struck me how contradictory it is to talk of anything in the Black Hills as glamorous."

Rebekah found Columbia's grin contagious. "Perhaps, but you're our best hope."

"At one time, that mattered," Columbia sighed. "But now . . . what beauty I have fades a little more with each child. And you know what, Rebekah? I don't mind one bit. It's a good trade."

"You haven't lost a thing, Columbia." Rebekah reached over and held her friend's hand. It was very warm, almost moist. "You just gained a blush that makes you even more enviable."

Columbia patted Rebekah's hand. "You are a most charming liar. I'm fat, miserable, short-tempered, and horribly grouchy. If you don't think so, just ask my Jim."

Rebekah sat back, allowing her arms to rest on the arms of the wooden rocker. She started to rock, glanced at the sleeping baby, then stopped. "Your Jim figures you're the reason God made the earth."

Columbia glanced at the baby. She brushed her eyes with a corner of the sheet. "He spoils me something terrible," she murmured.

"That is not the way he sees it," Rebekah said.

"This is much too maudlin a conversation." Columbia brushed her black bangs out of her eyes. "How are my other children? When do I get to see them again?"

"Dacee June hovers over them. She guards them like they were the treasure coach on its bimonthly run. She said she'd bring them over before going to the Raspberry Festival."

"Why doesn't she leave them home with me during the festival?"

"Quintin would be crushed. He insists on devouring an entire pie tonight. Besides, Quiet Jim said he was coming home right after the auction. We'll send them then, if you feel up to it."

"Yes, yes, please do. I miss them dearly. I just want to make sure I don't wear out my dear husband." Columbia propped herself up on her elbows.

"What can I get for you?" Rebekah asked.

"That damp cloth would be nice."

Rebekah scurried across the room for the damp green cloth. "I've never heard Quiet Jim complain of anything you and the kids do."

Columbia wiped her face, then her hands. "My Jim never complains. He comes from a generation of men that believe complaining is a sign of weakness of character and lack of trust in the Lord."

"Not a bad trait," Rebekah said.

"It's wonderful." She handed the damp rag back to Rebekah. "My Jim has his weaknesses, but I wouldn't want him to change."

"Quiet Jim has weaknesses?" Rebekah raised her eyebrows. "Whatever could those be?"

"He's too tranquil sometimes," Columbia reported. "He believes that he doesn't have anything important to say, and the truth is, he makes more sense than any man I've ever met. But sometimes I have to beg and plead to get him to give me his advice."

"He definitely lives up to his name."

"And then, of course, there are 'the boys.' Daddy Brazos, Yapper Jim, and Grass Edwards. I feel in constant competition. My Jim acts as if he couldn't survive a day without them. He was broken hearted when he couldn't go with them."

"Does that make you jealous?" Rebekah questioned.

"Oh, sure . . . sometimes. I would like to think I am all my husband needs. They remind me it just isn't so." She reached over and ran her fingers through little Sarah's fine, light-brown hair. "But that's not much to complain about, is it?"

"I suppose not."

"Yes, that's about all I can say about my Jim . . . oh, sometimes his incessant generosity peeves me."

"Helping anyone who comes along?"

"Yes. There are so many who seem to take advantage of him."

"Todd and I have the same struggle with Daddy Brazos," Rebekah said. "What is there about the boys of the Texas Camp of '75? They figure they owe every drifter in the Black Hills a grubstake."

Columbia glanced out the north window at the bright, clear June day. "I've just left it all to the Lord. I'll have to trust Him that we won't go broke and have nothing left for the children."

Rebekah sighed. "We have to let them be what they are down inside."

Columbia glanced across the room. "Yes, and that includes these dreary Black Hills."

"Don't tell me you tire of the gulch?" Rebekah tapped her fingers on the wooden arms of the rocking chair.

"I don't know about you, Rebekah Fortune, but this is not my idea of a perfect locale." Columbia sat up slowly and stretched her arms and neck. "Stamp mills boom day and night . . . dirt hangs in the air all summer, unless it's raining . . . there is violence in the street, and no level place for the children to play . . . do you know what I mean?"

FIVE

"Yes, I do. Have you and Quiet Jim ever talked about moving elsewhere?" Rebekah asked.

When Columbia lay back down, she gently rubbed her round stomach that pressed tight against her robe.

"Are you all right?"

"Mrs. Fortune, I look forward to you having children . . . then I won't have to try and explain what this feels like."

"You might not have to wait too long," Rebekah answered.

Columbia sat back up. "Really? When?"

"It's just my intuition now, so don't you go tell a soul."

"You cheered up my whole day!"

"You just want someone to share the misery."

"I'll come and visit you, and I promise not to say you're fat. Oh, my . . . this is such good news I forgot what we were talking about."

"I asked if you and Quiet Jim ever considered moving to a better place for the children?"

"Oh, no! My Jim has an almost sacred attachment to these hills. It would break his heart and his spirit to leave here. Of course, when we first got married and I was expecting little Quint, I fussed about moving out to Spearfish or Miles City . . . or Cheyenne."

"What did he say?"

Columbia laid back and gingerly turned on her side, facing Rebekah. "His lips said he'd go anywhere on the face of the earth, just as long as he could be with me. But his eyes told me he would shrivel up and die without these hills. It was through sacrifice, pain, danger, and the blood of his friends that these mountains were settled. He feels like a caretaker. It dawned on me one day that these hills are part of what make my Jim the way he is. And I don't want to change one thing about him. No, we'll never leave."

Rebekah rocked back quickly, causing the chair to squeak. *Lord, did you send her just to shame me? But Todd's different. He isn't one of the boys of '75. He didn't get run out of the hills by General Crook, nor did he fight the Sioux with his pards alongside. That makes it completely different, doesn't it, Lord? Would he be a different Todd if he was forced to leave the hills?*

Sarah blinked her wide eyes open and immediately sat up, pointing to Rebekah.

"Mrs. Fortune came to visit us, dumplin'," Columbia cooed.

"Pretty," Sarah squealed.

Columbia turned to Rebekah. "Where in the world did you get that silk dress? I want one just like it. That is, when I'm not so fat."

Rebekah held out her arms to model the dress. "I borrowed it from a friend."

"Well, I get to borrow it next! Which friend? Who in this town has such a elegant dress?"

"Her name is Mrs. Gordon, but she goes by the stage name Abby O'Neill."

"At the Gem?"

"Yes."

"I didn't know you knew her."

"It's a rather new friendship."

"Well, how cordial, Mrs. Fortune. Now, I really feel homebound. I've never known an actress in my life."

"I've never seen her act, but the newspaper said she carried the cast. I don't know her well."

"Well enough to borrow a dress."

"And baby-sit," Rebekah added.

Sarah crawled over and poked at her mother's stomach. "Baby," she announced.

"Yes, Darlin', and let's rock the baby to sleep." Columbia's left arm engulfed Sarah, and they rocked back and forth on the feather mattress. "Now, I want to know all about your friend the actress that has children whom you baby-sit."

"It's a rather long story."

"Good! The one thing I have, Rebekah Fortune, is plenty of time."

Todd's coat lay across the crate of pipe fittings. His vest was unbuttoned, his tie pulled loose, the top button on his white shirt unfastened. He was wiping his hands on a flour sack rag when two ladies and a young girl walked into the store.

The older lady had very dark, almost black hair with streaks of gray flaming through it.

"Abigail! Is this your mother and daughter?" he asked.

Abigail Gordon wore her "Douglas, Douglas, Tender and True" brown dress. "Mr. Fortune, may I introduce to you my daughter Amber . . . and my mother Mrs. O'Neill."

"Oh, my, which one is which?" Todd teased.

"I'm the daughter," the five-year-old announced. "And that's my grandma."

"Pleased to meet you, Mrs. O'Neill. You'll have to excuse the informality." Todd rolled down the sleeves of his shirt. "I've been unpacking freight."

"Oh, heavens, I didn't expect to find city dandies in Deadwood," the older woman offered. "This is a very hard-working town."

"You're right about that." Todd glanced at Abigail, who seemed to be waiting for him to say something. "Eh, did you get settled into Abigail's apartment?"

"Yes, it's a quite nice hotel. Then, it's just the kind of place I would expect my daughter to live."

Todd squatted down by the young girl with round cheeks and curly, light-brown hair that tumbled to her shoulders.

"Do you have candy in this store?" she quizzed.

"Amber!" Abigail cautioned.

Todd noticed the same fiery brown eyes as her mother's.

"Sorry, honey, we don't have one thing to eat in the whole store. I hear you're coming up to my house for a while tonight."

"Yes, but my mother said it was only for a short while. Are you having lima beans for supper? I don't eat lima beans," Amber announced.

Todd stuck out his tongue and made a face. "Neither do I!"

A smile broke across the girl's face, and Todd stood back up. "Are you headed up to the house now?"

"Yes. Is Rebekah home yet?" Abigail asked.

"I believe so. Very nice to meet you, Mrs. O'Neill. I trust we'll get to visit more later."

"I'm sure we will. Gail has told me so much about you and your wife."

Abigail scooted over to Todd as they walked to the front door. She spoke under her breath, leaving a toothy smile on her face. "If you ever call me Gail, I'll rip your tongue out."

"I'll remember that," he grinned. "Tell Rebekah I'll be home shortly."

A trio of cries greeted Todd as he entered his house on Williams Street at the top of the Wall Street stairs.

He had arrived in time to witness Quintin bop Amber in the back of the head with a wooden spoon. When she let out a cry, all three children began to wail.

"Quintin, put down that spoon!" he called. "Where's Dacee June?"

"Bye-bye . . ." Fern whimpered.

"Dacee June went bye-bye? Where's Rebekah? Where's Aunt Rebekah?"

"She's not really their aunt," Amber announced.

"Yes, well . . . that's not the point. Where is Mrs. Fortune?"

"I'm in the kitchen," Rebekah called out.

"What are you doing in there?"

"Trying to wipe molasses out of your good boots."

"My what?"

"Quint likes to play with molasses. I'm not sure everywhere he poured it."

"Where's Dacee June?"

"She went home to change."

A crash and a tinkle sent both of them scurrying to the parlor.

"Uh, oh!" Quintin gulped.

"What happened?" Rebekah called out.

"He hit the glass dove with the spoon," Amber reported.

"Uh, oh!" Quintin repeated as if it was sufficient to explain why the dove's left wing was now separated from its body.

"It's OK. Come on, you three, let's wait out on the porch for Aunt Rebekah to finish cleaning my boots," Todd insisted.

"What are you going to do with them out there?" she asked.

"I'll tell them a story, or something," Todd snatched up Fern and plucked the wooden spoon from Quintin. "Did you ever hear the story of when Stuart Brannon captured the train robbers using nothing but a barrel of molasses and a wooden spoon?"

Amber shook her head.

"Todd Fortune, don't you fill their heads with lies!" Rebekah called out.

"Certainly, dear," he hollered back. "Why don't you come entertain the orphanage, and I'll get ready for the Raspberry Festival."

"On second thought," she called out, "that Stuart Brannon molasses story would be delightful."

"I thought so."

The dining hall at the church at the base of McGovern Hill was built to hold seventy-five. Well over a hundred were now packed into it. Dacee June sat at the pump organ and played a tune that was somewhere between "Soldier's Joy" and "Goodbye at the Door." Amber Gordon sat beside her on the small wooden bench, watching Dacee June's every motion.

Fern was content to rest in her father's arm as he toted her through the crowd. Quint looked permanently attached to Quiet Jim's pant leg. Todd squeezed his way through the crowd to check on Rebekah in the kitchen.

He was greeted at the door by Thelma Speaker.

"Todd Fortune, your Rebekah is simply a marvelous hostess. Why, I wish my sister Louise was here to see this."

Mrs. Speaker clutched his arm and towed him by three ladies who were slicing pie. "Look at this display. Your Rebekah called it a Cascade of Fruitful Delight. Isn't that poetic?"

Todd caught a glimpse of his wife rolling her eyes to the ceiling. "She's an amazing lady. I think I'll step out for a little air. It's a tad crowded in here."

"You'll come back for pie, won't you?" Mrs. Speaker insisted.

"I wouldn't miss it for anything."

Several men loitered at the back door of the church. The conversation was light, the pipe smoke thick. In the evening shadows, Todd recognized most by their hats. The round hat and pointed crown of Seth Bullock caught his attention.

"Evenin' Sheriff."

"Todd, you get chased out?"

"It's a might bit crowded. But that's a good sign for a fund raiser."

A rider galloped up to the front of the church. Todd and Sheriff Bullock moseyed around to Sherman Street.

"Sheriff Bullock?" The man called from the horse. "You got to come down to the Piedmont Saloon. Nevada Jack done shot himself dead!" the man called out.

"Committed suicide?" Bullock questioned.

"Yes sir."

"Then you don't need me; you need an undertaker."

"But there's going to be some more dead if you don't come down. We was playin' a big poker game, and Jack bet the Piedmont Saloon on his cards. But after he drew a final card, he whipped out his pocket gun and blew his brains out. When that happened some of the cards spilt across the table. Well, some is declarin' a misdeal, and others sayin' the pot belongs to them. They're about ready to shoot each other."

The sheriff glanced across the street. "I'll borrow one of these carriages and be right down. What did they do with Nevada Jack?"

"He's still layin' there in his chair. At least, what's left of him."

"Fetch an undertaker." The sheriff turned back toward the church. "I'd better take someone with me. Maybe Quiet Jim would . . ."

Todd reached out and took hold of the sheriff's shoulder. "Quiet Jim's got family chores. I'll go with you."

"Appreciate it, Todd. I don't realize how much I count on those old cronies until they ain't around."

Todd marched across the street where several rigs were parked. "Must have been quite a lousy hand to want to kill yourself."

"Nevada Jack didn't commit suicide," Bullock announced.

"How do you know?"

"No professional gambler ever killed himself over a poker game. Over a woman, maybe, but not on losin' a poker game. That's their business. They don't expect to win every hand."

Todd held the bridle of the lead horse. "What are you saying?"

Seth Bullock climbed up into the rig and Todd handed him the reins. "I'd say someone shot him, and they won't say who until the fate of the pot is decided."

Todd swung up into the carriage beside the sheriff who handed him a short-barreled shotgun.

"Did you know that ol' boy who came ridin' up with the news?" Sheriff Bullock asked.

"It's dark, but he didn't look familiar."

"I've never seen him," the sheriff reported.

"It's soundin' stranger by the minute."

The trigger of the shotgun felt cold against Todd's finger. "You think they are tryin' to cover up something?"

"Maybe." The sheriff slapped the reins of the rump of the lead horse. "Maybe the whole story is jist bait."

CHAPTER SIX

The Piedmont Saloon and Gambling Emporium boasted it was the building most often burned down in all the Black Hills. No one contested that claim. In four years of notorious business, it had been leveled six times by fire and one time by a man named Slappy McMack. In a fit of revenge, he drove his ten-ox team and two freight wagons straight through the front door and out the back, to the shock of the raucous occupants.

The current owner was Nevada Jack, a slight man with a huge mustache that dwarfed his face. His greatest achievement was firing his six-foot one, black, lady bartender—Mabel MacQueen. She immediately hired on as the chief cook at the Hallelujah Gold Mine and gained a reputation overnight as the best cook in the Black Hills.

The saloon had a high-pitched roof with rafters of uneven lengths stretching past the walls and protruding halfway to the ground. No one bothered to saw them off at the eaves. This made the thirty-foot by seventy-foot building look partially finished in the daylight, and a dangerous maze at night.

Sheriff Bullock parked the rig alongside Whitewood Creek near where Main Street and Sherman Street joined. "Get around to the back," he ordered. "As soon as you hear me talking, step up and block the door. I don't want anyone running out."

Todd inched his way by each protruding rafter along the west side of the building. At the open doorway at the base of the mountain behind the saloon, he heard the roar of a room full of drinking and gambling men. He crouched in the shadows to survey the crowd. Lanterns flickered. The top third of the room was engulfed in a cloud of cigar smoke. Several men looked familiar. Most did not.

I don't see a body sprawled across the table. No one is too concerned about Nevada Jack's demise.

Todd backed up and stumbled over something tossed out in the dirt. He caught himself, then looked down. *Someone tossed the back door out into the yard? I don't suppose they will need it until winter.*

So, the sheriff's stuck with 'Young' Fortune. He's not the only one that wishes Daddy was here. This is not my type of predicament. It's for men of another generation.

The noise inside the Piedmont lowered as Todd heard a man call out, "Sheriff, what are you doing down here?"

Todd stepped up, shotgun in hand, and blocked the door. An unshaven man in a torn buckskin shirt and a huge knife strapped to his waist darted toward the back. He halted midstride when he spied the shotgun.

"Let me out!" he snarled.

Todd turned the barrel toward the man. He could feel his sweaty fingers on the trigger. "Just wait until the sheriff does his work."

"I cain't wait." The man glanced wildly back at the sheriff who hadn't spotted him yet. "I need to go to the outhouse!"

"Not right now you don't." Todd cocked both hammers on the double-barreled shotgun.

For a minute Todd thought the man was going to pull the knife and charge at him. *Lord, I don't want to shoot a man on his way to the outhouse.*

The man muttered a few words that Todd was sure had never been articulated in any of the homes on Forest Hill, then slunk back into the crowd near the rustic counter that served as a bar.

Seth Bullock sauntered into the middle of the room. Most of the crowd migrated back to give him space. "Nevada Jack, it's interesting that you are the one to ask me that. I came down here to bury you." Todd noticed several men, including the one in buckskins, hunched and hidden along the wall.

SIX

Nevada Jack, in the back corner of the unpainted bare wood building, stood up. His chair set against the wall. He displayed no injuries. He brushed back his drooping mustache. Todd could see several men rest their hands on holstered revolvers.

Like the professional gambler that he was, Nevada Jack had his sleeves rolled up halfway to his elbows and kept his hands in front of him. Todd could see no gun, but he knew there were at least two tucked away somewhere.

Nevada Jack carefully laid face down five bluebacked poker cards. "Bury me? I've got to commit a crime if you're going to bury me."

Bullock scrutinized the crowd. "I didn't say I was going to shoot you. I said, bury you. Word came uptown that you blew your brains out over a poker game. We just came down to drag off your body."

Nevada Jack glanced at the back door. So did the other thirty men in the room.

The sheriff waved his revolver. "You boys know young Fortune, don't you?"

Todd kept the shotgun pointed toward the center of the crowd.

Nevada Jack rested his thumbs in his vest pockets. "Ain't nothin' sillier than someone takin' a poker game that serious. You should know me better than that."

"That's sort of the answer we was expectin'," the sheriff replied. "But I thought maybe someone shot you in the back and was tryin' to say it was suicide."

Nevada Jack slowly grinned. His elbows gradually pulled against his sides. "That's always a possibility. Wouldn't put it past anyone in the room. That's why I won't turn my back on 'em. Appreciate you takin' concern for me, but it looks like a false call."

The sheriff pivoted toward the crowd at the bar. "Any of you know of someone so anxious to see me they'd send a messenger to lie to me at the church?"

There was no reply.

Nevada Jack pulled out a cigar. "I ain't dead, that's for sure." He bit off the tip and spat it on the floor.

"The night's still young, Jack!" one of the men at the bar hollered. The tension checked the laughter for a moment, then it burst loose.

"Sheriff, if you would like to stick around and see if I croak, you're welcome. Just don't block the doorway for my customers. As for me, I don't intend to waste a good poker hand." He plucked up his cards and plopped back down in the faded green wooden chair.

The man in the buckskin shirt slipped through the crowd again toward the back door, the large double-edged unsheathed knife by his side.

"I need to get out now," he snarled at Todd.

"Fortune," the sheriff called out, "we'll head on back up town. Bring Dubois with you. I've got a wanted notice out on him from Sidney, Nebraska."

Todd surveyed the crowd. "Who is that?"

When he turned his head, the man with the buckskin shirt and knife lunged at him. Todd jerked back and raised the barrel of the shotgun to the ceiling. The wooden stock swung across his midsection. The point of the large knife stuck into the walnut wood of the shotgun stock and jammed the stock into his stomach.

Todd leaped backwards through the doorway. The knife yanked out of the man's hand and remained lodged in the gunstock. The man dove after the knife handle. Todd swung the stock out of the man's grasp, and in doing so, the barrel of the shotgun slammed down into the top of the man's head.

He sprawled, unconscious, across the doorway.

Todd took a deep breath, pushed his hat back, and scratched his neck. *I'm not sure how this happened.* "Which one's Dubois?" he asked as he tugged the big knife out of his gunstock.

"Shoot, Fortune, why don't you just cold-cock all of 'em? We'll sort them out later," the sheriff bellowed. He holstered his revolver, then loosened his black tie.

A roar of reaction flooded the room.

"Junior is as tough as his old man," a gray-bearded man with an empty shot glass declared.

The sheriff drove the carriage up Main Street. Cigar Dubois slumped, still unconscious, in the back. "It's like someone didn't want me around the church," Bullock mused. "Were they plannin' on stealin' a raspberry pie? I figured maybe someone wanted to bushwhack me down in the badlands . . . but nothin' happened down there."

"They succeeded in getting both of us away from the church meeting," Todd added.

"They weren't after you. Nobody had any idea in the world that I'd bring you along. 'Course, they know better now. They all know you're the one who sat down Mr. Cigar Dubois. You got a reputation now, Boy. Some will respect you for it . . . others will want to test your toughness."

"It happened so quick. I didn't think much about it. I was lucky to stop that knife."

"Nothin' lucky about it. You reacted quick. That's just the way your daddy is. He don't sit around contemplatin' what to do. Must be something inherited." The sheriff pulled up in front of the jail. He handed the reins to Todd and jumped down. "You drive this carriage back to the church. I'll be up shortly." He loaded Dubois over his shoulder, "soon as I lock up this ol' boy and check around town a spell."

The crowd at the church had begun to thin out by the time Todd returned. He slipped in the back door where Rebekah and Thelma Speaker divided the remains of the Cascade of Fruitful Delight into glass jars.

"Looks like I missed out on the auction." Todd was surprised by a confidence that crept into his step and defied his tiredness.

Rebekah's wide brown eyes lit up when she saw him and, as always, her smile was magnetic. "I understand you and Sheriff Bullock had some business in the badlands." She tilted her eyebrows. His heart beat a little faster.

"It turned out to be a false report. I just went along with Seth for the ride."

"Nothing happened?"

"Not much. The Piedmont rolls on as usual."

"You went into that horrid hovel?"

"I just stood at the back door and watched, mainly."

"You just looked around and left?"

"The sheriff spotted a man wanted down in Sidney, Nebraska. We hauled him in. That's about all."

Dacee June traipsed over, Amber Gordon at her side. The five-year-old sported a raspberry-colored smile.

"Well, Lil' Sis, did anything exciting happen while I was gone?" Todd probed.

"I ate three pieces of pie," Amber admitted. "And I haven't even throwed up yet."

Dacee June's hair had fallen out of its combs and lounged across her left ear down to her shoulder. "Did you hear that Mr. Olene showed up and bid twenty dollars for Mrs. Speaker's raspberry cobbler?"

"Twenty dollars for a pie?" Todd glanced over at the older lady with the grayish-yellow hair. "I'd say you caught his eye, Mrs. Speaker."

"Well," Thelma blustered, "it was a little embarrassing." A wistful smile broke across the smooth skin of her face. She looked ten years younger.

"Rumor has it Mr. Olene's been negotiating on Ayres and Wardman's Hardware," Dacee June said.

"Where did you hear that rumor?" Todd asked.

"From Mr. Olene himself. Said if he couldn't buy Fortune's, he'd have to acquire second best and start from there."

"He seems like a very nice man," Thelma added. "But then, I don't know very much about him. I don't know where he lives, where he went to school, what his first name is . . . why, I don't even know if he's married."

"He was the last time I was in Chicago." Rebekah scanned a disappointed Thelma Speaker. "But that was several years ago. Besides, I thought you had made up your mind about your next husband."

She tossed her head. "I am getting quite tired of waiting for a certain old Texan to get inspired."

Todd slipped his arm around Thelma Speaker's shoulder. "You know you have our blessing to capture him, if you can. But latching onto Daddy Brazos would be like roping an old grizzly bear. You might be better off if you never caught him."

A wide, easy grin broke across Thelma's face. "I'm beginning to agree with you. Your mama might have been the only woman on earth to tame him."

"Half-tame him," Todd said.

"Well, it didn't seem quite right for him not to be here to crown the Raspberry Festival queen, like he normally does," Thelma said. "Did you tell Todd about the festival queen voting?"

"I don't want to talk about this," Dacee June blurted out, brushing her hair behind her ear.

"Oh?" Todd retrieved a wedge of pear from a glass jar and popped it in his mouth.

"If you're going to talk about the queen contest, I'm going into the other room," she pouted. Dacee June grabbed Amber's sticky hand and scurried to the social hall.

Todd turned back to Rebekah and Mrs. Speaker. "I take it she didn't win?"

"She did finish third," Thelma offered. "That was nice, don't you think?"

"How many were nominated?" he asked.

"Four," Thelma reported.

"No wonder she was a little crushed."

"She beat out Irene Seltzmann by one vote. Of course, Irene has a touch of ague and couldn't come tonight. Little Amber Gordon won second," Thelma Speaker continued her report. "It was Dacee June who nominated her. My, how that little girl can dance and sing."

"And who was the lucky woman who gets to reign as queen of the church Raspberry Festival for a whole year?" Todd asked.

Thelma Speaker smiled like a midwife delivering a baby to its mama. "Why, your Rebekah, of course!"

"What?" Todd exclaimed.

Rebekah bit her lip and tried to hide a sheepish grin.

"You were elected queen and I wasn't here to see it? I didn't know you were even running," Todd said.

"Neither did I. Mr. Olene nominated me at the last moment," she reported. "I thought it would be discourteous not to go along. Besides, I was confident that I had no chance of winning."

"And young Mr. Toluca seconded Mr. Olene's nomination," Thelma piped up.

"He did? No wonder Lil' Sis doesn't want to talk about it." Todd slipped his thumbs into his brown leather belt. "She'll take it as a conspiracy."

"It was this dress that did it," Rebekah added. "Anyone who wore this dramatic, raspberry-colored dress would have won. I imagine we could have sold a dozen of these dresses tonight. Don't you think so, Mrs. Speaker?"

"Oh, yes. I'd love one myself." Thelma dried her hands on a limp tea towel. "However, I have a good idea I'd look fifty years old, no matter what I wore."

"This is the first time I've ever been selected queen of anything," Rebekah said as she fastened lids down on the jars of fruit.

"I find that hard to believe," Mrs. Speaker replied.

"Well, it's the first time I ever ran for queen of anything. I have a difficult time relaxing and enjoying something like this. So, I have always avoided getting involved. I take things far too seriously. Perhaps that's my mother's influence." *'Save your best beauty for your husband. The rest of the world has not earned the right to enjoy it.' Dear Mother, I still do not know what that means.*

Thelma patted Rebekah's hand. "How long has she been gone, Dear?"

"About five . . . five-and-a-half years." Rebekah's voice was very soft.

"It's a shame she never got to see you in this beautiful dress. It's one of the things I miss about my daughters living in the East. I don't get to stare at how they look. Isn't that funny? They are both grown and married, and I miss looking at them. I suppose that's a mother's heart, don't you think, Dear?" Thelma looked at Rebekah's face. "Oh . . . my . . . that was inappropriate, wasn't it? You'll understand some day, I'm sure." Thelma Speaker tapped her hands nervously in front of her. "She does make a beautiful queen, doesn't she, Todd?"

He sensed Rebekah's ill ease, too. "Did you know that Mrs. Speaker was the county fair queen of Coryell County, Texas?"

Rebekah let out a deep sigh and relaxed her shoulders. "It doesn't surprise me a bit," Rebekah mused. "Many a younger woman in Deadwood has told me they hope to look as nice as Mrs. Speaker when they get . . ."

"When they get elderly?" Thelma proposed. "Do you know why I'm not offended? Because every last one of you cute young ladies will get old some day. We all have our turn."

SIX

Thelma Speaker glided out into the social hall to retrieve more dishes.

"That was a very nice compliment you gave Mrs. Speaker." Todd stepped up next to Rebekah and slipped his arm around her waist.

"It was true," Rebekah added. "Now behave yourself, young Mr. Fortune. We're still at church."

He gave her a squeeze and stepped back.

"Don't you think it's true that Mrs. Speaker is an attractive woman?" Rebekah pressed.

"And it's also true you look beautiful tonight."

Rebekah rolled her eyes. "That's what you tell me every day, Todd Fortune."

"I have to tell the truth. It's a law in the Fortune family."

"Good, then you can tell me what those two men wanted."

Todd squinted his narrow eyes and leaned closer to her. "What two men?"

"The tall one with blond hair. And the shorter dark-complected man with the thick beard."

Todd glanced around the narrow church kitchen as if looking to find someone lurking on the shelves. His hand slipped to the revolver holstered at his side. "Where are they?"

"Is something wrong?"

"Where are they?"

"I have no idea. They stopped at the church right after you and the sheriff drove off. I told them you'd be back soon, but they didn't want to wait. Did they come and find you?"

Todd rubbed his mustache and goatee with his fingers. "No. What did they want?"

"I think they wanted to pay off an account, or something. They said something about a debt they owed to Brazos Fortune and they were looking for his kid."

"Did they know you were my wife?"

"They left before I could introduce myself."

Todd paced the gray-painted wooden floor of the church kitchen. "Did Quiet Jim see them?"

"I don't think so. They came to the back door and asked for Brazos Fortune's kid. I assumed they meant you. Quintin got sick at his stomach and Quiet Jim took both the children home early." She pulled him out of his pacing and slipped her arm in his. "Who were they, Todd?"

"It sounds like the two . . . ," he stammered and turned his head away.

Rebekah's hand shot up to her mouth. She released his arm. "The escaped stage robbers? The ones who busted the window at the store? But they were soft-spoken and polite. I can't believe I stood right here and talked to them."

"I'm going to Quiet Jim's. You tell this story to the sheriff when he shows up. No, maybe I'd better wait for you, then we'll all go together."

Dacee June waltzed back into the kitchen with Thelma Speaker, both carrying a stack of dirty plates. "I'm going to take Amber home and clean her up before Abigail and her mother return," she announced.

"No!" Todd barked. "You aren't walking home in the dark." He marched over to the back door of the church kitchen and locked it.

Dacee June rolled her large round eyes and folded her arms across her flat chest. "It's not that far to walk."

He marched straight at her, pointing his finger. "We are all going together. Stay in here; I need to check around outside." Todd hustled into the social hall.

Dacee June looked over at Rebekah and scowled. "Oh, brother, what's eating him?"

Rebekah set the last stack of dirty dishes into the sink full of water. "He thinks maybe those two stagecoach hold-up men who busted the window at the store are back in town tonight. They stopped by the church looking for him."

Dacee June rushed over. "Really? It's a good thing I'm carrying my revolver." She patted her dress pocket.

"You are?" Rebekah snatched the teapot off the woodstove and coursed the boiling water over the dishes in the sink.

Dacee June dropped a handful of dirty forks into the scalding water. "Aren't you?"

"Of course not!" Rebekah replied. *The day I have to start carrying a gun is the day we move!*

"Don't worry. Stick with me," Dacee June insisted. "I'll protect us."

Carty Toluca carried a huge, empty punch bowl into the kitchen. "Mrs. Speaker said this never got used. Where do you want me to put it?"

"Dacee June, show him where that goes," Rebekah instructed.

"I do not wish to associate with that traitor," Dacee June pouted. "He betrayed me."

"I jist seconded Rebekah's nomination. I thought I was bein' polite."

"You can tell him it goes on the big shelf above the plates."

"She said that . . ."

"I heard her. I ain't deaf. And I ain't stupid, neither. The sooner she starts treating me nice, I reckon I'll do the same."

Dacee June's face grew as red as her lacy blouse. "That's the most absurd thing I've ever heard. Tell Mr. Toluca I treat him just the way he deserves. I'm going home."

"Todd said to wait for all of us," Rebekah cautioned.

"Well, he's my brother, not my father. I'll walk home if I want to," Dacee June stormed. "I have not enjoyed this evening nearly as much as I thought I would."

Carty strolled over next to her. The wispy whiskers on his chin made his face look soiled. "I'll walk you home and protect you," he offered.

Dacee June's small round nose was pointed in the air. "And who will protect you?"

There was indignation in his voice. "Who do I need to be protected from?"

"From me," she exploded as she pushed Carty back.

Thelma Speaker carried a large pitcher to the sink.

Rebekah's voice resounded across the room like an irate mother. "You'll wait for Todd like he asked."

Dacee June stomped toward the social hall door.

"Where are you going?" Rebekah called out.

"To finish clearing the tables. Is that all right, Queenie?" Dacee June sneered.

Thelma Speaker slipped her arm around Dacee June and ushered her back to the social hall. "Snootiness does not become you, Dear. Righteous indignation is always good. And if you can't come up with that, you might try laughter. Laughter shows how generous you are with sharing honors. It makes quite an impression. Trust me. But a selfish pout ruins one's complexion. And you have such a lovely complexion."

The adjoining door swung close. Rebekah stared down at the jars of fruit. *Lord, I think I've entered my last queen contest. She'll pout for a week, just like she did after our wedding. Why did I ever let them enter me? This is just what I've always tried to avoid. If I hadn't entered, then Dacee June could have ended up . . . in second place! Oh, my . . . wouldn't that be disastrous.*

The voice of laughing ladies brought Rebekah out of her contemplation as Abigail Gordon and her mother entered the church kitchen.

"I'm surprised to see you so soon," Rebekah called out as they approached.

"We finished a delightful supper in Central City, then took a ride up to Lead and back around to Deadwood," Mrs. O'Neill reported. "The Black Hills are so beautiful, even at night. It's such a peaceful area. I'm quite impressed."

"Except for the stamp mills, some spots are more peaceful than others," Rebekah concurred as she continued to wash dishes. "I'm pleased you had a nice time."

"How was my Amber?" Abigail probed.

"She and Dacee June were inseparable." Rebekah glanced at Abigail's soft, easy eyes. *Just two ladies at church, visiting about children. That's a little shocking for both of us.* "She is very precocious and outgoing. She is quite at ease visiting with adults."

"I'm afraid that is mostly my fault," Mrs. O'Neill added. "There aren't many children in my neighborhood in Omaha. She spends most of her time talking with me and my friends who come over to play hearts. She's quite a good player herself."

Mrs. O'Neill reminded Rebekah of a gray-headed Louise Driver Edwards. "I've been busy in the kitchen most of the evening, so I didn't get to spend as much time with her as I wanted. Your Amber won second place in the Raspberry Queen contest. She charmed the entire crowd. You would have been proud of her, Mama. She's got actress in her bones."

"I certainly hope not. It's a dreadful disease of which one is never cured."

"You love every minute of it," Rebekah prodded.

"See how dreadful it is?"

"Well, little Amber certainly got my vote."

"I wish we could have seen it," Mrs. O'Neill added. "By the way, who was selected queen of the festival?"

Rebekah hesitated.

"It was you, wasn't it?" Abigail blurted out.

Rebekah pulled her hands out of the dishwater and spun around modeling the outfit. "It was your dress that did it. I've never been queen of anything."

Abigail took her hands. "Nor have I," she added.

"I'm shocked. With your stunning looks, I would have guessed otherwise."

"She was a very, very thin girl," Mrs. O'Neill reported. "If I would have let her bob her hair, she could have passed for a boy until she was eighteen."

"Thank you, Mother, for bringing up those painful memories."

"You're welcome, dear."

Rebekah released Abigail's hands and stepped back. "Well, no one would make that mistake now."

Mrs. O'Neill straightened the cuffs of her dark purple dress. "Certainly not the men at the Zachary Jaque's."

Rebekah raised her eyebrows. "They flirted with you, no doubt."

Abigail twisted her sparkling violet necklace. "Not all of them. Some of the older ones seemed to find mother quite the dish."

"I do like this country," the gray-headed woman blushed. "Perhaps I should move to Deadwood."

A controlled panic flashed across Abigail's face. "I'm sure she's teasing. I keep telling mother I'll move on to a larger town where there are more opportunities for acting, and I'll send for her and Amber then. Anyway, we thought we'd pick up that precocious daughter of mine from the church and save a hike up to your house."

"Did you want to cancel our teatime tomorrow since your mother is here? She and Amber are invited to come, of course."

"Tea?" Mrs. O'Neill asked.

Rebekah glanced at the older woman. "Oh, Abigail and I like to have a little tea in the afternoon and visit, but I know it's a steep hike. We can certainly miss one day. I'm sure you two have much to talk about."

"Oh my, I don't want to interfere with my daughter's routine with her good friends. I'd be delighted to come," Mrs. Gordon added, then turned to her daughter. "What time do you have tea, dear?"

As if delivering a line on cue, Abigail turned stage left toward Rebekah and smiled. "The usual time?"

"Yes," Rebekah said, "3:30 P.M. seems to work best for both of us."

"We'll scoot along now." Abigail hugged Rebekah's shoulders, kissed her on the cheek, and whispered, "You're a better actress than I am, girl. Thanks."

"Your Amber should be with Dacee June. Probably over at the little pump organ. That Amber is so talented. When she sang and danced at the festival, it brought the house down."

"She did what?" Abigail turned to Mrs. O'Neill. "Mother?"

"Alright, so I taught her a few things besides hearts. She has natural rhythm and timing. Just like you, Dear."

"And I have told you I didn't want her growing up to sing and dance."

"Oh my, I hope we didn't start something," Rebekah said.

"We will discuss this matter later," Abigail lectured.

"I do believe Grandma's in trouble." Mrs. O'Neill turned to Rebekah. "Do you have a spare guest room, Mrs. Fortune?"

"Mother!" Abigail huffed.

Mrs. Gordon waved weakly to Rebekah as they left the kitchen.

With the dishes done, Rebekah began hanging the tea towels to dry. *Lord, I really like Abigail. I believe she would make an excellent friend. Perhaps that is why you had me stay in Deadwood to this point. But I don't know anything about her commitment to You.*

Abigail poked her head back into the kitchen. "We can't find Amber and Dacee June. Where did you say they were?"

"They aren't out in the social hall?"

"No."

"Did you check the sanctuary?"

"They aren't there either."

Rebekah hung her last towel and unfastened her full-length apron. She led Abigail back out into the church social hall. She glanced around at the few people left milling in the room full of benches and chairs. "They aren't out on the front step?"

"No, I'm sure we would have seen them," Abigail reported as they approached Mrs. O'Neill.

"Carty?" Rebekah called out to the young man who was waving his arms and telling a story to two younger boys near the silent fireplace. "Have you see Dacee June and Amber?"

Carty removed his wide-brimmed hat and meandered toward them. "Yes, ma'am, Mrs. Fortune. Dacee June and Miss Amber walked home."

"What do you mean?" Rebekah could barely control her voice. "I distinctly told her to wait for the rest of us!"

Carty Toluca hung his head. "Yes, Ma'am, you did."

"Well . . . well . . ." Rebekah clenched her fists tight enough to turn them white. "Why didn't you walk with them?"

Carty rolled the brim of his hat and stared at his feet. "I started to, Mrs. Fortune, but she pulled a gun on me."

Mrs. O'Neill's hand flew up to the top of her plum-colored straw hat. "She what?"

Mr. Toluca kept his chin buried in his chest, but peeked up like a scolded puppy. "She told me she'd shoot me if I tried to walk with them."

"Oh, she and Carty play games like this, Mrs. O'Neill." Rebekah waved her arms about as she tried to explain.

"My word, they play with guns?" Mrs. O'Neill gasped.

Abigail seized the moment. "It is the frontier, Mother. I did warn you."

"Sometimes we use knives," Carty added with a sly grin.

"He's teasing," Rebekah insisted.

Carty pushed up his flannel shirtsleeve and flashed a two-inch scar. "Dacee June stabbed me once."

"Carty . . ." Rebekah grabbed him by the tie and tugged him toward the door. "Would you please leave now?"

He glanced back at the stunned Mrs. O'Neill. "She stabbed me by accident. She was just mad because I punched her."

"Carty!" Rebekah yanked the tie above the young man's head like a noose, then released him.

"That was years ago when we was just kids!" he called back as he staggered, then trotted out of the room.

"I'm afraid Dacee June's a little obstinate tonight," Rebekah tried to explain.

Mrs. O'Neill let out a deep breath and color returned to her cheeks. "No need to apologize. I had a teenage daughter much the same myself."

"Dacee June didn't exactly like being third in the queen contest," Rebekah reported. "But don't worry about her. She's very careful with children. Besides, she knows her way around town better than anyone else in Deadwood."

Rebekah walked with both ladies out to the porch of the church. Flickering lantern lights sprinkled the gulch.

"We'll walk up to your house for Amber." Abigail adjusted her white felt hat and took her mother's arm. "After a big French supper, the climb will be good for us."

"If you'd like to wait, Todd will be back soon and we can all go together." Rebekah stared through the night up and down Sherman Street. *Todd . . . I wish you'd come back and deal with your sister. There are times when I really miss Daddy Brazos.* "In fact, I'll walk with you, now." Rebekah called to a young man sulking in the shadows. "Carty? Could you tell Todd that we went on home?"

"Yes, Ma'am . . . do you need me to escort you?"

"I want you to stay here and give Todd the message."

"You can count on me," he called out from the darkness.

Why is it, Mr. Toluca, that your promise doesn't give me a great deal of assurance?

All three women were huffing by the time they hiked six blocks, then climbed the seventy-two steps up to Forest Hill. Rebekah could see a lamp lit in her parlor. *Dacee June deserves a spanking! Too big to paddle, and too young to act mature. It's a wonder any sixteen-year-old survives to adulthood.*

She thrust open the door. "Dacee June? Amber's mother and grandmother are here."

There was no answer.

Rebekah led them into the entry, then the parlor. "Dacee June?" At the foot of the stairs, she glanced up to a darkened second story.

"Dacee June, are you upstairs?" *If she's pouting and hiding from me, I'll spank her backside no matter what her age.*

"Maybe they walked up a different route and we passed them," Abigail suggested.

"She must have been here; the lamp is lit. Oh, perhaps they had to go next door." Rebekah turned to Mrs. O'Neill. "Dacee June and my father-in-law live next door. Daddy Brazos is gone hunting for a couple weeks. They probably went over there. I'll step over and fetch them. You ladies sit down and rest a minute. I'll be right back."

Rebekah scampered out the door, down a dozen steps, over to the neighboring house and up the steps. *I have many more important things to worry about than to play hide-and-seek with you, young lady.*

There were no lamps lit at Daddy Brazos's house. Rebekah stuck her head into the entry and called into the dark, "Dacee June?" *Lord, I'm getting peeved with this behavior.* "Dacee June, you come out, and you come out right now!"

A shirt-clad arm reached out of the shadowy entry, and a man's strong, grimy hand grabbed her arm. Rebekah's heart felt like it would explode. She was yanked into the darkened entry of the house, too terrified to talk, too stunned to pray.

A hand went over her mouth.

Her hands were yanked behind her back.

The front door slammed.

But she was not thrown to the floor.

Her clothes were not torn.

Finally, her spirit squeaked out a silent *Lord Jesus, no!* It was a pitiful prayer and she knew it.

Her eyes fought to adjust to the faint evening light that drifted into the house.

"Who did you get?" a man's deep voice demanded.

The other voice sounded higher, more tense. "I don't know, but it ain't the girl. This one was lookin' for the girl."

Rebekah labored to extract her hands, but only succeeded in paining her shoulders. *They're looking for Dacee June? Everyone's looking for her.*

The man who clutched her arms reeked of tobacco and whiskey. "Lady, I'm goin' to take my hand off your mouth and I don't want you to scream. Now, listen to me. I don't know who you are. I have no intention of hurting you, but if you scream, I swear I'll put a blue lump on your head with the barrel of my revolver. Now, nod your head up and down if you promise not to scream."

Rebekah nodded.

He didn't loosen his grip on her arms, but he did ease his other hand off her mouth.

One time when Rebekah had been eleven, she was in front of her home in Chicago when a milk wagon ran over a puppy of hers called Little Mister. In panic, she screamed so loud her father had always teased that the Chicago-Milwaukee Railroad jumped its tracks.

But it was nothing compared to the scream she now let loose.

Immediately the man's dirty, greasy tasting hand was stuck into her open mouth. She bit into the first finger she could reach, tasted blood, then dropped to her knees.

The man cursed. "This she-devil done bit me!"

A revolver barrel crushed nothing but the straw of her hat, sending it flying into the darkness.

But then she was thrown face down on the hardwood floor. A knee buried itself in the small of her back. Rebekah thought her ribs were crushed. There was a cramp in her lungs. She couldn't catch her breath. *I'm going to die right here! I'll turn blue and die with a hideous expression on my face!*

There was a knock on the front door. The man on her back eased his knee.

Rebekah sucked in a breath. Tears rolled down her cheeks.

"This ain't workin' right," one man whispered.

"Maybe it's the girl," the other replied.

"Knocking at her own house?"

The knocking continued, this time followed by a tentative voice. "Rebekah? Rebekah, are you all right?"

Rebekah struggled forward on the floor where the knee was on the small of her back, not her lungs. *Abigail? No . . . no . . . go away!*

The front door swung open and all Rebekah could see in the moonlight were the shoes of Abigail, her mother, and a man in tattered boots.

"Oh, my word!" Mrs. O'Neill gasped.

"Get in here," he demanded, "or I'll use this gun."

"Rebekah!" Abigail cried out.

The door slammed shut and a sulfur match flared. The candle on the entry table flickered to life. The shadows revealed two men in dusty trail clothes and wide-brimmed hats. One was tall and blond. The other short and dark bearded.

"This is the lady at the church kitchen," the blond one muttered.

"What is the meaning of this?" Mrs. O'Neill demanded. "You release that woman immediately!"

The barrel of a revolver was waved alongside the temple of Mrs. O'Neill. "I'll do what I want to do, Old Lady!" he growled.

The other man backed his knee off Rebekah and yanked her to her feet.

"Did they hurt you?" Abigail asked.

"Her? Look at this." The blond man with the gun held up a bleeding finger. "She nearly bit my finger off!"

Abigail stepped toward Rebekah with a handkerchief she had pulled from her sleeve and wiped blood off her lip and chin.

"I'm OK . . . ," Rebekah fought not to break down and start crying. "Once he got his knee out of my back."

The blond-haired man grabbed the handkerchief from Abigail's hand and threw it on the floor. "Where's the girl?" he demanded.

"Amber? They want her? Dr. Gordon would stoop to this?" Abigail swung a clenched fist at the dark-haired man, but he caught her arm before it struck him.

"Who's Amber?" he demanded.

The other man yanked on Rebekah's arms. "How many girls does Brazos Fortune have?"

The pain was so severe, Rebekah struggled to form words. "Why are you doing this?" Rebekah was shocked at how hopeless and whiney her voice sounded.

"We've got a house full of women and none of them is the right one." The dark-haired man with a full beard held Abigail's clenched fist in one hand, his revolver in the other. "This is Brazos Fortune's house, ain't it?"

"Yes, and as soon as he gets here you two stagecoach outlaws will be hung?" Rebekah managed to mumble.

"How did you know who we was, church lady?"

"Because Sheriff Bullock is looking for you."

"The sheriff's down in the badlands on a wild-goose chase. Maybe we could take all three of them," the dark-headed man proposed.

"We want one to be a Fortune or it won't work."

The man holding Rebekah's arms loosed his grip a bit. "What are we going to do? Maybe we ought to just shoot them."

Rebekah's knees buckled. The man's tight grip on her arms kept her from collapsing to the floor.

"We cain't shoot 'em. That would rile the whole town, no matter who they are. They'd call the troops out from Fort Meade and comb the hills. We want 'em to chase us, not catch us."

"I don't understand," Rebekah whimpered.

"You church ladies ain't supposed to know anything. Jist thank the Lord that we didn't put a bullet in all of your brains. Now, let's tie 'em up. Maybe it'll take them a while to discover 'em. That might be fear enough to send out a posse."

A dirty bandanna was tied in Rebekah's mouth. *Fear enough for what?*

Within minutes all three women were gagged and shoved to the floor of the entry hall, their hands tied behind them with a curtain sash.

Then the blond man blew out the candle and they left.

In the dark, Rebekah closed her eyes. *Lord, here I am, bound, hurting, and scared. But that's a lot better than I thought a few minutes ago. Daddy Brazos, these men are mad at you and plan to take it out on your family. And you aren't even here! Todd Fortune, I really, really need you right now. It's time for you to come home. Lord, protect us . . . oh, Lord God, deliver us all from evil.*

Todd drove the borrowed rig recklessly up Shine Street. It was so steep that most of the residents of Forest Hill usually walked to and from their homes. He turned abruptly right at the corner. The right wheels of the carriage raised off the ground. He whipped the two horses on down the dirt path of Williams Street to the front door of the house. He knotted the reins to the hand brake, leaped off the rig, and sprinted up the steps to the front door.

Dacee June sat on the couch, a sleeping Amber Gordon stretched out beside her, head in her lap.

SIX

"Dacee June, where's Rebekah?" His voice was almost a shout.

"She hasn't come home," she replied. "Are you mad at me, too?"

"What do you mean, she hasn't come home? Carty said the three ladies walked home nearly an hour ago."

Amber sat up and blinked her eyes at the light.

"What other ladies?" Dacee June asked.

"Abigail and her mother." Todd paced the room.

"I've waited and waited for them."

"You were supposed to wait for me at the church," he brayed.

"Well, I got to acting really stupid and marched home. But it's OK, now," she announced.

He stopped in front of her and looked down. "What do you mean it's OK?"

"When we got here, Amber was sick and needed to go to the privy so I . . ."

"My tummy hurts," Amber mumbled in a barely audible voice.

"Anyway, I went up on up the hill and talked to the Lord. And now I need to come back and apologize to Rebekah for being such a pill. So I've been waiting for her. I'm sorry I took off like that, Todd. Don't be mad at me."

"I'm not mad at you," he shouted.

"Well," she murmured, "it certainly sounds like you're mad."

Todd paced the room again. "Dacee June, this is getting crazy. Quiet Jim's been shot."

"What?" Dacee June flinched at the words so drastically that Amber clutched her arm and began to whimper.

"I found him wounded along Lincoln Street."

Dacee June cuddled Amber. "How about Quintin and Fern?"

"If they ever stop crying, they'll be alright. They weren't hurt."

"Is Quiet Jim . . . dead?"

"No, the doc's over at their house now. Columbia is beside herself, and the kids are all crying. I've got to get back and help. I need Rebekah to come with me," he fumed.

"Maybe she stopped by the Gem Theater."

"Why on earth would they do that?"

"I don't know. Perhaps Abigail wanted to show them something. I don't know, Todd . . . I don't know anything . . . I wish Daddy were here."

"Well, he's not here, Dacee June, and we've got to pull together." *The old man gone a week and the whole world falls apart. Lord, this isn't good.* "Lil' Sis, I need you to help me out. Rebekah's not here, and I've got to count on you to fill in for her. I don't need a twelve-year-old sister; I need a twenty-year-old one."

"What do you want me to do? I can do it, Todd."

"You take Doc's rig and drive over to Quiet Jim's. Just barge in and take the kids off to one room and try to settle them down while Columbia and the doc look after Quiet Jim. I'll be right over as soon as I find Rebekah."

"How about Amber?"

"Take her with you."

"Would it be good if I brought all the children back here?"

"If I haven't shown up in a half hour, have Carty help you bring them all home."

"I won't need any help."

"Dacee June, I don't have time for a sixteen-year-old's vanity. Do you understand?"

"I know . . . I know you're right. I'll ask Carty," she mumbled.

"I'm going to backtrack Rebekah to the church. Maybe . . . maybe she stopped by to show them the store . . . or something." He waved toward the entry. "Take the shotgun."

"I have my revolver."

"I said, take the shotgun. I'm tired of you not doing what I ask!" He could see Dacee June start to tear up again.

"I'm sorry, Lil' Sis. I didn't mean to snap like that. I'm worried. I'm really worried. My wife and two other women are missing. Quiet Jim's been shot . . . there are men roaming town looking to shoot me . . . I'm sorry."

Dacee June hugged her brother. Amber hugged his leg. "It's like the tribulation in Revelation, isn't it?"

"There is a likeness." He brushed her bangs out of her eyes. "Maybe the Lord is coming back soon."

"That would be nice." Dacee June pulled away and retrieved the shotgun near the front door. She led a startled Amber Gordon to the porch. "It's OK, Todd. I mean, it's OK to yell at me. I deserve it sometimes. I know I do. I'm trying to grow up. I really am."

Todd stepped out on the porch and gave her another hug. "Take care of yourself, Lil' Sis. If two strangers come up to you, point that shotgun at their midsection and ask them what they want. I'll see you in a few minutes. Do whatever you can to help Columbia."

"May the Lord have mercy on us, Todd Fortune," Dacee June called out as she and Amber trotted out into the night.

He watched her whip the team and spin them in the narrow road, then disappear down Williams Street. *Have mercy on us . . .* Todd glanced back at the house with the lantern still lit in the parlor. *I ought to turn it off . . .* Then he glanced at the house next door. *Dacee June didn't close Dad's front door all the way . . . I ought to . . .* He turned and looked down the steep stairs down to Wall Street. *No, I've got to find my wife!*

Todd took the steps two at a time, swinging on the wooden handrail. *"Be merciful unto me, O God, be merciful unto me; for my soul trusteth in thee; yea, in the shadow of thy wings will I make my refuge, until these calamities be overpast."*

He ran down Wall Street, all along Main past the Grand Central Hotel, Stebbins & Post Bank, and the hardware, then down Deadwood Street to the church. He turned on Sherman Street and sprinted back to the Gem Theater.

Then he retraced the entire route, checking every hotel, café, and theater. Finally, he ran back up the Wall Street stairs to find Carty Toluca with a shotgun over his shoulder sitting on the front porch.

"Did you find Mrs. Fortune?" he called out.

"Not yet. She didn't come home?" Todd pressed.

"No, sir. Dacee June's inside with the passel of children. I'm standin' guard."

"Carty, you take Doc's rig back to him at Quiet Jim's, then hike back and check with anyone you meet in the street about Rebekah and the other ladies."

"You want me to leave the shotgun?"

Todd took the shotgun from his hand and barged through the door. The parlor was empty. "Dacee June?"

"We're all upstairs, Todd!" a mature-sounding teenager called back.

He tramped up the stairs. Amber, Quintin, and Fern were lined up and tucked underneath the covers. Amber was asleep, and the other two were wide-eyed and motionless.

"I don't know why, but I just felt safer bringing them upstairs. Columbia insisted on keeping Sarah."

"Does the doctor have anyone with Quiet Jim?"

"Their neighbor, Mrs. Osburne, came over, but her husband's working the night shift at the DeSmet Mine, and she can't be away from her children too long. Plus Sheriff Bullock's there."

"What did Seth say?" Todd asked.

Dacee June came closer to her brother who was seven inches taller. "He figured it's the same two that took a shot at us the other night. But he doesn't know how they can appear and disappear so easily. You didn't find any trace of Rebekah or the others?"

"Not yet."

"Are you scared?" Dacee June slipped her arm in his. "I'm really scared."

"I'm not as scared as I should be."

"What do you mean?"

"It's a terrifying predicament . . . but somehow I believe the Lord's still in control."

"Good. Then you can sit with the kids." Dacee June released his arm.

"I've got to find Rebekah and get over and check on Quiet Jim."

"Well, let the peace of Jesus keep you right here for two minutes because I've got to run next door and get my nightgown and robe."

"I'll get it for you," he offered.

"I will not have you digging through my private dresser, even if you are my big brother. Just give me two minutes."

"Take the shotgun."

"To go next door?" she protested. "This is Forest Hill!"

His glance silenced her complaint.

"OK . . . OK . . . I'll take it . . . and I'll fire a blast if I'm in trouble."

"Hurry! . . . wherever Rebekah is, I'm sure she needs me."

Rebekah had heard Todd come home twice . . . and she thought she had heard him talking to someone on the front porch. She had tried to shout, but the best sound she could muster was a muffled hum.

Finally, there were steps on the porch. The partially open door flung open as someone carrying a gun rushed in. Rebekah pulled her feet back, but the person stumbled and crashed to the floor. The report of the shotgun slammed against her eardrums, and a long red flash of gunpowder momentarily lit up the face of the gunman.

Dacee June?

Then another person, with gun drawn, was at the door.

His silhouette was the most wonderful sight Rebekah had ever seen. He struck a match and squatted down by the three tied ladies.

When Todd's eyes met hers, she began to sob.

CHAPTER SEVEN

A thick overcast sky hugged the entire gulch from White Rocks to Forest Hill. Heavy, dark clouds sagged like an old mattress on a broken bed frame in a cheap hotel. Yet, there hadn't been a drop of rain. Main Street still corralled a stampede of dust from the heavy traffic.

Small black-winged goldfinches sat on top of the wooden guardrail, watching with beady dark eyes, too tired or too startled to fly off, or even let out a familiar "per-chik-or-ree." It was as if all of creation held its breath, waiting to see what would happen next.

Dacee June called out to Todd from the front porch as he crossed Williams Street. "I don't know why I have to stay cooped up like this! I can take care of myself," she said.

Todd tipped his crisp, brown felt hat to a short, broad-shouldered man who sat on the porch of Daddy Brazos's house next door, a shotgun across his lap. Todd patted the side of his suit coat and felt the .45 holstered on his belt. When he reached the top of the stairs, he threw his arm around Dacee June's shoulders. Her white cotton blouse was buttoned high at the neck, but the sleeves were pushed halfway up to her elbows. Her long brown hair was stacked neatly on top of her head.

The determination in her eyes caused him to hesitate.

"Why are you staring at me?" she prodded as he approached.

"For just a moment, you looked a lot like Mama."

"Really? Really, Todd? Do I look like Mama?" She greeted her brother with a hug and brushed a kiss across his cheek. "That's the highest compliment I've ever received from any of my brothers. Of course, Robert doesn't compliment, he only teases. And Samuel, well, it's getting where I can hardly remember him, Todd. Isn't that sad? I remember Mama, though sometimes I forget what she looks like. I still miss her every day. Do you miss her, Todd?"

He wiped tearless eyes. "Yep. I miss her, Lil' Sis."

"I believe she was the best mother in the whole wide world."

Todd brushed back her bangs and kissed her forehead. "I believe you're right about that."

She leaned over and kissed his cheek again.

"If we don't stop smooching, Rebekah will get jealous," he laughed.

"Well, if I don't practice on you, how will I ever learn?"

"I have a feeling that you've had some practice before."

"Did he tell you that?" she challenged.

"Who?"

She tilted her nose and studied his eyes. "Never mind. Now, why can't I sit out here with a shotgun like Lars?"

"Lil' Sis," he spoke in a quiet, firm voice. "I need you in the house. I've got Lars guarding things in front of both houses, but he's only one man." He led her over to a bench and sat them both down. "Those men proved they're not bashful about intruding into our homes. Rebekah and the other ladies took quite a scare. I want you to keep your gun in your pocket and an eye out for anything suspicious."

"Wouldn't it be better for me to be out here?" The lace yoke of her dark green dress stretched from shoulder to shoulder and bounced as she talked.

"I need you inside, to help Rebekah with the children." He caught a strong whiff of her petunia perfume. "Besides, you're our secret guard. I don't want them to know how dangerous you are."

"Yes!" Dacee June's round eyes sparkled again. "I'm the treacherous ace up the sleeve!"

"You're the ace alright, Lil' Sis." Todd stood up to enter the house.

SEVEN

"You want me to stay at your house?" she asked.

"You just go about a normal routine, only don't leave Forest Hill. We don't want to give away your role."

"Right. I'll . . . I'll go home . . . Abigail and Mrs. O'Neill took the children over there. I'll check and see if they need help."

"That's good."

"But that means me and Lars will be over at Daddy's house, and there will be no guards here."

"I'll be here." He patted his holstered revolver.

"Right. I forgot." She bounded down the steps, then spun back. "Should I keep a journal of anything suspicious, or will an oral account be sufficient? I read that spies always keep journals."

"Keep a journal if you want to."

"I will! Maybe I'll write a book someday. I'll call it *Dacee June's Deadwood*." She trotted to the house next door.

He found Rebekah was in the kitchen. "How's the prettiest gal in Dakota?" he asked.

She peeked under the lid of a huge blue kettle on the kitchen stove. "Merely in Dakota?"

Todd tugged off his tie and draped it around her neck like a backwards necklace. "Well, I don't remember much else in the world."

She tied the tie like a scarf around her neck, letting the tails drape down across the front of her white blouse. "I'm doing very well," she replied.

He touched her shoulder and spun her around. "I want an honest answer."

She dropped her chin and scowled at him. "My arms ache, my back cramps up if I get in the wrong position, and my wrists are so stiff I have to soak them in hot soda water. But . . . on the inside, I'm doing a whole lot better than that. I apologize for breaking down like that last night."

"Darlin', none of you ladies need apologize for enduring such a horrible ordeal. I can hardly force myself to imagine it." He gently tugged her shoulders tight against his chest. "I intend to do everything I can to see that it never, ever happens to you again, even if it means we move out of the Black Hills."

Rebekah relaxed. There were times when she felt that being in Todd's arms was the most peaceful place on earth.

This was one of those times.

"How are things around town?" she asked as she returned to the stove.

"Things are tense, but Quiet Jim is better this morning."

She removed the kettle lid. The kitchen filled with the aroma of beef and rice soup. "Does he have any movement in his legs?"

"Not yet." Todd leaned his backside against the counter. "But the doc says it's still too early. At least it looks like those bullets are not going to kill him. Doc said finding him quickly and getting the bleeding stopped probably saved his life."

Rebekah handed him the wooden pepper grinder. "Would you unscrew this? My wrists are quite useless today."

Todd opened the top and handed it back to her.

"Why would someone ride by and shoot him in the legs?" Rebekah searched her kitchen shelves.

"They were either bad shots, in a hurry, or . . ."

"Or just wanted to wound him?" She scooped a handful of peppercorns from a small brown burlap bag, then funneled them into the grinder.

"It's getting downright frightful."

Rebekah opened the oven door with a folded towel and slid out a pan of biscuits. "How's Quiet Jim taking it?"

"Like always. He never complains." Todd reached over and pinched one of the steaming biscuits and received a soft slap on the fingers.

"But how is he really doing?"

Todd folded his arms across his chest. "I think he's scared he might never walk again."

"That makes me so mad I want to scream." She darted into the pantry and emerged with a jar of wild blackberry jam. "Why . . . why? Why would anyone want to do that to such a gentle, respectful man? They wanted to grab Dacee June, cripple Quiet Jim, bust up our store . . . it's like they wanted to rile the whole town."

Todd brushed biscuit crumbs from his chin whiskers as she reentered the kitchen. "Or at least one man."

"And Daddy Brazos is out of town." Rebekah glanced over at the hole in an otherwise full pan of biscuits. "I know . . . I know when we make a stand for righteousness we attract the forces of evil. But evil still makes me angry. I want to scream. I want to stomp on it. I want to bash evil up alongside the head."

"Good," Todd asserted. "If we ever become complacent, we've lost the battle."

Rebekah pulled the biscuits apart and placed them in a linen-napkin-lined basket. "How's Columbia?"

"She is shocking everyone." Todd followed her out to the dining room. "She's been bedridden for two weeks. Now she jumps up, tugs little Sarah around with her, and waits on Quiet Jim."

"I bet he's upset with that." Rebekah covered the biscuits with another white napkin.

"Only for a minute. I was there when she told him that she meant it when she promised to take care of him, for better and for worse. She said bluntly that whether she lived, the baby lived, or Quiet Jim lived, was all in the Lord's hands, but she had no intention of allowing someone else to take care of her man."

Rebekah laced her fingers and could feel the lace cuffs on each sleeve rub together. "What did Quiet Jim say?"

Todd tugged at her apron strings until she backed over to where he stood. "Quiet Jim just mumbled something about there being a lot of dust in the air and wiped his eyes."

She leaned her head against Todd's chest and closed her eyes. For a moment there was no pain in her arms, no cramp in her back. *Sometimes it takes the tough times to remember the important things, doesn't it, Lord?* She opened her eyes and glanced across the room. "Can you set down the porcelain soup tureen?"

Todd scooted out from behind her and retrieved the large white soup bowl.

"Do you have a guard stationed at Quiet Jim's?" she asked.

"Pete Whip is there," he said.

"It was a good thing all those treasure coach messengers were in town this weekend."

"I've got six of 'em takin' turns guarding the houses and the store. Seth took the other six with him."

"I don't suppose Mr. Lander at Wells Fargo likes having all his treasure coach messengers unavailable."

"They don't ship bullion until Monday. Of course, if the sheriff isn't back by then, they'll just have to postpone."

"Can they do that? Isn't there a schedule to keep?"

"Some things are more important than schedules."

Rebekah jammed a slightly wrinkled green apple into the peeler and began to crank. "Can you crank this for me? I feel helpless."

Todd stepped over and spun the peeler.

"Are they going ahead and displaying the gold bars in the bank window?" she asked.

"They said they weren't going to break tradition of the past four years."

"Did the sheriff think he had a trail to follow?"

"He picked up their sign just up Whitewood Creek."

"If he's on their trail, why do we need to continue this self-inflicted quarantine?"

"Because the trail was too easy. They might be setting an ambush."

"Or perhaps they're really dumb."

"Did they sound dumb to you?" he asked.

"They sounded like men with a plan, a plan to get even." She waved an arm toward the front of the house. "Would you bring the deacon's bench in for a couple of the children to sit on?"

Todd reemerged with the straight-backed, dark wooden bench. "I don't figure we've seen the last of them. That's a frightening thought, isn't it?"

"Not nearly as terrifying as it would have been last night."

"Something's different?" Todd quizzed.

"I've been chastised a little," she admitted.

"By whom?"

"The Lord," she said. "For several days I've wanted to talk to Abigail about where she stood with the Lord. Well, last night I had a wonderful opportunity to demonstrate the peace of Jesus . . . and I failed horribly. She and her mother did better than I did."

"But that was an extreme test."

"And I extremely failed. This morning I prayed the Lord would give me another chance to demonstrate that peace."

"You don't mean you want to be tied up and threatened again?"

"You know what? I told the Lord it didn't matter."

"It matters to me," he insisted.

"Listen to me, Todd. I told Him I would be willing to go through anything at all, if it meant I could demonstrate His love in such a way to reach Abigail."

"She means that much to you?"

"She does. And the funny thing is, I don't know why. Why her and not some other person in town? It's like the Lord said, "It's time to put your faith into practice." Then He sent Abigail my way. Next time, I know I'll do it better. And I'm not nearly as frightened as I thought I should be."

"If you don't mind, I'm praying those two never come within a hundred miles of Deadwood again."

"That's all right, too. Did you tell Columbia we'd be bringing lunch?"

"Yes, and she pitched a fit, but finally gave in to my astute logic and charm," Todd declared.

"Oh, what logic and charm was that?"

"I said she couldn't stop me from bringing it over and if they didn't want it, they could take it out and dump it in the street."

"Take it or dump it? You call that logic and charm? I don't think any Fortune man was ever accused of having charm," she laughed. "Todd Fortune, you're beginning to sound just like Daddy Brazos!"

"Now, that's a challenging thought. But you're wrong about no charming Fortune men."

"Samuel?"

"Sammy can charm a mama bear into giving away her cub for a huckleberry."

"I would love to meet him someday."

"I know. I know. Last time Robert came up with Jamie Sue, we talked about the two of us just riding down to the Indian Territory and finding Samuel. We figured we'd just hog-tie him and bring him here to the hills."

"Maybe you should."

"He's got to want it, honey. He's got to want to see Daddy."

"It's sad."

"Yeah, you can see it eat away on Daddy's face every day of his life."

"That and the loss of your mother. He has such sad eyes when he's thinking about her."

"You know, it never crossed his mind that he would ever have to spend a single day of his life without her. Now, after all these years, there are days when he still seems stunned."

"You're getting melancholy, Todd Fortune."

"You're the one that said it. I'm getting more like Daddy every day."

"That's alright with me. I married you just because of your daddy."

"What?"

"I said to myself, 'If the kid turns out like the old man . . . well, I have myself a winner.' " She took his hands and pulled him close. "That and the fact that your kisses melt my shoes."

The front door opened. They stepped to the parlor as Abigail Gordon entered the house.

"Sorry to interrupt." Abigail wore the same dress as the previous night. There were dark semicircles under her eyes. "I know you two would probably like more time together. I do remember what it's like to be married."

"You are not interrupting anything," Rebekah reassured.

"Are you complaining?" Abigail winked.

"Only a little!" Rebekah replied. "Anyway, it's time to eat. Do you want to go get the gang next door?"

Abigail brushed a few wisps of her errant dark hair behind her ear. "Yes, that's why I'm here. Quintin is quite sure we've missed a meal or two."

"I'll go round them up." Todd scooted out the front door, leaving it open wide.

Rebekah turned back to the kitchen, and Abigail trailed after her. "What have all of you been doing over there?"

"Mother and Amber are teaching Quintin and Dacee June to play hearts."

"How's your mother doing after last night's ordeal?" Rebekah quizzed.

"She calls it the adventure of her life and can't wait to get home and tell her friends."

"I'm so thankful no one was hurt . . . at least, not seriously." Rebekah scooted the large pan off the stove.

"The others were busy with hearts. How about you and Little Fern?"

"She wanted me to read to her."

"Did you find anything over there to read?"

"I eh . . . I hope this is all right . . . I was reading Mr. Fortune's big Bible."

"I'm sure he wouldn't mind a bit. He's got his small one with him on the hunt, no doubt."

"I presume that's a picture of him and Todd's mother in the front."

"Yes, that was taken down in Brownsville after the war."

"She was a beautiful woman."

"According to Todd, she was as tough as nails, and as tender as a feather bed. Her faith and her family was the absolute center of her life. Heaven help anyone who threatened either. She and Daddy Brazos communicated with just a nod, a glance, a shout of the eyes. She was his girl . . . and that's about all he ever really wanted in life."

Abigail raised her sweeping eyebrows. "I'm surprised Mr. Fortune didn't take that photograph with him."

"He couldn't get her image out of his mind if he wanted," Rebekah said.

"Do you find it's a hard image to live up to?" Abigail scooped up a handful of spoons from the polished oak box and set one by each soup bowl.

"At first it was a challenge. Deceased people are perfect. They never make any more mistakes and their former ones seem to fade as the years go by. But then it dawned on me that Todd was struggling to live up to his father's image. I suppose we all try to copy someone else. And Todd's mother is as good an example as I could find. I think everything's ready. Where's that gang from next door?"

"I'm sure Mother won't let them adjourn until the hand is over." Abigail surveyed the orderly table settings. "You know, that was one of Amber's father's problems. The way he was headed, he was going to be just like his father."

"Was his father a doctor?" Rebekah asked.

"Oh, yes . . . a doctor . . . a racehorse owner . . . and fairly addicted to Tennessee whiskey and Tennessee women. At last count he had been married four times. I suppose we all live in someone's shadow."

"Maybe the secret is getting under the right shadow."

"You, Rebekah Fortune, are my new shadow."

Rebekah straightened her shoulders and stared into Abigail's dark eyes. "Me? You can do much better than this!"

"In the Black Hills?"

"Yes. You saw me last night."

"And I see you work it through today."

"I'm sure there are some older women who . . ."

"Older women? I want to see someone my age do it right," Abigail said.

"Do what right?"

"Life . . . love . . . marriage . . . kids . . . faith . . . everything."

"Children?" Rebekah grinned.

"Sooner or later."

"Perhaps sooner."

"Really?"

"I think so, but I'll have to have you help me with child raising."

"I'm not a good example of a mother. Having Amber with me reminds me how much I've never learned."

"Maybe we'll just learn together."

Abigail took Rebekah's arm. "Do you mean that?"

"What I mean is as long as we're living in the same town . . . well, I'd like very much for you to be my best friend and prayer partner," Rebekah blurted out.

"Prayer partner? But I . . ."

"If I'm going to be your example, you have to pray for me."

"I'm not sure God wants to listen to my prayers," Abigail murmured.

"Abby-girl . . . I'm going to have fun schoolin' you."

"Schoolin' me? Are you starting to drop your g's? You sound like a Deadwood old-timer."

"Now that, Mrs. Abigail Gordon, is an astonishing observation."

A line of hungry children and adults paraded into the dining room.

"I won the last hand," Dacee June reported. "I had a whole bunch of middle hearts, the toughest to get rid of, but I did it. I didn't take one point."

"I don't want any raspberry pie," Amber announced.

"Are we having peas?" Quintin probed. "I don't like peas."

SEVEN

"I like mash'tatoes," Fern added as she struggled to pull herself up onto the deacon's bench.

"I like beefsteak," Quintin said. "Can I have two?"

The inside of Fortune's Hardware was gloomy when Todd returned to work. He couldn't tell if it was the overcast day, the armed guard by the front door, or the mood of most of the customers and clerks. Everyone seemed to be looking over their shoulders, expecting something disastrous to happen.

"Do you want me to run these boiler valves up to the DeSmet?" Carty Toluca asked. "We could wait until they send someone to town."

Todd glanced around the store. "I want you and Dub to take them up to the mine. I promised to send them up as soon as they came in."

"It ain't more than a crate full," Carty mused. "I reckon one man should be able to handle it."

Todd rested his hands on his hips and could feel his holstered revolver under his suit coat. "One of you ride shotgun. We aren't taking any chances." Todd paced the aisle, but kept his eyes toward the front door.

Carty waved his shirt-clad arm towards the badlands. "The whole town is takin' this personal. Talk is, if them two show up below the dead line, they will be shot down on sight. Folks down there can be mighty protective of ladies up on Forest Hill, too. Nevada Jack is offering to give the Piedmont Saloon to any man who kills them both."

Todd parked himself by the open front door and surveyed the rigs and riders in the street. "He said that?"

"Yep. That's how the regulars feel. The drifters and bummers . . . well, they're hopin' ever' lawman and treasure messenger leaves the gulch. But that type is no account." Carty opened a small folding knife and cleaned the dirt from under his straight-cut fingernails.

Two men galloped up the street and Todd slipped his hand on the grip of his holstered revolver. "I reckon we'll all be jumpy for a while."

"Kind of reminds you of '76, right after the battle at the Little Bighorn."

After the horsemen passed the hardware store, Todd dropped his right hand to his side. "When we closed the roads and put up barricades to fight the Sioux and Cheyenne?"

"Yep. But they never came." Carty's grin revealed a slight gap between his upper two front teeth.

"Well, Mr. Toluca, I hope that's the way it is this time, too. It's just hard to imagine those two not coming back to complete whatever it is they are aiming at."

Todd had just watched Carty and Dub Montgomery drive off when Elijah Lander strolled through the front door shaking his finger as a prelude.

"Elijah, what are you doing over here during banking hours?"

He bounced his finger in the air three times before he replied. His full lips formed an oval, mimicking the shape of his bald head. "Fortune, when is your father coming back?"

The banker rocked forward on the toes of his black patent leather shoes, slightly elevating his five-foot-four-inch frame. "I reckon it will be another week or so," Todd replied. "Don't suppose I can help you with anything?"

Lander's sideburns were about as thick as Grass Edwards's, but with a bald head, they were clown-like. Again, his hands waved before he spoke. "I've decided to take the gold bars out of the window."

Todd glanced back out at the open front door. He watched Madame DuFur whip her ox team that struggled to pull two loaded freight wagons toward Lead. "Sounds prudent to put the gold in the safe."

"But I've got to ship it on schedule on Monday. I've got to get the bullion to the train in Sidney, Nebraska, on time. I just got a telegram from the secretary of the treasury personally saying they must have our shipment on the train to Philadelphia as per schedule."

"You actually got a telegram from the secretary of the treasury?"

Elijah Lander pulled a square piece of paper out of his pocket. "Right here!"

Todd looked it over. "Whenever you need Lars, Pete, and the boys, you take them. We'll make other arrangements for guards."

"Thanks, but even then I hate to ship at half strength." Now Lander shook his right hand so hard, he seemed to be having an attack. "I trust the sheriff will be back soon. I'll need to hire some additional messengers if he delays. I don't suppose you could spare a few days . . ."

"I just can't ride off and leave my family. If I hadn't had that trouble up at the house, and if . . ."

"If you hadn't had that trouble, all my messengers would still be in town."

"If you're asking me to choose between protecting my family or your gold, then my choice is easy," Todd said.

Lander bounced his index finger in the air. "Quite so. I must agree." He finally pointed out to the armed guard on the boardwalk. "Do you think you could really spare Princy Black and the others?"

"If you have to ship the bullion Monday, we'll figure out something. Is Handsome Harry well enough to drive the coach?"

"No, but I've got this new man, Tweed Bucklan, lined up. Handsome Harry heard tell that he's an outstanding driver."

"So now you're rounding up extra messengers?"

Lander glanced around before he spoke. "Well, I'm not going to make a general announcement down in the badlands. I thought I'd hire a half dozen at the last moment, mix them in with the regulars that are left, and send 'em off. It's good pay, and they wouldn't have time to get greedy."

"I think you ought to wait for the sheriff's bunch. They force you to change plans, and you're playing into someone's hands."

"I have to ship on Monday. You saw the telegram."

"What could they do if you shipped one day late? Or two? They will not refuse the gold."

"No, but they could contract someone else to handle the transactions." Lander waved his arms in the air, then folded them across his chest. "Maybe Brazos will be home by Monday."

In his mind, Todd imagined his father and Yapper Jim scampering up and down some tiny creek in the Bighorns, panning for gold. "We never know about him."

"That reminds me." Lander's mouth chewed air, then continued. "I opened a rather substantial account this morning in the name of Olene Steel Company."

"I've met Mr. Olene."

"I know. That's why I figured you'd be interested in his account."

"Did he decide to buy out Ayres and Wardman's Hardware?"

"No, he bought the old Langrishe Theater," Lander announced.

"A theater? What for?"

"He's going to tear it down and build a flat-iron and brick hard-ware store."

"He said that?"

"Yes, and he's transferring sixty-five thousand into a new account."

Todd glanced out at the sky above the gulch. He was surprised how much darker the clouds had become. "That will be the fanciest building in the Black Hills."

"Certainly the nicest hardware building in all of Dakota. He said you turned him down when he offered to buy you out."

Todd paced the floor next to a rack of nine-pound sledge hammers. "I told him we'd think about it and let him know in a few weeks. I suppose that's the same thing as turning him down."

"What will Brazos say when he returns?"

Todd could envision his father's flushed face and clenched fists. "He threatened to put us out of business if we didn't sell. I don't fig-ure Daddy will be too pleased with that. Is Olene still in town?"

"He's not leaving until tomorrow. Are you going to talk to him?" Lander quizzed.

"What is there to say? He's free to do what he wants, and we're free . . . well, we would be free if these two outlaws get captured."

"I suppose so. I don't think I've known of a time in the past three years where so many good men in this town were either absent or preoccupied."

"Mr. Lander, I still say you should jam those gold bars in your best safe and leave them there until you get your regular messengers back."

"But, the Secretary of the Treasury said . . ."

"You can stall him for a day or two. He won't send in the troops . . . which wouldn't be a bad idea. Maybe you should ask for an army escort from Fort Meade."

Lander windmilled both hands with limp wrists. "I couldn't do that. That would be an admission that we can't look after ourselves in the Hills. That's an image we've tried so diligently to overcome.

SEVEN

How will we achieve statehood if we have to rely on federal troops to conduct our regular business?"

Todd rested his hand on the shorter man's shoulder as they walked to the door. "Elijah, we aren't ever going to have statehood until the folks in Yankton and Bismarck decide to get along with each other."

"Yes, quite so." Lander continued to wave his hands. "The fact remains, we have to handle this ourselves and prove that we can keep a schedule."

After Mr. Lander left, Todd surveyed the store from the staircase at the back of the building.

It's just a hardware store.

A mining camp hardware.

Goods, parts, mining supplies.

Nothing fancy. Nothing special.

Except memories.

Memories when there were only a dozen tents in this gulch and those that wintered out were convinced they would freeze, starve, or get slaughtered by hostiles.

But businesses come and go. A big eastern store . . . it would bring prices down . . . for a while. They must be counting on the railroad coming in soon. That could be five, ten years away.

But prices would be cheaper. For some. For a while. After they drive off competition, it will be difficult not to raise prices.

Todd hiked up to his second-story office, then strolled to the Main Street window to glance over at the Wells Fargo office. He thought he could see a few sprinkles dripping into the dusty street from the dark clouds.

The whole reason for building Fort Meade was to protect the Black Hills. I can't figure why Lander is so dead set against rousing out some troops for the treasure coach. Stubbornness is what it is, mining camp stubbornness. "We don't need any help, and we'll put a fortune in gold on the line to prove it." If I can convince him to just wait two days, the treasure messengers will be back and they can ship out like normal.

The Secretary of the Treasury? I think Daddy knows the Secretary of the Treasury or is that the Secretary of War? Doesn't matter. Even if he were pals with President Rud Hays, Daddy's just like Mr. Lander. He wouldn't send for troops no matter what.

Todd caught up three days of bookkeeping and made out his orders for the following week. He heard someone sprint up the stairs but didn't bother to turn around and look.

"You get those deliveries made, Carty?"

"How did you know it was me?"

"No one else has the energy to race up the stairs this late in the day. Did you have any trouble?"

Carty looped his thumbs in his suspenders. "None, but the mines have the guards out and armed to the teeth. People drivin' up the road ain't friendly until they see who you are. It's like everyone's expecting somethin' terrible to happen."

"As soon as the sheriff brings in those two ol' boys, it will quiet down."

"I surely do wish Daddy Brazos was home," Carty added. "He'd get things settled down in a hurry."

"He'd probably enjoy the whole thing a lot more than we do. The old man thrives on adversity."

"I have an idea," Carty blurted out. "Why don't you send a telegram to Buffalo . . . or Fort McKinney . . . and see if they know where Daddy Brazos and Yapper Jim happen to be? They could be home in three or four days if they knew we were in trouble."

"We do not need to send for Daddy Brazos," Todd said.

"I thought you said . . ."

"What I said was, we all would enjoy having them home," Todd snapped. "But that doesn't mean we can't handle this ourselves."

After Carty slunk down the stairway, Todd stared across the room and out the window at the low-hanging clouds that blocked his view of Mount Moriah and White Rocks.

I guess I'm as stubborn as Landers. But I've got to know. Can I make a decision . . . carry it out . . . protect my family . . . lead the community . . . without my father around? A man has to learn that sometime.

Perhaps this is my time.

If it's not, may the Lord have mercy on us.

Todd spent the rest of the afternoon going over detailed drawings of an addition to the Hallelujah Mine's stamp mill building. His desk was piled high with bolt catalogs, charts of stress tolerances, and wholesale steel company price lists. In the milk bucket used for a trash can was deposited the twenty-five-page price guide for Olene Steel Company. He was calculating a bid on the hardware and had just tallied his final sums when Carty Toluca poked his head up the stairs.

"That attorney fella is downstairs wanting to talk to you."

Todd kept his thumb on the total at the bottom of the page and glanced down at Carty's head. "What attorney?"

Carty scooted close so his thin face was between the perpendicular wooden rails of the stairs. "Mr. Watson Dover."

"He's still in town? I thought he left."

His hands on the rails, Carty looked caged, or jailed. "He came back."

"Why?" Todd fastened the top button on his shirt and straightened his tie.

"There's another man with him. A doctor."

Todd pushed back from the desk and marched toward the stairs. "Doctor Gordon? Did he bring Abigail's husband with him?"

Carty remained halfway down the stairs, his head peeking up into the second-story room. "I don't know. I just told 'em I'd announce they was here. I told 'em you was busy."

The man standing next to the Chattanooga attorney was six feet tall, broad-shouldered, with premature, solid white hair. With tailor-made, charcoal gray suit and four-in-hand forest-green tie, he dominated the dusty hardware filled with grubby prospectors and white-aproned clerks.

Todd marched right up to them. "Mr. Dover, I really didn't expect to see you so soon."

A wisp of dark hair shot out from under the attorney's round hat, drawing attention to his furrowed forehead. "The doctor was waiting for me in Spearfish."

"He came all the way to Dakota and then sent you into the hills to do the dirty work?"

"I think I do a good job of representing my client." He turned to the white-headed man. "Dr. Gordon, this is Mr. Fortune, who I have described."

Neither man exhibited much enthusiasm in the handshake.

"Fortune's a younger man than I thought." Gordon's complexion was pale, but he looked like the type that could easily redden. "I understand you are representing my daughter's mother?"

Todd surveyed the well-dressed Tennessee doctor. "I'm a friend of Abigail's, that's all, not an attorney." *I wonder if he feels as out of place as he looks?*

"I would like to know where she is; I don't intend on staying in this wretched hole in the ground any longer than possible." The doctor's bushy eyebrows narrowed, his lips tightened. "I understand she has not been in her room at the Gem Theater, nor the hotel room she rented for her mother and daughter."

Todd Fortune stared at the scowling steel-gray eyes of Dr. Gordon. "I'll be quite happy to pass the word along. Did you want to meet with her?"

The doctor tugged at the starched French cuffs and tweaked the gold and onyx cuff links. "I didn't come this far to enjoy the scenery."

Todd folded his arms across his chest and nodded toward the hills. "That's too bad. It's nice scenery."

Gordon pulled a gold pocket watch from his silk brocade vest. He flipped it open, closed it, then dropped it back into his pocket without glancing at the time. "Will you assist us, or should I turn to the sheriff?"

"The sheriff's out in the hills trying to catch some bushwhackers. You have my permission to try and track him down. I presume your words were meant as a veiled threat."

Impatience swept across the doctor's face. "Perhaps that was a poor choice of words."

"Perhaps it was," Todd said. "Here's a primary rule of life on the frontier: every threat, veiled or not, will be taken seriously and challenged. Now, if you would like to schedule a meeting with Abigail, give me a time and location, and I'll see what I can arrange."

Gordon looked over at the attorney, then back at Todd. "How about in one hour at my room in the Merchant's Hotel?"

Todd pointed back over his shoulder in the general direction of Forest Hill. "How about in one hour on the front porch of my house? Mr. Dover is well aware of where it is."

The doctor reached into his coat pocket as if to retrieve something but pulled his hand out empty. "On the front porch?"

SEVEN

"Mr. Dover has been banished from entering our home by my wife. Surely an attorney that represents his client well told you about that."

With a tone like he was instructing his staff, Dr. Gordon announced, "We need to find a more neutral place. I have important matters to discuss with her . . . alone."

"You mean, Mr. Dover will not be there?" *Does this man always get his way?*

"Of course, I'll be there. There are legal matters to decide." Dover patted the coffee-colored leather briefcase at his side.

"Good," Todd added, "I was afraid you meant just the Dr. and Mrs. Gordon. I understand the last time they were left alone, the doctor threatened to give Mrs. Gordon a broken jaw."

Dr. Gordon clenched his fists at the accusation. "I'll have you know that I never intentionally struck that woman." The air in the hardware was a stale mixture of oil, leather, and cold iron. Gordon's large round nose widened as his face flushed. "I do not intend to stand here and be accused by a complete stranger."

Todd took a deep breath. He could feel his heart race. *Lord, help me not to say and do what I very much want to say and do.* "I'm sorry," he added. "I know it is my Christian duty to be more charitable. I just have a difficult time being civil when I'm in the presence of some-one who mistreats women. In the West, such actions are considered by most men to be a capital offense. My wife and I will, of course, be with Abigail, if she chooses to meet with you."

"I said I wanted a private meeting," Dr. Gordon huffed.

"What you said was, you wanted your attorney with you so that you two men could badger one lone woman. I will not insult Abigail by taking such a request to her. I will tell her you agreed that we should come along. Now, as far as a neutral place is concerned, how about the private banquet room of the Merchant's Hotel, providing it's not in use this evening?"

Mr. Dover, shorter than either of the others, stepped between them. "That sounds fine. Shall we say, in one hour?"

Todd rubbed his temples in an attempt to force himself to relax. "If we are not there in an hour and a half, Mrs. Gordon has rejected the arrangement."

"I want to know one thing, Fortune." Dr. Gordon jabbed his well-manicured finger at Todd, stopping only inches short of his chest. "What is your interest in this matter? Why are you interfering with my former wife's business? I presume she's living at your home. Could it be you have a romantic interest in her?"

The short-barreled .45 Smith and Wesson that normally stayed concealed under Todd's suit coat was yanked out and cocked so fast, Todd could hardly believe it himself. With the barrel prodding his midsection, Gordon lost all color, and his face was almost as white as his hair.

"Wait!" Dover called out, his hand on Fortune's left arm.

Todd's heart throbbed through his temples, shot down through his arm, and pulsated in his trigger finger that pressed the cold steel of the .45. "Dr. Gordon, you have insulted the honor of a fine lady, and cast a shadow on my marriage and my morality. This is the frontier. Men have died in this town for much less than that, and I assure you no Deadwood jury would hold me guilty of a crime if I pull this trigger." He backed away one step, turned his head toward Dover, but left the gun pointed at the doctor. "Get him out of here, Mr. Dover. Get him out of here . . . now!"

With sweat beaded on his forehead and trembling hands, Watson Dover tugged at Dr. Gordon's arm. "Mr. Fortune is right in some of what he said. This is a different country out here. It would be expeditious for us to adjourn now."

Dr. Gordon, color returning to his face, said nothing. He shuffled along under Dover's tow.

The banquet table did not have a centerpiece. Nor did it contain place settings, glasses, or a tablecloth. It was a bare, round, quarter-sawn oak tabletop with pillar and paw feet. Along one side were three straight-back wooden chairs. Across from them, two chairs with well-dressed, slightly nervous men standing behind them.

Todd tipped his hat toward them. "Dr. Gordon, this is my wife, Rebekah."

He nodded, but did not take his eyes off Abigail. She stared back at the doctor. Her face poised, her voice steady. "I do not intend to shake your hand, Doctor, if that is what you are waiting for."

"I did not expect you would."

Todd held the middle chair for Abigail, the left one for Rebekah. After the ladies were seated, all three men sat down.

Dr. Gordon rapped his long fingers on the tabletop. "Mr. Dover says you absolutely refused my offer. Is that right?"

Abigail's hands lay in her lap. "Yes, it is. And I'm sure that you didn't journey all the way here from the train by stagecoach to hear me say that. So, why this meeting?"

"I have a few more delicate matters that have come to my attention since we last spoke," Mr. Dover asserted. "I believe it strengthens the doctor's contentions."

"I trust you are talking about legal matters. I do not intend to sit here and listen to anyone dispel my character and castigate my choice of professions," Abigail asserted.

Watson Dover yanked a handful of papers from his briefcase. "I will do what I am paid to do."

"Well, go ahead Mr. Attorney, earn your keep," Abigail encouraged.

"In light of new evidence," Dover announced, "I would like for you to reconsider Dr. Gordon's offer."

"What new evidence?" Abigail asked.

Dover handed her a piece of paper with a detailed list of allegations. "First, through some diligent work of some investigators hired by Dr. Gordon, we have received a telegram from Omaha, Nebraska, and learned that you have not raised your daughter, but she is, even as we speak, staying with your elderly mother. Second, you have chosen to work at a place called the Gem Theater. Its private boxes are notoriously known for being impromptu brothels."

Todd jumped to his feet. "Are you accusing Abigail of being a soiled dove? Because if you are, you haven't even begun to see what I would do when I get angry . . ."

Abigail held out her hand and gripped his coat sleeve. "Wait, Todd. I would like to hear the conclusion of these accusations."

Todd clutched his holstered gun.

"Daddy Brazos," Rebekah commanded, "sit down!"

The words spun Todd's head around. *Well . . . well, perhaps I do sound like him, but . . . but . . . he's right! This is untenable!* Todd left the gun holstered but continued to stand alert.

"I have a strong suspicion," Abigail continued, "that it will become even more repugnant. Please sit down, Todd."

A red-faced Todd Fortune reluctantly sat on the edge of his chair. "I presume you will get to the point," he inserted.

The doctor cleared his throat. "The point is, unless you agree to this settlement, I will be forced to go to a court and seek to remove my daughter from your inferior custody and place her in a foster home where she can be properly cared for."

This time it was Abigail who leaped to her feet. "You came here with papers disinheriting your daughter, and yet you accuse me of providing improper care?"

Dr. Gordon stood, his face a cold mask of fury. "I'm only saying that there are several options here, and I want you to understand the implications of your decision," he shouted.

Rebekah and Todd raised up beside Abigail. "Mr. Fortune," Rebekah's voice quivered with rage, "this might be a good time to go ahead and shoot Dr. Gordon."

"Wait!" Dover called out. "I believe my client perhaps had a poor choice of words."

"Dover, we had no idea how articulate you were until we heard the doctor rant and rave," Todd grumbled.

"I believe there is a better way to phrase this. May I continue, Mrs. Gordon?" Dover asked.

"With that man in the room, I have nothing to discuss." She pointed at Dr. Gordon.

"This is preposterous," he blustered.

Dover, a good eight inches shorter than the doctor, swelled up his chest and shoved the bigger man toward the east wall of the room. "Dr. Gordon, you are interfering with my negotiations. Go over and sit in that chair near the door, or exit the room immediately."

"Do what?" he roared.

Dover again shoved Dr. Gordon. "I do not tell you how to perform surgery. I do not need you to tell me how to negotiate. Go over there and sit down."

"I can fire you," Gordon threatened.

"And that would leave you alone with Mr. Fortune and his revolver, a situation that I am seriously considering. However, I

SEVEN

believe you have threatened to fire me for several years. Somehow your threats seem far less enforceable in Deadwood than they do in Chattanooga. Now go over there and sit down. I know far too much about your life and practice for you to ever fire me. Shoot me, perhaps. But you will never dismiss me."

Todd Fortune stared at Watson Dover as Dr. Gordon shuffled to the east wall and slumped into a captain's chair. He leaned across the table and spoke in hushed tones. "Dover, I'm proud of you. Spoken like a man."

"Yes, well," he replied in a whisper, "it must be this Deadwood air that makes a man both foolish and brave. I suspect I have not heard the last of this."

Dr. Gordon called out, "I expect to hear what's going on. No secret negotiations."

They all sat down.

"Here is the point," Watson Dover continued. "My client is extremely concerned about getting a quitclaim on his estate signed and will pay handsomely for it. If it is not signed, he will try to achieve a similar result, albeit by different methods."

"Methods of character assassination, slander, and threat to children?" Rebekah quizzed. "Is that the way you operate, Mr. Dover?"

"I believe Mrs. Gordon and I both know the doctor is capable of just that," Dover suggested. "I will attempt to keep this something that must be proved in a court of law. I will resign if I cannot. The doctor, however, will not quit until he gets his way. That much I can assure you. However low you think of me for suggesting them, the courts will view the quality of child care and character of the mother as serious concerns, no matter who the attorney might be."

"Mr. Dover, I'm sorry your practice is in such shape that you feel the need to have to work for such a man as Gordon. Under all this chicanery, I believe you're a good man. This is bringing out the worst in you." Todd realized that he was no longer angry with the attorney. "I presume such a case would be tried here in Deadwood."

"I believe the child resides in Omaha, so the trial will be in Nebraska," Dover corrected.

"Your information is insufficient in that regard," Rebekah declared. "Mrs. O'Neill and Amber live here in Deadwood with Abigail."

"What?" Dr. Gordon called out from across the room.

"That's right," Todd added, "they live in a home next to us up on Forest Hill. So the trial would have to be in Deadwood."

"No matter," Dover added. "However distasteful the subject matter, I will represent my client well."

"Perhaps you'd like for me to introduce you to Judge Bennett. I believe I saw him out in the dining room. Judge Bennett believes in awarding all children in a custody case to the mother. He is a firm believer that even a poor mother is better than no mother. So, let's remove the threat of court action," Todd continued. "Now, what do we have left?"

"Then I must appeal to your Christian charity," Dover shrugged. "The doctor wishes only to go on with his life unhampered by the past."

"There is no Christian grace in that woman," Dr. Gordon shouted from across the room.

Abigail stood. Her hands quivered so violently that even clutching them together didn't quiet them. "Dr. Gordon knows very little about me and absolutely nothing about his daughter. As far as my faith in the Lord is concerned, it is all very new to me. But it is real. And here's the first proof of charity and trust in His leading. I will sign the quit claim."

"You see," Dr. Gordon shouted. "I told you threatening her would work."

Dover wiped the sweat from his brow that was no longer so severely furrowed. "Thank-you, Mrs. Gordon. And I will prepare you a draft for ten thousand dollars," Dover assured.

"Five thousand dollars," Dr. Gordon called out. "I rescinded the ten-thousand-dollar offer after it was rejected the first time. She only gets five thousand dollars."

Abigail shook her head. "Thank-you, Dr. Gordon, for that graphic reminder of why life with you was absolute hell. But, it doesn't matter what is offered. I will refuse any money. Only, I want it written in the contract that Amber is Dr. Gordon's oldest child. And when she reaches eighteen, she may decide for herself whether to pursue her rightful place in her father's estate."

"Absolutely not!" Dr. Gordon shouted. "That's the whole purpose of this matter!"

SEVEN

Dover marched over to the doctor and mumbled some words. They both nodded, then Dover returned to the table. "We will accept your offer. I will have an agreement drafted by morning."

"Undoubtedly you both feel that you can convince Amber otherwise when she is eighteen." Abigail's tightly clasped fingers whitened under her grip. "But that will be her decision. And that is my whole point. She should decide, not you and me."

Dacee June burst through the door, trailed by Amber, Quintin, and Fern. "Sorry to interrupt. Todd, Carty came up to the house and announced that Columbia's having her baby. Mrs. O'Neill went back with him and I said I'd look for Dr. Spencer."

"Did you find him?" Rebekah asked.

"He's sick in bed. Everyone who ate at the Oyster Bay lunch counter turned up vomiting sick today. What are we going to do?"

"We'll go right over. You take the children home." Then Todd turned to Gordon. "Doctor, your services are needed."

"I am not practicing medicine in the Black Hills."

"To the relief of everyone in this room." Todd drew his gun. "However, today, you are going to assist a birth."

"You are forcing me at gunpoint to deliver a baby?"

"I'll do whatever it takes, Gordon. It's Deadwood. Things are done different here. Columbia has had some complications and we are going to need professional assistance."

"It will cost you a pretty penny."

"That sounds like a fair price," Abigail snapped.

"That was hyperbole. I charge at least twenty-five dollars to deliver a baby."

"I changed my mind," Abigail told Dover. "I'd like to have twenty-five dollars when I sign that quitclaim."

"This is outrageous," the doctor fumed as he paced the room. "What are those children doing staring at me? Make them quit staring at me!"

"I'll tell you what is outrageous." Abigail choked the tears back. "That beautiful little girl in the violet dress is your daughter, and you had absolutely no idea who she was."

If the entire earth did not rotate around the happenings at Quiet Jim's house in the Ingleside district of Deadwood, Dakota Territory, it was unknown to those inside. For two hours and thirty-six minutes no one in the house thought about revengeful hold-up men, impending business failure, restlessness, business executives, gold shipments, or who reigned as Raspberry Festival queen.

They didn't even think of the father, gun shot and paralyzed from the waist down.

But they did think of the mother.

Through pain, agony, and panic, James Jr. was brought into the world.

Mrs. O'Neill took care of baby Sarah.

Todd sat by the bedside . . . of Quiet Jim.

Rebekah and Abigail worked alongside Dr. Gordon.

Two minutes after he arrived, the doctor pulled off his coat, tossed his tie aside, rolled up his sleeves, and went to work. He spoke hardly a word. And for two hours Rebekah forgot about how much she despised him.

Her dark-blue dress was soaked with sweat. Her light-brown hair dangled from its combs. She waltzed into the room where Quiet Jim lay, Todd standing by his side.

"Well, Daddy, I thought you might like to see young Jimmy!" She swung the blanket-wrapped bundle around and laid him on the bed next to the smiling father. "Isn't that round red face about the cutest baby you ever saw? Todd, look at this little boy," she sighed. "I believe he already looks like his daddy, don't you?"

Quiet Jim stared at the baby.

Todd reached down and laid his hand alongside the infant's head. Then he looked up at Rebekah. *There's mama in your eyes, Rebekah Fortune. I do believe we will have children soon, no matter where we live.* "Yep, he looks like his daddy. He's a treasure, that's for sure. Do we call him Quiet Jimmy?"

The baby whimpered and Rebekah snatched him up. "We can definitely call him Jimmy, but it remains to be seen whether he's quiet. So far, he's more like Uncle Yapper Jim." Rebekah glanced at Todd, who seemed mesmerized by the baby. *I see your silly grin, Todd Fortune. I know what's in your mind. I'm thinking the same thing. I want one of these, Lord. Even after watching Columbia's agony, I want one of these and I want one right away. On second thought, perhaps in about eight and a half months would be fine.*

SEVEN

"How's Columbia?" Quiet Jim asked.

"Tired. And she's bleeding a little," Rebekah reported.

"I'd like to see her."

"I think she's sleeping now. The doctor said the bleeding should cease in an hour or so. He also said this should be the last child for her. Of course, she scoffed at the idea," Rebekah reported.

Quiet Jim looked down at his listless legs. "Two bullets might have answered that matter already." He turned to Todd. "I need to go see Columbia."

"You'll be getting better," Todd encouraged. "By next fall you'll be out huntin' with those old men and making up more stories about the Black Hills."

Quiet Jim pushed himself up on his elbows. "I don't care if you carry me, drag me, or throw me on the floor and let me crawl, but I want to see my Columbia. And I want to see her now."

CHAPTER EIGHT

The dual rows of tiny pearl buttons ran straight as a plumb line up Rebekah's teal green dress as she raised up in reaction to Todd's news. "She just got off the stagecoach and announced that she was looking for a job as housekeeper and nanny?"

Todd hung his suit coat on a peg and whisked it down with a hickory handled brush. "Something like that."

"Don't you think that's strange?"

"Quiet Jim thinks it's Providence."

"Does she have any references?" Rebekah held the folded tea towel in front of her.

The aroma of strong coffee drew him to the pot on the cookstove. "Yes, but all her papers are from Boston, or the old country."

Rebekah refolded the clean towel. "Ireland?"

"Katie O'Callum. How much more Irish do you want?" Todd poured the boiling coffee into a black ceramic mug with gold foil rim.

"It sounds too Irish." She started to refold the towel again, but checked herself and tossed it down.

The coffee scalded the tip of Todd's tongue. He gulped it down and it burned his throat as well. "What is that supposed to mean?"

"Look, a woman comes to Deadwood, marches into the lumber mill . . . not the hotel, mind you, but a lumber mill that happens to be owned by Quiet Jim . . . and offers her services as a housekeeper and nanny. And you encouraged them to hire her?"

Todd rubbed his squinting blue eyes. "She seems like a gift from God. It's hard to find domestic workers in a boomtown. Look how long you've been looking. She's exactly what they need and you know it."

"And I say things don't happen that smoothly, even when the Lord's involved." Rebekah poured her coffee into a thin china cup with purple violets painted on the side.

"I checked over there this morning, and the report is that Katie is doing wonderful." Todd took another gulp and winced.

Rebekah diluted her coffee with several tablespoons of clean water. "And I say there is potential for real trouble. We'll stop by and check it out after church."

"No, we won't." Todd fastened the top button on his white shirt.

Rebekah felt her neck stiffen. "What do you mean, we won't?"

"We have a trip to take, remember?" He raised his light-brown eyebrows.

"A trip?" Her words came out like a spear, aptly thrown.

"To Rapid City." He attempted to knot his short black tie. "I promised you a trip to Rapid City on Sunday, and we're going."

Rebekah's white lace cuffs framed her thin waving hands. "But that was . . . before all this and . . ."

He leaned over and stuck out his neck. "You still want to go, don't you?"

She fidgeted with his tie. "Well, yes, but we can't go off now. What about those men on the prowl?"

Todd stepped back. "They are either halfway to Texas, with Seth Bullock on their tail, or they will circle back to town, still looking for Daddy Brazos. It wouldn't hurt for us to be gone. We'll spend the night in Rapid City. We can come home tomorrow after we've looked around."

Rebekah prowled the kitchen looking for anything out of place. "Todd Fortune, I can't believe you'd desert your little sister to such uncertainty. There is no way I'm going off and leave Dacee June by herself."

A sly Fortune grin crept over his face. "Lil' Sis is coming with us."

"She is? Well, then this won't exactly be a quiet little respite." She spun her wedding ring around on her finger.

"Oh, that's not all . . ." Todd refused to look her in the eyes. "Abigail, her mother, and Amber wanted to see Rapid City, so I invited them along."

"You did? What kind of carriage did you rent?"

"Mert Hart's three-seater."

"For the six of us?"

"Actually, there's eight. But Carty's bringing his new gelding and is going to be the outrider. I told him he could be the scout."

"You said eight?"

"Thelma Speaker is coming along too."

"You're kidding me!" Rebekah spun around so quickly that her dress flagged away from her. "This whole thing is a joke, right?"

"No. Thelma's been cooped up here in the gulch ever since Louise and Grass Edwards went to California. She offered to bring a box dinner for all of us. We'll leave straight from church."

A fire of curiosity danced in her eyes. "Abigail's going to church?"

"She said she wasn't joking about what she told Dr. Gordon about her faith. She mentioned that you were going to teach her everything."

"I can . . . tell her what I know."

"Sounds like a spiritual opportunity."

"You really think it's safe to travel?" she pressed.

"We can't let this bunch tell us how to live our lives. If we're hiding in the house every day, they've won already. We're going to Rapid City. I will live wisely, but I will not live in fear," he declared. "At some point we have to trust the Lord."

"But this trip is crazy. You don't even want to go to Rapid City," she protested.

"I do now."

"Where will we spend the night?"

"If there are no rooms, we'll camp out," he said.

"In the rain? Those clouds look ready to drop."

"It will be an adventure."

"Todd Fortune, this sounds like something Daddy Brazos would do . . . not his sensible, clear-thinking, oldest son."

"Rebekah Jacobson Fortune, I promised you a trip to Rapid City, and you're going to get it . . . whether you want it or not!"

"I had envisioned something a little . . . less hectic. I'll need to pack."

"We can just brush out what we're wearing and head back tomorrow," he suggested.

"Todd Fortune, I said I'll need to pack!"

Mert Hart's three-seat surrey had a top that was meant to keep the sun off the passengers. But halfway to Sturgis, it began to sprinkle. The leather top took on the role of rain barrier as well. Since there were no sides to the big carriage, those who sat windward soon got wet. Todd drove the rig, Rebekah beside him. In the middle seat were Thelma Speaker and Dacee June, right behind her brother. In the third seat were Mrs. O'Neill and Amber and Abigail Gordon.

Carty Toluca, his yellow oil cloth duster flapping in the storm, rode his bay gelding ahead of the rig. With Winchester '73 carbine across his lap, he gave his best impression of a frontier scout but looked more like a late entry in the kids Fourth of July parade.

"This sure is fun, Todd Fortune!" Dacee called out from the seat straight behind him. "I'm soaked!"

"Not much more water than a Presbyterian baptism," he mumbled. "Besides, it's a warm rain."

"It's not all that warm." Rebekah added as she tugged a gray blanket with black stripe across her lap.

"I'm hungry," Amber piped up from the back seat.

"We can eat anytime," Thelma Speaker announced. "The food is all cooked."

The cloud cover suppressed the noise of the carriage. The slightly muddy road took the clomp out of the horse's hooves. It was not wet enough yet for the gumbo to pack the iron rims of the wheels. Each voice sounded crisp, clear.

"I thought we were going to picnic?" Dacee June said.

"We aren't stopping in the rain," Todd insisted.

"Perhaps we could just snack as we drive along?" Abigail suggested.

"There's an old deserted tollhouse at the top of Boulder Canyon. I thought we could pull off the road and drive up there," Todd announced.

"It doesn't have a roof on it," Dacee June replied.

Todd wiped rainwater off his forehead. "You're thinking about the one at Bullfrog Meadows."

"I ought to know the difference between Bullfrog Meadows and Boulder Canyon Tollhouse," Dacee June fussed.

"Carty!" Todd shouted to the young man on the wet bay horse. "Ride on up and see if we can take dinner at the old tollhouse."

"It doesn't have a roof on it!" Dacee June repeated.

By the time Carty came back, Todd's wool trousers were damp. Most of the rest of the passengers had blankets up to their necks. It was a steady, light drizzle that seemed to seep into the dusty roadway but puddled up on faces and laps. Todd wiped the moisture off his goatee and eyebrows. "What did you find out?"

"It has a roof . . ."

"It does?" Dacee June sputtered. "But . . . but . . . well, maybe I was thinking of Bullfrog Meadow."

"It has a roof, smoke in the stack, and three ponies saddled outside," Carty announced.

"What are we going to do?" Rebekah asked.

"How about Redbud Cave?" Dacee June suggested.

The lead line to the team of horses was starting to soak up water from Todd's hand. "It's way off the road."

"We're too wet to care," Rebekah reminded him.

"I think I'm going to starve to death," Amber murmured.

"Could we build a fire at that cave?" Abigail asked. "I need to dry out my dress a bit."

Todd kept the rig moving at a walk. "That means it'll be almost dark when we get to Rapid City."

"Why don't you send Carty to the cave to check it out before we drive too far off the main road?" Rebekah suggested.

Carty Toluca pushed back his soggy, drooping hat. "I . . . eh . . . don't really know where it is."

"Well, I do," Dacee June inserted. "You ride in the carriage, and I'll take your pony . . ."

Carty sat straight up in the saddle. "Oh no you don't. I ain't ridin' in the wagon with the women. I'm the scout on this here trip."

Dacee June straightened her drooping straw hat. "Well, you're not much of a scout. You don't even know where to find Redbud Cave."

"Dacee June, why don't you ride with Carty and check it out for us?" Todd suggested.

"You mean ride double?"

"Sure."

"I'm not riding double with Carty Toluca."

"Yeah, this horse is hot-blooded. He might buck a little too much for the inexperienced rider," Carty asserted.

"Too hot for me? I can outride you any day, Carty Toluca. And everyone in this surrey knows it. Now, ride over here so I can climb aboard. Scoot back; I get the saddle."

"You get the saddle? This horse is soaking wet. I've been keepin' the saddle dry myself."

"Thank you. I appreciate it."

"I cain't believe this. Are you sure this is the way Kit Carson got his start?"

"Carson, Cody, even Stuart Brannon had to scout doubled up with beautiful women," Todd teased.

"Beautiful women?" Carty grumbled.

Dacee June stuck out her tongue and climbed aboard the bay horse from her position on the wagon. She straddled the saddle horn, both legs hanging down the off side.

They crested a muddy hill before Todd started up the carriage.

"Why does Dacee June treat Carty so pitiful?" Abigail called out from the backseat.

Todd leaned back. "Overexposure, I reckon. They've known each other too long. They just built a habit of tormenting one another."

"That will be quite a ride," Rebekah remarked.

The warm June rain picked up some. The blankets got heavier. Rebekah stared off at the low-hanging clouds. *This is crazy, Todd Fortune. I can't believe we're riding off into a summer squall. We should just turn around right now. You won't, of course. You're a Fortune. Fortune men are never wrong, so they can never quit and go home. It's your virtue and your vice. If a Fortune says we're going to have a picnic, were going to have a picnic . . . no matter what storm, tornado, or riled Sioux nation gets in our way.*

Todd glanced to the middle seat. "Mrs. Speaker, are you all right?"

"Oh, my yes. This is a nice diversion. It reminds me of my first trip to Dakota when Dacee June, Jamie Sue, Louise, and I rode off across the prairie with a blackguard and a blizzard."

"Sounds like you've had a life of adventure," Mrs. O'Neill added. "All I do is sit around my boring little house and play hearts. Why, being tied up by those men the other night was the most exciting time of my life. Does that sort of thing happen often?"

"I should hope not!" Thelma chuckled. "But sometimes life in the gulch gets so turned in on itself we hardly remember what it's like to be anywhere else. That's when we need to get out and about. Louise and I used to take a lot of trips. That was before she married Mr. Edwards." Thelma turned to the ladies in the backseat. "My sister married Professor Edwards. He's lecturing in California this month on Rocky Mountain weeds."

"He sounds like quite a learned man," Mrs. O'Neill replied.

"Self-educated, mainly . . . but he's written a definitive book. Robert Fortune's brother-in-law did the illustrations."

Rebekah waved toward the muddy trail ahead. "Isn't that Dacee June . . . riding by herself?"

"Oh my, I trust she didn't do him in," Thelma cautioned.

"What?" Mrs. O'Neill gasped.

Mrs. Speaker chuckled. "I was joking, dear."

"Lil' Sis, where's your pard?" Todd called out as she approached.

"He's not my partner," she insisted.

"I do believe she 'doth protesteth too much,' " Abigail said.

"Quite so . . . quite so . . . ," Thelma mused.

"Where is Carty?" Todd demanded.

"At the cave. He wanted to have a fire going when we got there."

"That's thoughtful. He is a pleasant boy, Dacee June," Thelma chided.

"He's a boy, alright. He acts about twelve."

"Well, I think it's quite mature to stay and get us a fire going," Abigail added.

"He just wanted to look at some old horses."

"What old horses?" Todd asked.

"Next to the cave in a cluster of aspen. There's a string of ponies grazing in a little rope corral."

"Is someone running cattle up there?" Todd said.

"We didn't see any cows. Anyway, the cave's wide, deep, and dry."

"I believe we should warm up and dry out. Then eat, turn around, and go back to Deadwood," Rebekah suggested.

"Nonsense," Todd added. "I'm not going to let a sprinkle change our plans. I promised you a trip to Rapid City, and that's what you'll get. Besides, it will probably stop raining in a few minutes."

"Daddy said it rained every day for over two months in the summer of '75," Dacee June reported.

"Thank you for that word of encouragement," Rebekah added.

"You're welcome." Dacee June plastered on a smile. "I think I'll ride on up to the cave and get out of this drizzle."

Todd turned around to the others. "Do you really think she's just going back to get out of the rain?"

"Honestly," Dacee June pouted, "I wish my own brother would give me credit for having better taste than Carty Toluca."

Thelma Speaker tugged at her black gloves. "I believe she's right. Young people today have high standards. Why, it could be that even Mr. Toluca has higher standards than we give him credit for."

"What do you mean by that?" Dacee June gasped.

"Nothing, dear. You'd better ride along. That straw hat of yours is starting to sag something pitiful," Thelma urged.

Located on an eastern slope of limestone-crested Red Mountain, Redbud Cave offered a panoramic view of the Dakota plains that stretched east of the Black Hills. The cave stood no more than ten feet high, twenty feet at the mouth, and barely fifteen feet deep. Old-timers called it the Smile in the Mountain.

Travelers fighting the arctic storms of a Dakota winter called it a gift from God.

During a mild storm, summer tourists called it a picnic.

A blazing fire roared at the cave entrance. Inside, Amber played with bites of one of Thelma Speaker's thick bread and pot roast sandwiches. Dacee June propped a coffee pot on rocks and huddled close, waiting for the tea water to boil.

"This is absolutely perfect!" Abigail declared. She, Rebekah, and Mrs. O'Neill lounged on a blanket and snacked on a jar of pickled asparagus spears.

Thelma Speaker took it on herself to see that everyone's tin plate was constantly refilled.

Todd and Carty stood at the cave entrance, north of the campfire, and stared out at the drizzling storm.

"What do you think?" Carty asked.

"About the storm? Or those horses?"

"Either one."

"The storm has me puzzled," Todd reported. "If it's going to rain hard, Rebekah's right. We should warm up and then race back to Deadwood. There's no reason to get sick in a summer deluge. On the other hand, if it blows clear in a half hour, we'll be looking mighty weak rolling back into town. Nothing worse than an indecisive storm."

"And the ponies?"

"They are saddle ponies, shoed well, left here either last night or this morning."

"The corral isn't big enough for more than one day's grazin'," Carty said. "You think it's someone on the prowl?"

Todd stepped closer. "That's my guess. It's too far up the mountains to be used for anything legal. But don't alarm the ladies. We'll pack up and roll out of here as soon as they're done picnicking."

"Did you notice that three of 'em are bigger than the others?"

"What do you think that means?" Todd pressed.

"If I was carryin' meat, I'd use them bigger ones as packhorses. You reckon it could be a huntin' party?"

"No telling, Carty. But, if you were to rob a bank in town, you could ride hard about this far, then trade off horses."

"And stash your loot on the big horses?"

"Maybe. But if I were an outlaw, I would have struck the bank when the gold bars were out in the window."

Carty pulled off his red bandanna and wrung water out of it. "Is the treasure coach going out on schedule tomorrow?"

"That's what Lander says."

"Is he goin' out with only six messengers?"

"He was lookin' to hire more."

"You think these are relay horses for someone holdin' up the treasure coach tomorrow?"

"That thought crossed my mind. I think we'll head back to Deadwood, so I can tell Lander about this."

"What about these ponies?"

Todd rocked back on his heels and could feel his wet trousers grind into his leg. "If that rope corral got busted, the horses would scatter. Then it would only be neighborly to round them up and drive them into the corrals at Deadwood. The owner could claim them there."

"And if someone was plannin' a heist, it would slow 'em down a bit." Carty glanced over at Todd. "But that rope corral ain't busted."

Todd pulled out his folding knife, opened the three-inch blade, and strolled out into the rain.

"But it's a beautiful afternoon. The clouds have broken. The dust is settled. We're all warmed and fed," Rebekah protested. "You convinced me. Let's drive on over to Rapid City."

He slapped the lines, and the carriage rumbled down the hill. "I told you we need to run these ponies back to Deadwood."

"Todd Fortune, what is going on here? For half the afternoon, you wouldn't let anything, not even a thunderstorm, keep you from this trip. Every time I mentioned going back you would laugh it off. And now, the weather breaks and a rope corral falls apart and you feel responsible for someone else's horses?"

He put his arm around her stiff shoulders. "That's the way we are up in the hills. We have to look after each other's belongings."

"So I packed my suitcase for a cave picnic? That's it?"

Todd looked around at the rest in the wagon. "We had a fun time, didn't we?" he called out.

"Rapid City is more rapid than I thought," Thelma Speaker quipped.

"I feel like I'm going to thrup," Amber admitted.

"You're going to what?" Todd called to the backseat.

"Thrup," she grimaced.

"She's going to throw up!" Dacee June explained.

"Perhaps you could slow down," Rebekah cautioned.

Todd kept the horses at a trot. "I need to keep those horses following Carty."

"But we don't need to stampede back into Deadwood. Why don't you just leave them at the old tollhouse corral? They have plenty of corral space. Then we could turn around and head on down to Rapid City."

"Someone's staying at the cabin now. Besides, we've got to get back to Deadwood." His words rolled out like a general commanding his troops.

Rebekah didn't reply. *You've told me that. What I want to know is what you aren't telling me.*

A bright Dakota sun broke through the clouds as they followed the narrow roadway straight west toward Granite Peak. The loose band of saddle horses followed Carty's lead. The carriage pushed the stragglers. There was no dust, and the recent sprinkling made the roadway seem quieter.

"I must say, the West is certainly peaceful," Mrs. Gordon called out from the backseat, Amber curled in her lap. "We can't hear the stamp mills and there has hardly been any traffic all day."

"There should be a stagecoach soon," Todd said. "The Sunday coach isn't usually very crowded, but they do keep a schedule."

Abigail retied the violet ribbon of her straw hat under her chin. "I enjoyed our trip, even though it was cut short. Sitting back here with mother has given us some time to talk. And we have an announcement to make." Abigail's voice turned dramatic. "Mother and Amber are going to stay in Deadwood through the summer, and I'm going to see if we can find a place and settle down."

"That's wonderful," Rebekah cheered.

"There just seems to be a lot to do in Deadwood," Mrs. O'Neill suggested.

"Oh, but I'm sure there are more opportunities for a social life in Omaha," Rebekah challenged.

"Not that kind of busyness. Cities are full of people doing things. What I meant was, there are a lot of needs in Deadwood. A person would feel very useful," Mrs. O'Neill explained. "Mrs. Speaker has been such an inspiration to me."

"I have? Oh, my, I wasn't trying to attract attention," Thelma sputtered.

"I'm talking about your everyday life. You have a lending library in your living room. You cook meals for most everyone in town. You work at your church. You teach piano lessons. You are constantly doing things for other people," Mrs. O'Neill said.

"And she mothers everyone who comes within a hundred feet," Rebekah added.

"Oh, dear, that sounds so nosey." Thelma picked some loose threads from her long black dress.

"The point is . . . I would like to do more good with my life, and Deadwood just might be the place."

"I want to be an actress just like my mother," Amber piped up.

"Oh no you don't," Abigail cautioned.

"Dacee June said that if we stay in Deadwood this summer I could be in the church play!" Amber pouted.

"The church has a play?" Mrs. O'Neill asked.

"I write and direct a play every summer and every Christmas." Dacee June's full lips parted in a wide smile.

"You write and direct it?" Abigail asked.

"Lil' Sis also stars in it. She's a quite versatile gal," Todd grinned.

Rebekah reclined on the back of the carriage seat so she could view those behind her. "Abigail, I'm thrilled that you might be making a more permanent home in Deadwood."

"I have a confession to make," Abigail announced. Her voice seemed in time with the jostling of the carriage. "Now that we've turned around and are not going to Rapid City today, I have to tell Rebekah why I pitched a fit and talked Todd into bringing us along."

"I thought it was his idea," Rebekah said.

"Oh no, I insisted we come. I wanted to point out how horrid it would be to move to Rapid City. I want to do some things different with my life, and I know I'm going to need your help. It would ruin everything if you moved. Isn't that selfish?"

"Perhaps, but it's honest," Todd noted.

Rebekah folded her hands in her lap. "I feel like this whole excursion has been arranged just to coerce me. Are you in on this too, Mrs. Speaker?"

"Oh, not me," Thelma offered. "I had no intention of running down Rapid City. However, I did think about faking a heart attack before we got there. We all really want you to stay, dear. I might add it would certainly break Louise's heart too, if you moved. She has always said that you will be the next president of the women's association at church. But I don't mean to put any excess pressure on you."

Rebekah began to laugh.

Thelma Speaker swatted a black-gloved hand over her mouth. "Did I say something amusing?"

"In the midst of the most threatening and most trying week of my entire life, I'm finally happy to live in Deadwood," Rebekah mused. "Everything I was afraid might happen to me . . . did. And now I'm ready to stay."

Todd pushed the horses out to a full trot. "You are?"

"For a while, anyway," she replied.

"Maybe that's the reason," Abigail suggested. "You faced your worst fears and realized you can survive."

"I'm not afraid of anything," Amber declared. "Except maybe spiders . . . that's all. Spiders . . . and snakes. I don't like snakes. I'm not afraid of anything except spiders and snakes . . . and falling down a mine shaft into a dark hole and getting stuck and no one is around to hear me scream."

Carty circled the half-dozen horses back toward the carriage. "The stage is parked up at the old tollhouse. What do you suppose it's doing up there?"

"Maybe a horse lamed up or something," Todd suggested.

"Should we ride up there and help them out?"

"If they need a horse, one of these big boys might be a driving horse," Todd said.

As they turned off the road and drove up the hill, Todd noticed there was no smoke in the stack and no horses in the corral. *I guess those others waited out the storm and rode on. Someone could be sick. Why else would they make a stop and leave the horses all harnessed up?*

Todd parked the rig beside the stagecoach. No one came out of the door of the square-cut log building of the ramshackled tollhouse. As Carty corralled the string of horses, Todd tied the reins to the hand brake and swung to the ground.

"Dacee June, get up here and get ready to drive," he ordered.

"Why? What's happening?" she said.

Todd reached under the seat of the carriage and pulled out a shotgun.

"What's wrong?" Rebekah challenged.

"There's got to be a stage driver and passengers somewhere."

Dacee June's eyes grew wide. "You think there's trouble?"

"It's a strange sight. If there is trouble, you drive straight to Deadwood and get help," Todd told Dacee June.

"Without you?"

Rebekah slipped to the ground. "Give me your revolver," she told Todd. "I'm going in that building with you."

"No, it could be . . ."

"Todd Fortune, I don't have a life if it's not with you. I'm going in. Do I get a gun, or do I go in unarmed?"

He handed her the revolver.

"Daddy Brazos says all Fortune women are bulldogs," Dacee June explained. "He's right, you know." She slipped to the ground. "I'm going in, too, and I have my own revolver."

"I think we'll all go in." Abigail climbed down and offered her hand to Amber. "We're all in this together."

"My word, yes," Mrs. O'Neill added. "I'm not about to miss out on the adventure. This is so exciting!"

Todd surveyed those lined up behind him. "This is crazy."

"This is the Black Hills, Big Brother." Dacee June pointed her small revolver in front of her.

Todd led the crew around the parked stagecoach, then approached the front door. "Ho! In the tollhouse! Anyone in there?" he shouted.

"I think I heard someone moving around," Dacee June said. "I sure wish Daddy was here."

The weather-ravaged tollhouse door sagged open an inch or two. All Todd could see was shadows and darkness inside. He pushed the door slowly open with the barrel of the shotgun.

"Anyone home?" he called.

There was a muffled response.

Dacee June scooted next to Todd.

Carty trotted close behind.

EIGHT

Rebekah slid up behind Todd, a hand on his shoulder, her revolver clutched near his right ear. "What do we do now?"

"We go visiting." Todd stepped through the open doorway, alone.

Several bodies were strewn on the dirty, broken floor of the bare room. Todd knelt by the one nearest the door, face down on the floor, a puddle of blood beside him. *Elijah Lander? What are you doing on the Sunday stage?* He searched and found a weak pulse.

"Todd, can we come in? Is it safe?" Dacee June hollered from the porch.

"No!" he yelled back.

"No, we can't come in, or no, it's not safe?" Rebekah queried.

"Just wait . . ."

He scurried to a second man, hands and feet tied, a gag in his mouth. He tugged down the red bandanna and started untying the thick rope.

"Mr. Dover, what happened?"

"Oh, Mr. Fortune, you couldn't have been a more welcome sight if you were the angel Gabriel! When I heard horses outside, I just knew they came back to shoot the rest of us," Dover rattled on.

"Who else besides Lander got shot?"

"Dr. Gordon." Dover pointed to the man crumpled in the corner.

Todd tugged on Dover's ropes. "Did they hold up the Sunday stage?"

"Oh, yes, the driver was in on it. He drove us right up here where the other two were waiting."

"A tall blond-headed man and a dark-headed one with a beard?"

"My word, yes," Dover replied. "Do you know them?"

"They've been on the prowl for a week. I just didn't know what they were up to."

"You go check on the doctor." Todd let Dover untie his own feet as he scooted over to the next bound man to remove his gag.

"Mr. Olene?"

"My word, Fortune, I can't believe it's you. I had said my final prayers and bid this world adieu."

Todd worked to untie the man's hands. "Sorry to delay your final trip."

"Oh no, that's quite alright. I do trust this doesn't make me beholding in a business deal," Olene muttered.

"I can assure you, Mr. Olene, the hardware business is far from my mind."

"Mr. Fortune," Dover called out. "Dr. Gordon's seriously wounded!"

Todd scampered to the corner of the building. Dr. Philip Gordon, Jr. was propped against a wall, clutching his bloody vest.

"Fortune!" Dr. Gordon sputtered. "I trust you have a posse with you." He looked toward the doorway. "Where did they all come from?"

The entire gang, from Mrs. Speaker to Little Amber, lined up inside the room, staring at the men on the floor.

"This is my posse. Actually, we were all out for a picnic."

"What?" Gordon roared. "You purposely endangered the lives of women and children."

"It seemed like a safe day for a ride. But who would be dumb enough to rob the Sunday stage? There's never any money in the box and seldom many travelers." Todd tugged off his bandanna and swabbed it on Dr. Gordon's wound.

"There was treasure this time," Olene quipped from across the room.

"What do you mean?" Todd barked as the doctor took over his own care.

Dover waved toward the unconscious Lander. "There were three gold bars. I saw them."

"This isn't the treasure coach," Todd protested. "It goes out tomorrow, with armed messengers. What are you talking about?"

Olene hunkered down next to Elijah Lander. "Oh, there was treasure, alright. We didn't know it, but Lander did. And the outlaws did. Wells Fargo will definitely hear from me about this. They endangered the lives of passengers, without proper protection."

Todd, still on his knees, sat back on the heels of his boots. "Why was there gold?"

"Maybe Lander was worried about not having his regular messengers tomorrow, and decided to slip it out early," Dacee June offered from the lineup across the room. "Maybe he figured no one would suspect the Sunday coach."

"Todd, what can we do to help?" Rebekah called from the far side of the room.

Todd felt the eyes of everyone on him, waiting his decision. *No . . . I'm not the one. I'm the wrong Fortune. You want the old man. He'll whip things into shape . . . doctor the injured . . . chase down the outlaws . . . take care of the women and children . . . oh, Lord . . . what am I doing here?*

"Todd?" Rebekah reiterated.

"OK, look . . ." For a moment he felt like a lone wolf cornered in a box canyon. But he knew it was time to turn and run right at them. "Here's what we have to do. Doc, you're goin' to have to tell us how to patch up you and Lander. You got a kit?"

"On the stage. The black valise," he replied, all arrogance whipped out of him.

"I'll go get it," Carty offered.

"You don't know a thing in the world about assisting a doctor," Abigail said, "but I do. I'll dress the wounds."

"You'll need some help."

"I'll help her," Rebekah said.

"You can't . . . ," Todd cautioned. "You don't like the sight of blood."

"I can change," she murmured. Rebekah grabbed the bag from Carty and scampered over to Abigail.

"OK, folks," Todd offered. "This is a day for doing new things. Mrs. O'Neill, perhaps this is a good time to take Amber for a walk."

"Oh . . . my, yes . . . would you like to assist me, Mrs. Speaker?"

"Most definitely. I believe I spotted some *Frasera speciosa.*"

"What's that?" Amber asked, clutching both of the older ladies' hands.

"It's what Professor Edwards calls a monument plant," Thelma announced as they scooted out.

Todd waved at the short man with the crumpled suit. "Mr. Dover, search the stagecoach and see if there's a lantern. We'll need more light in here."

"What can I do?" Carty called.

"You check out the other room in this building and the stage. See how many saddles we can find."

"We going after them?" Carty grilled.

"If we have enough saddles."

"My word," Olene groused, "we can let the lawmen ride after them, can't we?"

"Mr. Olene, we are the law. By the time the sheriff gets back and makes his way out here, these men can be hidden in the real Badlands." He waved his arm toward the northeast. "Olene, go through the bags on the stage and get anything clean we can use for rags."

Todd crawled over to Lander. "Lil' Sis, come hold your hand on this wound."

Dacee June scampered over and clamped her hand down tight on the bloody chest of Elijah Lander.

Todd went back to where Rebekah and Abigail knelt by Dr. Gordon. "How did this happen, Doc?"

"They knew the gold was there. Lander pulled out a gun to protect it, and they just shot him."

"How about you?"

"I, eh . . . ," He murmured. "I acted rather foolish. They demanded my wallet, and I . . ."

"You pulled a sneak gun?" Todd questioned.

"I attempted to."

"How much was in the wallet?"

"A hundred dollars, I suppose."

"Hardly worth it, was it?" Todd motioned to the unconscious Elijah Lander. "As soon as the ladies patch you up, maybe you could tell them what to do with Lander."

"Drag me over there; let's take care of him first."

Todd stared down at the doctor. "Are you sure?"

"Just get me over there."

Dover lit a lantern.

Olene stacked a half dozen revolvers, a shotgun, and a pile of shirts on the floor.

Carty Toluca stuck his head in the doorway. "We got three regular saddles and an old McClellan," he reported.

"Carty, come with me. The rest of you stay here and do whatever the doc tells you," Todd instructed.

"You aren't going after them without me," Dacee June protested.

"We're just going to look for signs. We'll be right back."

EIGHT

Todd and Carty circled the corrals twice, getting a clear picture of the outlaws' trail. All the time he kept expecting Carty to say, "I wish Daddy Brazos was here."

He never did.

When they got back to the porch, Dacee June, Watson Dover, and Tobias Olene waited for them.

"Carty, saddle up the four best ponies," Todd ordered.

"Who's going to ride?" Carty asked. "I'd like to go with you. I ain't never rode with a Fortune before. I'd sort of like to have somethin' to tell my grandchildren about someday."

"Grandchildren?" Dacee June hooted. "That's being very presumptuous, isn't it?"

"Thank ya, Dacee June. I was hopin' you'd see it my way."

"What way? You had no idea what I . . ."

"Carty, you're going with me. Olene and Dover, I need you to grab a weapon and ride along."

"That's absurd," Olene protested. "I most certainly will not endanger my life over a matter that does not concern me."

"They shot two men in front of your eyes. It concerns you a lot" Todd insisted.

"I will not endanger my life," Olene insisted, raw panic in his eyes.

"I'll go," Dover offered. "I am not much of a horseman, but I'm a fair shot with a target rifle."

"Thanks, Dover. Go help Carty saddle the horses," Todd instructed.

"You've got to let me go, Todd. Let me ride in that fourth saddle," Dacee June pleaded.

Todd stared at Olene, "It isn't much of a man who'd let a girl do his fighting for him. Are you riding with us, Olene?"

"Absolutely not!"

"Wash that blood off your hands and ride with us, Girl. Daddy will never forgive me if you get hurt."

"But he'd take me with him if he were here."

"You're right about that. Go get the others. We need to talk."

Todd gathered the whole crew into the tollhouse. *It's like a play and everyone is waiting for me to say my lines. Only, I'm not sure what my lines are supposed to be. This is Daddy Brazos's part. I'm just the understudy.* He pushed his hat back and cleared his throat. "How are the wounded?"

"We've got the bleeding stopped in both men," Abigail reported. "Dr. Gordon wants me to try and remove the bullet from Lander first. He think's he might pass out when we remove his bullet, and he would be of no help to Mr. Lander."

"How's your helper? Has she fainted out yet?"

"I'm doing alright," Rebekah offered. "The doctor carries smelling salts in his case."

"Mrs. O'Neill and Mrs. Speaker, keep Amber on the porch, but don't wander off just in case the ladies need a hand."

Thelma Speaker fidgeted with her gloves. "And perhaps we could build a fire and boil some tea?"

"Eh . . . yes . . . that would be helpful." Todd watched Olene cowering at the door as he spoke. "The outlaws took off in the general direction of Redbud Cave. I reckon we have their relay horses. We missed them riding down, because we swung down to the Sturgis Road. They were countin' on loadin' the gold on the three big horses and ridin' the others. They'll ride their ponies into the ground, thinking they have remounts. So we should be able to catch up with them. Dover, Carty, and Dacee June and I will see what we can find. At least we can mark the trail for the sheriff to pick up later."

"What about Mr. Olene?" Rebekah asked from her kneeling position beside Elijah Lander.

"Olene refuses to ride."

"What?" Rebekah gulped.

"I'll ride, alright." Olene stomped to the middle of the room. "I insist on driving the carriage back to town immediately. I will send others back to help."

"You'd drive off and leave the women and the wounded?" Carty asked.

"They may come along with me, if they so choose. I am not remaining here so that the brigands can return to shoot the rest of us."

Todd's fist caught the Cleveland businessman in the stomach. He staggered back, slammed his head on a doorpost, and dropped to the floor.

"Todd!" Rebekah called out.

"Tie him up, Carty. I'm not having anyone drive off in that carriage by himself. We'll be back in at least two hours. But I want you to load up the wounded men in that carriage and drive back to town whenever they are able to ride. If you're gone when we return, we'll meet you in town. Meanwhile ladies, keep one of these revolvers close-by, for protection."

"What are we protecting ourselves from?" Rebekah asked.

"Pure, unadulterated evil," he replied.

Todd volunteered to use the old McClellan saddle. Carty led the way along the muddy tracks. "Ain't going to be hard to track 'em. Heavy loaded horses in the mud leave lots of signs."

Todd crammed his tie into his coat pocket, his white shirt still buttoned at the top. "We have two advantages. We know we're on their trail. They don't. Second, they think they have relay horses stashed. We know better." He rode the long-legged black horse whose only gait seemed to be a gallop.

Watson Dover bounced on a wide-rumped bay horse, the stagecoach shotgun perched on his lap. "I can't believe I'm doing this . . . riding in a posse after stagecoach robbers and killers. It's like I'm living out one of those dime novels. I don't know whether to shout or wet my trousers."

Dacee June insisted on straddling the horse with her long skirt. Todd banished her to riding at the back. She offered only mild protest.

Todd signaled a stop at Boulder Creek to water the horses.

Carty rode up alongside Todd. "I cain't figure this out. Them two was terrorizing town, then they took off goin' south, leadin' the sheriff away from town, then sneakin' over here to the east and robbed the stagecoach. Why was they hasslin' us in town?"

Todd slipped to the ground. "Part revenge. Part diversion. If they kept us in our houses and the treasure messengers preoccupied, they could pull off a robbery with none of us expecting it. Especially when Lander decided to try this fool stunt of his and shipped unguarded bullion." Todd yanked the cinch tight on his saddle. He inspected the cracked leathers of the old McClellan.

Dover rode up, half standing in the stirrups, to the relief of his tender backside. "What's our plan if we do catch up with them? Are we actually going to have a shoot-out? I find this incredible. Watson Dover riding with a posse chasing stagecoach robbers."

Todd surveyed his posse of two teenagers and a Chattanooga lawyer. *Alright, Daddy Brazos, this is not exactly your type of gang.* "Personally, I'm praying they throw down their weapons and surrender. Aren't you?"

From the ponderosa pines below the cave entrance, all four surveyed the Smile in the Mountain.

"You see anything?" Carty quizzed.

"Nope," Todd said. "If they are up there, they are hiding at the back."

"Why would they do that?" Dacee June asked.

"Because they spotted us and want to set an ambush."

"That's a happy thought. I would rather not end up shot like the doctor and that Lander fellow," Dover added.

Todd Fortune slipped down out of the saddle. "Dover, take your shotgun and slip around there to the left. Dacee June, you do the same on the right. Carty, help me pull the saddles off the horses."

Carty Toluca jumped to the ground. "What are we going to do?"

"You and I will stay behind the horses, but try to herd them up the hill a little. If you were restin' in that cave and glanced down to see the missing horses grazing down below, you'd come running down after them, wouldn't you?"

"I reckon so."

"We've got to sucker them out of that cave."

Todd and Carty, guns in hand, pushed the horses out of the pines and up the meadowed slope.

Carty's voice was low. "Do you see anything yet?"

"Still looks empty from here."

"We push these ponies any higher, they'll be able to spot us," Carty stewed.

Todd cocked the hammer on his .45 Smith and Wesson. "I'm going to take a peek."

"What do you want me to do?"

"Pray."

Todd stepped out from the protection of the horses and hiked slowly toward the cave entrance. There was nothing between him and the cave entrance. *Lord, this is either the bravest thing I've ever done or the stupidest. But I have to do it. It was my home they broke into, my wife they tied up, my store they busted up, my friend they shot. This is the moment of destiny where I take care of my own, where I remove the threat. No longer dependent on my father, but I trust in You to lead me . . . and protect me.*

His boot heels made no sound in the wet ground around the scattered sage, but his revolver hung heavy in his hand, his finger turned cold as it clutched the trigger. He spotted Dover on the left, Dacee June on the right. His hat, pulled low over his eyes, caught the heartbeat throb in his temples. He held the pistol straight out in front of him, peering down its sights as he aimed it at the cave. His eyes searched for any sign of movement. He took a deep breath, crested the sloping hill, and stared inside the cave.

He let out a long . . . slow . . . sigh.

Lord, I might of overdramatized this a tad. The absolute turning point in my life ends up being an empty cave? Like the rest of my life, this was just a dry run, a practice.

"What do you see?" Carty shouted from below.

"No one's here!" he called out.

All four resaddled and mounted, then circled the cave for signs. Carty spotted the tracks first. "Did they have a wagon? They seem to be trailing this wagon track."

"That's our carriage tracks," Todd exclaimed. "They're trailing us! They figured people in the wagon hauled off their horses, so they're going to track them down."

"All the way back to the tollhouse?" Carty asked.

"They don't know where the wagon tracks lead. They'll follow them out to the Sturgis road. But our carriage is obviously headed back to Deadwood, so they won't follow it far. They'll have to ride out into the real Badlands, broken down horses and all."

"Will we follow them out there?" Dover asked.

"No, we'll mark their trail, then break off and go back to town. At least we'll be able to send the sheriff in the right direction."

"No gunfight?" Dacee June whined.

Todd's stern glance silenced his sister. He led them in a canter down the trail they had covered earlier in the day. The sun dropped behind the hills as they skirted the eastern edges near the Sturgis road. Scattered clouds and evening dimmed visibility, even though it was a couple of hours until dark. The rain had taken away the advantage of dust clouds that followed riders in a Dakota summer. Todd slowed down to a trot, knowing it's always possible at any moment to come upon the outlaws.

When they reached the road breaking off to Sturgis, Todd reined up. The others pulled alongside.

Carty read the tracks. "They didn't go to Sturgis! That means . . ."

"The tollhouse! They're still following the carriage." Todd slammed the heels of his boots into the flanks of the black horse and wished for spurs. He knew the other horses were dropping behind, but he didn't turn to look or slow down. Somewhere down the road, a gust of wind caught his hat and blew it off his head. He didn't slow down a step.

Lord, this is exactly what I didn't want to happen. Send Rebekah and the others off to Deadwood. Lord, get them out of there before these men show up. I was up at an empty cave thinking myself heroic. Lord, I'm not a hero. I don't care if I'm ever a hero. I don't care if I have to live in the shadow of Brazos Fortune my whole life. I don't care if I live in Rapid City or Omaha or Chicago. Just don't let anything happen to Rebekah and the others.

For fifteen minutes he slammed into the bounce of the saddle and prayed hard.

Gunfire from over the next pass caused Todd to kick the already lathered horse and quit praying. When he reached the descent toward the old tollhouse, he could hear more gunfire. Gunsmoke drifted up from the stagecoach and the building.

He spied two gunmen using the parked stagecoach for cover. Todd couldn't spot a third outlaw but assumed he was nearby.

I need to wait for the others to catch up. But I can't wait. I've got to get them to stop. I'll get myself killed if I ride in there now. I could get Rebekah killed if I don't ride in there, quick. At least they're putting up a fight. I've got to do the same. Lord, I'm tired of thinking about it . . . fools rush in . . .

Todd's first shot was at the dirt in front of the lead horse of the stagecoach. The white horse reared, and he blasted another .45 bullet under the horses. As if on command, all six horses bolted the rig forward. Totally exposed, the two men scrambled for shelter.

A shot from inside the tollhouse clipped the dark-haired man in the thigh. He dropped his gun and screamed. Falling to the mud, he tried to drag himself to cover. More shots from the tollhouse's window and from the approaching posse stung the yard around him, and he collapsed, too wounded or too scared to move.

A tall, blond man with broad shoulders, hat dangling down his back on a stampede string, sprinted toward some boulders near a huge, rusted, abandoned winch. Todd galloped straight at him. His first shot sailed just over the man's head, and caused Todd's horse to jerk sideways. The second shot slammed into the boulders ahead of the man. Todd kept the horse at a gallop and jammed his gun back into his holster.

The man fired a couple of wild shots over his shoulder. He stumbled, picked himself up, then bolted toward the boulders. Leaning low next to the galloping horse's head, Todd continued straight at the fleeing man. He dropped the reins on the saddle and kicked his left foot free from the stirrup. He stood with all his weight in the right stirrup just as the man stopped running, spun around, and pointed his gun.

Todd was no more than fifteen feet away.

He saw fear in the man's narrow eyes.

When Todd leaped from the racing horse, he felt the dry, cracked stirrup leather bust. He dropped more quickly than he planned. Suddenly it was as if everything was enlarged and in slow motion. Flying through the air, he could see the finger pull the trigger. The hammer slammed against the cartridge.

Fire flew from the barrel.

Smoke swirled.

A report blasted.

Todd didn't think of dying.

Or the pain a lead ball could bring.

Or Rebekah dressed in widow's black.

At the moment, the whole focus of his attention was upon tightening his clenched fist and making sure it landed on the face of the gunman below.

The crash of knuckles into the jawbone, the collision of two men on the Dakota mud silenced the rest of the shooting.

The outlaw didn't move.

Todd did.

He scampered, gun drawn, behind the boulders that the unconscious gunman never reached. *Lord, I don't know where that bullet went. But I'm mighty glad it's not in me. Thank you for broken stirrup leathers.*

There were no more gunshots.

Carty Toluca, Dacee June, and Dover slowly rode up toward the tollhouse, their guns focused on the two downed men.

"Rebekah," Todd shouted. "Rebekah, are you alright?"

It was, for him, the sweetest song he had ever heard in his life. He wanted to mount a tall white horse and lead a giant parade when he heard Rebekah's voice call out. "We're safe!"

"I'm shot in the leg. You got to help me," the dark-haired outlaw screamed from the mud.

"You raise your head up one more time and you'll get it shot too," Todd yelled back. "Stay down. We'll get you some help."

"There is another one out there, Todd!" Rebekah shouted. "Be careful. I saw a third man."

Todd waved at Dacee June and the others to keep their distance. *The third one must be the new stagecoach driver. He should be with the stage but it rolled off.*

With gun pointed toward the stage, Todd stepped out from behind the rocks and marched across the yard toward the restless six-up team.

No one in sight . . . but the lines are drawn tight . . . Under the seat? If he's a little man, he could be under that seat.

Todd's shot splintered the back of the driver's bench. The horses lurched forward, and a short man with a long black beard unfolded himself from under the seat. He slapped the ribbons, and the stage bolted for Todd.

Pointing the .45 straight at the driver, Todd squeezed the trigger. Deafened by thundering hooves was the dull click of the hammer on an empty chamber. Todd holstered the empty gun as he jumped out of the way of the frightened horses. He vaulted for the iron railing next to the driver's seat.

What he grabbed was the long hickory stick of the hand brake. The impact jerked his feet off the ground. His right hand reached up and clutched the hand brake as well. The result was to throw all

EIGHT

hundred and seventy five pounds of Todd Fortune against the brake-levered brake pad. The stage jerked sharply left. The horses stopped instantly. The stagecoach driver tumbled out among the prancing hooves.

The short man hit the ground between the two wheel horses who danced and strained at the brake, terrified of what was lying at their feet.

"Get me out of here," the man screamed.

"Crawl out under the horse's belly," Todd instructed.

"He'll trample me!"

"They will all trample you if I let go of this brake. Crawl on your belly."

"I ain't crawlin'," he hollered.

"And I'm not hanging on any longer."

"Wait! I'll crawl . . . I'll crawl!"

On his stomach, his hand wrapped over his hatless head, the man scooted in the mud as the eleven-hundred-pound wheel horse pranced above him. When the man's muddy boots cleared the ground under the horse's belly, Todd released the brake. The nervous team rumbled the stagecoach up the trail.

Todd pulled his gun and started shoving cartridges into the cylinder from his bullet belt. "Carty, tie that blond one up before he comes to," he yelled. "I'll take care of this one. Dacee June, you and Mr. Dover tie up the injured man."

"You cain't tie me, I'm shot!" the man hollered.

"Tie him!" Todd replied.

Rebekah scurried out of the tollhouse, still holding her revolver. Abigail was right behind. Todd hugged Rebekah's shoulder but kept his focus on the stagecoach driver at his feet.

"Are you all really alright?" he asked.

"No one got shot. They had just got here when you rode up."

"Mr. Lander and the doctor aren't doing too well," Abigail added, "but we were all safe inside."

Watson Dover, with shoulders back, head high, and a new strut in his pace, marched into the tollhouse.

Dacee June scampered up to them. "Who shot this one?"

"I believe I did," Rebekah admitted. "I got angry and lost control."

"First, I don't win the beauty contest, then I don't even get to shoot anyone. But I did fire my gun! Rebekah Fortune, you're the luckiest woman alive."

Abigail folded her hands together under her chin. "I don't think I've ever been rescued by a handsome knight who rode up on a black horse and saved the day."

"You've been in too many theater productions," Todd mumbled.

"I've never been in a play where a man dove off a horse and put a man out with one punch, then walked straight up to a galloping stagecoach and shut it down like that. In fact, you couldn't even put that in a play; it would be too unbelievable," the actress reported.

"She's right," Carty called out. "For a minute there I figured I was watchin' a young Daddy Brazos."

"Some of it was mighty reckless and other sheer luck. The Lord was kind to me, that's all. It was nothing special, I can assure you." Todd finished tying the man on the ground, then holstered his revolver.

Rebekah stared at the creases around Todd's eyes. *You will make a handsome middle-aged man, Mr. Todd Fortune. And you aged ten years today.* "What made you think to do such a foolish and brave thing?"

"I prayed and prayed all the way up there that the Lord had sent you all back to Deadwood. But when I heard the gunshots, I figured it was something He wanted me to take care of. I just reacted. I think maybe I decided if you're where the Lord wants you to be . . . all a person needs to do is react. It's all we have time to do well."

"What about me?" The dark-haired man hollered. "Who's going to take care of me? You cain't leave me tied up like this!"

"There's your chance to shoot a man, Dacee June," Todd winked at his sister.

"Really?"

"What are you sayin'!" the man screamed. "You cain't shoot an unarmed wounded man!"

"Of course we can," Todd called out. "Dacee June, if this man tries to reach over for his revolver, shoot him. It he tries to crawl away, shoot him. If he moves a muscle toward you, shoot him."

"I ain't movin'. Look at me!" he screamed. "I ain't movin'."

"Shall we haul him in there and let the doc look at him?" Todd asked.

An ashen-faced Watson Dover appeared at the door. "He's dead," Dover mumbled.

"Who's dead?" Abigail quizzed.

"Dr. Gordon. He just died."

"No!" Abigail blurted out. "He can't die . . . not now . . . not like this!" She sprinted into the tollhouse.

The others followed.

Mrs. O'Neill sat in the corner of the room on the floor, rocking a whimpering Amber in her lap. Thelma Speaker fussed with a teapot at the cookstove, carefully keeping her back to the commotion.

The two wounded men were stretched out on the floor.

Neither moved.

On her knees, Abigail Gordon stared down at the lifeless doctor. Rebekah scooted up beside her.

"I didn't want him to die," Abigail wept.

Rebekah slipped her arm around her shoulders. "I know, Abby . . . I know . . ."

"I have never known a man who ever treated me better. And I never have known a man who treated me worse. When I first fell in love with him, it was the deepest I've ever loved a man in my life. And this week . . . this week . . . I have never hated anyone so thoroughly. But I never . . . ever wanted him to die," Abigail whimpered.

Todd hunched down between the ladies. "I didn't know his wounds were that serious. What happened while we were gone?"

Rebekah leaned her head on Todd's left shoulder. "He had us keep working on Mr. Lander. He kept saying he was alright."

"He knew he was dying," Abigail murmured. "He was a very smart doctor." She laid her head on Todd's right shoulder.

"May the Lord have mercy on his soul. For a man with obvious faults, he made a heroic stand at the end," Todd murmured.

"His poor wife in Chattanooga," Abigail sighed. "It will be a shock to her."

"Mr. Dover can explain the circumstances. Perhaps it will soften the grief a little," Rebekah suggested.

Abigail glanced over at her mother rocking little Amber. "Could I . . . eh, have a few minutes alone with my daughter? We need to say good-bye to her father."

Rebekah stood and clutched Todd's arm.

But she couldn't control the sobbing.

Somewhere out on the Dakota plains, the sun was up and summer bright. But not in Deadwood. White Rocks and the steepness of Whitewood Gulch kept the town in the shade. Recent rains had cleared the air of its summer dust cloud. The clear sky was prairie blue. But there was no sun. Yet.

Todd stood on the front porch of his Forest Hill house and sipped the final dregs of coffee. Rebekah scurried out of the door behind him. Her curly light-brown bangs tumbled precisely and evenly down both sides of her narrow face. Her long hair tucked under a straw hat with a white lace band. A wide, black felt ribbon circled her neck, just above the pointed collar of the white blouse.

"Are you still sick at your stomach?" he asked.

"It doesn't last long. I think it's something I'll just have to get used to."

"Are you sure you feel like going to Columbia's?"

"Yes, today is my day. Abigail took a turn yesterday."

Todd stepped back inside and set his coffee cup on the entry table, then slid his hat off the peg and plopped it on his head. He offered her his arm as they walked down the steps.

"Did you hear Wells Fargo hired a new stagecoach driver?" she asked.

"Who is it?"

"His name is Mink Carlton. He's about our age."

"Now, how did you find that out? Mr. Lander is still in Denver, recuperating. And Handsome Harry's driving the Cheyenne run."

Rebekah laced her fingers together. "A young lady gave me a complete description of him, including a dimpled smile that simply makes one's heart stop beating."

"Dacee June?"

"Yes, she's told me he was just the type of man that makes a woman want to settle down, get married, and have children of her own," Rebekah reported.

EIGHT

"She said that? She's only sixteen! How old is this guy?"

"Around thirty. Daddy Brazos has been gone for several weeks. She's feeling frisky."

"Not that frisky," Todd cautioned. "I'll have a talk with her."

"Todd Fortune, she is not your daughter. Perhaps you should give her credit for some wisdom."

He stared straight at Rebekah's wide brown eyes.

"OK," she grinned, "perhaps you should talk to her. At least until Daddy Brazos shows up."

Todd shook his head. "Poor Carty, I suppose I'll have a depressed clerk for a while."

Rebekah held tight on to Todd's arm. "Maybe this will be the time where he just finds someone less fickle."

"Not Carty. She's his one and only."

She brushed some crumbs from his goatee. "Did I tell you about the latest idea Abigail had?"

"The one about a jewelry shop?"

"No, that takes too much capital. She decided she wants to open a ready-made women's clothing shop, specializing in nobby attire."

"That will cost money, too."

"She has the financing arranged. It seems she's lined up some prominent citizens to back her."

"Anyone I know?" he asked.

"Mrs. Speaker, Mrs. Edwards, Mrs. O'Neill, Columbia, and, of course, Mrs. Fortune."

"Mrs. Todd Fortune?"

"Yes, you've no doubt heard about the courageous exploits of her brave and strong husband."

"It's all a rumor," he chuckled.

"Oh no, I assure you it's quite true." She held his arm tightly. They were almost skipping down the Wall Street stairs.

"You know this Fortune man well?" he asked.

"You might say I have him wrapped around my little finger." Rebekah's eyes danced.

"I hear he and the missus are moving to Cheyenne City," Todd said.

"Cheyenne City?" She stopped their stroll. "Where on earth did you hear that?"

"Or was it Virginia City? Or Rapid City?"

"Well, you can take it from me. She's going to stay in Deadwood for at least nine months."

Todd looked at her from head to toe. "Don't tell me she's great with child?"

Tears began to stream down Rebekah's face.

"What did I say?"

"I'm going to get fat and ugly, aren't I?" she sobbed.

"Fat, yes, but never ugly. Are you serious about staying in Deadwood?"

"Yes, I am," she wailed.

"What changed your mind?"

"A friend and a purpose."

"Are you through crying?"

"Maybe," she sniffled.

After wiping her eyes on a lace-embroidered handkerchief, they turned the corner west and ambled toward the hardware store. Sheriff Seth Bullock rode up on a yellow gelding with almost white mane. "That hold-up bunch is in the Yankton jail, waitin' for their trial," he said.

"That's a comfort to know," Rebekah said.

"They were a couple of the smartest and yet dumbest hold-up men I ever met," the sheriff continued. "They set us all up to be too preoccupied to keep track of the gold. They planned it all the way from wounding Handsome Harry, so they could replace the driver, to terrorizing town to get us hidin' in our homes. They even sent that bogus telegram from the secretary of the treasury. It was the driver that tipped them off about the Sunday shipment."

"So why would they ride back to the tollhouse and the scene of the crime?" Rebekah asked.

"I think that when you get away with things, you reckon you'll never be caught. Any gang that overlooks the Fortunes of the Black Hills is askin' for trouble." The sheriff tipped his hat to Rebekah and rode on down the street. Then he swung back in the saddle. "Todd, I owe you a steak dinner at International for doin' my work . . . you remember that."

"I intend to collect real soon," Todd called back.

EIGHT

They promenaded farther down the sidewalk. "Did you hear what the sheriff said?" she asked.

"You mean the part about the 'Fortunes of the Black Hills'?"

"Yes, I do believe you've been promoted."

"I think you're right. But I'm not my Daddy."

"That's the whole point. Todd Fortune, in and of himself, is a force to be reckoned with."

He patted her hand. "I think that's a wife talking. I don't know if I did anything all that special. I just sort of blundered us in a tight fix and stumbled my way out of it."

"Did you even think that maybe that's the way the Lord leads all of us? In the shadow of his wings."

"It keeps a man from getting a swelled head. I trust I never do anything that dumb again."

They stopped outside the hardware store. "The reluctant hero. It fits you well," she swooned.

"Would you like to come in and tell windy stories around the stove?" he offered.

"My word, no. I'm walking straight up to Columbia's house. We'll have some hot tea, and then . . . we'll tell some windy stories!"

He squeezed her hand. "I love you, Mrs. Fortune."

"And I do truly love you."

"Will we have lunch together, or shall I have that beef chop with Seth?"

"By all means, have lunch with the sheriff. I'll stay at Columbia's. That new gal of theirs is a truly great cook. I'm glad I talked them into hiring her."

"How about Dacee June? Where will she eat?"

"She talked Mrs. Speaker into eating Chinese food with her down at Ah Lee's."

"They're going into China Town?"

"Yes, what a pair. I understand a certain thirty-year-old stage-coach driver eats all his meals there."

"May the Lord have mercy on him and protect him 'until these calamities be overpast,' " Todd offered.

He walked through the front door of the hardware store and smelled hot coffee and heard familiar voices.

"Daddy?" he called out.

Brazos Fortune brushed back his long drooping mustache. "Now, here's a lad that has some explainin' to do."

Four men gathered around the stove . . . one in a wheelchair, one in a plaid wool suit, and two with three weeks of unshaven stubble and dirt sprawled across their faces. "When did you get in?" Todd asked.

Brazos peered over a tin cup of coffee. "Last night."

"But when?"

"We rode in about midnight and you can't imagine how surprised I was to find two women and a little girl livin' in my house," Brazos chided.

Todd thought his father looked a little shorter than he remembered. "That's Abigail Gordon, her mother, and daughter. What did you do for a bed?"

"I slept on the couch up in your office. It's a whole lot softer than those lousy Bighorn Mountains."

"I take it you two didn't have any luck . . . hunting."

Yapper Jim stood up and slapped his hands together. "There's two million people in those mountains already. You can't turn around without stepping on someone's claim. And there ain't no gold there, that's the funny part. Oh, they might find some up in Devil's Canyon, but we stumbled on a band of Crows that convinced us to come home."

Brazos rested his right hand on his holstered revolver. "Quiet Jim said you had a little ruckus while I was gone."

Todd glanced over at the man in the wheelchair. "He took the bullets. All I did was what had to be done. You know how that is, Daddy."

"Yep . . . I do. And I'm proud of you, son, for runnin' 'em down." Brazos turned away from the stove and rubbed his beard, slipping a finger up to the corner of his eye. "It was my job to take care of, and I wasn't here. I was out runnin' around like some gold rush fool. Good thing I got a kid who's smarter than me."

"Ain't nothin' you could have done that Todd didn't do," Quiet Jim added. "Besides, I got another healthy baby and Columbia's doin' fine. Are you telling me I had a bad month?"

Brazos took a long slow look at everyone around the stove. "No," he finally roared. "I'll tell you who's having a bad month. It's

EIGHT

Professor Edwards here. Have you ever in your life seen a more horrible looking suit?"

Grass Edwards frowned. "It's quite the style in San Francisco."

"It looks like curtains down at the Green Door," Yapper Jim blurted out. "Not that I've ever been there, mind you."

"You boys jist go ahead and vent your jealousy," Grass said. "As I was telling the governor of California . . ."

"The governor?" Brazos whooped.

"He and his lovely wife attended several of my lectures."

"Why? Is his life so boring that your lecture was more interesting?" Yapper Jim hooted.

Todd glanced at the four men, each one over fifty. "I know why Quiet Jim's sitting there with a big smile on his face. There are tall stories once again being told around the stove at the hardware. Things are back to normal in Deadwood."

Quiet Jim's smile peeked cautiously out of his leather-tough face. "Even in a wheelchair, it seems good, real good."

"I'll have to agree with you there, but I've got a store to run," Todd announced. "Whenever you run out of stories, I'll tell you about Mrs. Gordon . . . and the man who wanted to buy the hardware."

"I hear you cold-cocked old man Olene and now he's going to build a store and put us out of business?" Brazos said. "Quiet Jim filled me in some. I surely wish I could have been here to turn him down in person."

"You didn't see the offer."

Brazos glanced at the men drinking coffee. "There ain't enough gold in the Homestake to be worth the value sittin' around this stove."

"That was my appraisal, too." Todd had just reached the counter at the back of the building when a short man with a brown plaid suit, round hat, and crisp bow tie entered the store. He watched as the man marched up to Dub Montgomery. Todd strained to hear the conversation.

"Excuse me, I'm Hawthorne Miller, and I need to see . . ."

"*The* Hawthorne Miller, the writer of dime novels?" Dub quizzed.

The man pulled a long, almost black cigar from his vest pocket and bit off the end of it. "Yes, and I would like to speak to Mr. Fortune."

"He's back at the woodstove."

Todd's eyes followed the man toward the stove.

"One of you men Mr. Fortune?" Miller probed, looking each over.

"That's me," Brazos offered.

"Nice suit," Grass Edwards commented.

"Eh, yes . . . and the same to you," Miller mumbled.

"Thank ya," Grass beamed.

"You a drummer?" Brazos inquired.

"No, I'm a writer. Hawthorne Miller's the name. Perhaps you've heard of me."

Brazos shook his head. "Can't say that I have. What can I do for you?"

Miller hesitated while he lit the cigar. "I might as well come right out. I didn't think Todd Fortune was quite as old as you are."

"Todd's my oldest boy," Brazos announced. "He's the one over at the counter runnin' the store."

Miller glanced at Todd and tipped his hat, then turned to the men near the woodstove. "Nice meeting you, gents. I hope to write a book about Mr. Todd Fortune's recent exploits. It's certainly nice to meet his father."

Miller strolled toward the counter at the back of the store.

Todd's eyes locked briefly onto his father's.

You heard him, Daddy Brazos. You are Todd Fortune's father. You thought you'd never see the day that you were defined by who your children are, did you?

To tell you the truth, neither did I.

Look for Samuel Fortune's story in

Book Three

Fortune of the Black Hills

The Long Trail Home